THE BAKER'S DOZEN

L.E. WILLETTS

THE BAKER'S DOZEN

Copyright © 2022 L.E. Willetts

The moral right of the author has been asserted.

For: Boost and Scooby
Forever by my side

AUTHOR'S NOTE

The average person doesn't even notice them, but those who know me will testify, I often walk with one eye to the ground as I seek out my next manhole cover.

I'm not alone. Jeremy Corbyn of the UK Labour Party once famously admitted that he collected them, and Michael Palin made a reference to them in his book *Around the World in 80 Days*. ("In the middle of all this [Jeddah] I chance upon the nostalgic sight of a manhole cover made by Brickhouse of Dudley, impressively inscribed 'The Pennine Drain Cover.'")

Brickhouse Dudley was the result of a merger with Dudley and Dowell (co-founded by my great-grandfather) and the Brickhouse Foundry in 1967. The company sent more than one hundred tons of manhole covers a week to America alone and even had one at the top of the Rock of Gibraltar.

When I first visited Las Vegas, despite being faced with glittering casinos and flashing neon billboards, my eyes still inadvertently scanned the ground for another piece of family history. What I never stopped to consider, however, was that there could be people living in the drains beneath my feet.

In 2007, I became aware of a recently published book: *Beneath the Neon: Life and Death in the Tunnels of Las Vegas* by Matthew O'Brien. Armed with just a flashlight, tape recorder, and expandable baton, Matthew (then a journalist with *Las Vegas CityLife* newspaper) had decided to follow in the footsteps of a psychotic killer and enter the Vegas flood-control system.

He didn't encounter any homicidal maniacs during

his search for secrets, but he did strike upon a community living in the storm drains beneath the infamous Strip—a fact that appalled and intrigued me in equal measure. How was it possible—or even permissible—for one of the wealthiest cities on Earth to exhibit such extreme extravagance on the surface while harboring unfathomable poverty directly underneath it?

The fact that a person could effectively disappear underground nagged away at me—the first seed for this novel well and truly sown. Matt, thank you! Not only for the inspiration, but also for your ongoing help, advice, and guidance writing this book. It would only be half what it is without you (and all remaining errors are my own).

In 2009, Matt founded Shine a Light, a charity now led by Paul Vautrinot, a recovering addict who lived in the tunnels for three years. The organization has helped hundreds of people living in the drains by providing housing, support for drug addiction, job training, and other services. Financial and/or material donations, including bottled water, socks, underwear, batteries, and McDonald's and Target gift cards, are always gratefully received. If you would like to show your support, you can find them on Facebook (@shinealightLV) or by visiting www.shinealightlv.com.

CAST OF MAIN CHARACTERS

ELIZABETH ANGEL: Public defender

MARIO BROWN: Loan shark, casino fraudster, money launderer & overall crook

ALAN DUTTHIE: Edward Dutthie's son

NIGEL GOODMAN: Defense attorney visiting Las Vegas

DR. JOSEPH GRIFFIN: Licensed clinical psychologist for the Nevada Department of Corrections

BILLY JACKSON: Convicted for the first-degree murder of his father, Jacob

LORRAINE JACKSON: Billy's wife ("Lorrie")

MARLENE JACKSON: Billy's mother

BO PURDY: Visits Billy in prison with crucial information regarding his father's murder

MADDISON SCOTT: High-profile reporter. Ruthless. Made more than her fair share of enemies over the years

ALICE VITRIANO: Angelino & Ronnie's daughter

Las Vegas Metropolitan Police Department (LVMPD)

KARL ANDREWS: Homicide detective (previously worked as a death investigator for the Clark County Coroner's Office)

DENNIS BOYD: Homicide detective (newly promoted)

EDWARD DUTTHIE: Law enforcement officer

YORKIE FLETCHER: State trooper. Married to Elena

NOAH MASON: Homicide detective

BURT ("FISH") MYERS: Homicide sergeant. Married to Nancy. Godparent to Alice Vitriano

Midas Touch Enterprises

ETHAN GARDNER: Director of surveillance at the Lucky Plaza Hotel & Casino

ALFRED TURNER: Security officer at Foo Dogs Resort & Casino

ANGELINO VITRIANO: "Mister Big" and the brains and brawn behind Midas Touch. Married to Ronnie

PROLOGUE

SIN CITY (1998)

News item from the *Vegas Observer,* by Maddison Scott,
October 16, 1998:

SMILE, YOU'RE ON CAMERA
"Laughing Boy" Giggles His Way to Prison

DEFIANT TO THE END, BILLY JACKSON STOOD UP AND
smiled as the judge branded him cold and calculating
and sentenced him to life in prison for the murder of his
father, Jacob. Marched from the court in shackles, Jackson's laughter could be heard echoing through the corridors long after his departure from the courtroom.

Local law enforcement officer Edward Dutthie took
the stand and described under oath the events leading
up to that fateful night: "The O'Haras hold a party
every New Year's Eve and this year was no different,
except the boys—that's Jacob's kids—well, they never
showed up. Jacob was kinda bothered about that, but
my kid hadn't shown his face either, y'know? You ask
me, they were all big and ugly enough to sort themselves

1

out, but Jacob wasn't happy. Decided to head home and check if things were as they should be, only he never came back. I never gave it a second thought. Don't think his wife did either—quite the party animal was Marlene once she got going—but my wife… well, she had a bad feeling in her guts and said she couldn't sleep 'til she knew everything was all right, so I went round to be sure and that's when I saw him."

When asked to confirm exactly what he saw, Officer Dutthie told the court that Billy Jackson had been standing at the base of the stairs directing the muzzle of a gun at his father. Planning to take him by surprise, Dutthie attempted to tackle him from behind but as he stepped forward, the accused pulled the trigger. "Blood spilled everywhere," Dutthie told the court. "Jacob never stood a chance."

In a session that lasted less than fifteen minutes, the judge acknowledged that Billy Jackson had admitted culpability by entering a guilty plea to the courts. He also noted, however, that he had shown no remorse and had laughed throughout his trial, except for one brief interval where he interrupted proceedings to deny Dutthie's version of events.

Jackson was transferred to Nevada State Prison this afternoon, where he will spend a minimum of twenty years behind bars.

CHAPTER ONE

Sin City (2018)

"AND HOW DID THAT MAKE YOU FEEL?" THE PATIENT shrugged and refused to make eye contact as he scratched at an invisible mark on the table with a fingernail bitten down to the quick. Reluctantly dragging his eyes away from his subject, the doctor took advantage of the temporary silence to scribble a few notes on the page in front of him:

For all intents and purposes, an empty vessel sits before me. The container appears to be devoid of feeling or emotion, but beneath the surface lies a dormant volcano that threatens to erupt at any time.

In truth, his client bothered him. Dr. Joseph Griffin had seen enough cases pass through the doors of his office over the years to know that it was the quiet ones who normally represented danger. Which was why he would be recommending against early release to the parole board, although recently his opinions seemed to be falling on deaf ears. This was partly, he suspected, due to prison overcrowding and partly because prisoner's release plans tended to include the continuation of counselling with him at his private clinic. Not that they ever bothered to turn up.

The doctor absently twisted the hairs of his eyebrow between his thumb and forefinger as his eyes digested the distinctive, color-coded uniform that had been allocated to his patient so that guards and other inmates could identify how dangerous or unruly he was likely to be. Today, the prisoner wore blue. He was no longer considered to be a threat.

"You been working out, Billy?" He decided to change tack, keep to an even keel in the hope it would persuade him to relax and open up.

"Water bags," he replied sullenly. Free weights were prohibited in the prison gymnasium, the risk of prisoners using them as weapons too great. Trash bags filled with water were, however, permitted by the authorities in what they considered to be a happy compromise.

"They clearly work." The doctor nodded encouragingly.

"Picture this," the patient nibbled at a bloodied cuticle as he changed the topic. "You're stuck in your truck in a jam heading north on the interstate. Some retard is threatening to jump from the pedestrian bridge up above and no one's going nowhere 'til the cops and their people can talk him down."

Dr. Griffin felt a flutter of excitement in his chest at the realization that his client was finally starting to communicate.

"Just as it's starting to look like things can't get any worse," he continued, "your man on the bridge suddenly slips and loses his balance."

The doctor strained to hear above the rhythmic tapping of rubber sandals on the wooden floor as the prisoner repeatedly jigged his leg under the table. Pulling his chair closer and leaning forward, Dr. Griffin placed his elbows on the table and rested his chin on his knuckles.

"Nobody can get to him in time, and he plummets headfirst onto the asphalt below. You're pleased, right? Now they can clear up the mess and you can finally be on your way. Well, that was kind of how I felt."

"On the night of your father's murder?" Now that his patient had finally decided to talk, the doctor whispered the words for fear he might somehow interrupt his train of thought and stop him mid-flow.

"I spent my whole life in that jam waiting for some good to come out of the bad," he replied, "and I would have gladly pulled the trigger if someone hadn't beat me to it."

"Yet you entered a guilty plea?"

"That was the *liar's* idea. Said it'd secure me a lighter sentence." The doctor didn't doubt that the mispronunciation was intentional, but, nonetheless, he chose to address it.

"The lawyer, you mean?"

"Elizabeth Angel was a *LIAR!*" he roared. "I did *not* kill him!" The prisoner slammed his cuffed fists on the table, making both the contents and the doctor jump.

"So why not plead no contest?" he asked, his brow wrinkled in confusion. His client could have easily done so with no repercussions. Rather than admitting culpability, Billy could have simply conceded that the prosecution had sufficient evidence to prove his inferred guilt.

"The liar never thought to mention it." Billy shrugged defiantly as he spoke, reminding the doctor how young and naïve his client would have been at the

5

time of his conviction. Nineteen. Same age as the doctor's youngest. *Still plenty old enough to know right from wrong and be treated as an adult though*, he thought to himself.

"Doesn't mean I killed him." Billy pressed on insolently, as though determined to hammer the point home.

"A cop saw you fire the fatal shot," he gently reminded him as his eyes flickered to the clock on the wall behind the patient's head. The appointment had already run over by ten minutes, but they couldn't stop now. They were so close he could feel the full force of pent-up emotion—the magma building beneath the surface seconds before the volcano erupts.

"A cop *said* he saw me fire the fatal shot," Billy retaliated. "It's not the same thing."

"But the night of your arrest, you"—the doctor paused mid-sentence as the doubts that he could ever help his patient if he remained in a state of denial started to take hold—"said you were glad he was dead."

"It's true." The patient's sandals tapped aggressively on the floor as he jigged his leg with increased gusto. "I was pleased. He deserved it, but that doesn't mean I shot him."

"Pleased?" Dr. Griffin flicked through the papers in the file on the desk in front of him, his eyes finally settling on the relevant news article:

MIDNIGHT MASSACRE
"Laughing Boy" Sentenced to Life in Prison

"You were a little more than pleased, Billy." The words bounced uncontrollably from the page as he scanned the story. "You giggled like a rebellious schoolboy throughout your trial."

"Nerves do that to some people. I couldn't have stopped myself laughing if I wanted to." The patient's words spilled into the doctor's brain. "And why would I? Want to, I mean? It was piss funny." He let out a throaty chuckle.

"How was it funny?" The doctor cocked his head to the side and looked at his patient encouragingly, determined to get to the truth after all this time.

"I guess you needed to be there." Billy smirked. It wasn't a pleasant smile, more the rictus grin of the Joker. "New year, new start," he scoffed when the doctor neither spoke nor reciprocated the humor. "While everyone else joined hands and formed a circle to sing 'Auld Lang Syne,' our father lay in a crumpled heap at the base of the stairs, legs buckled beneath his fat ass and bits of his brain spattered on the wall behind him." He started to giggle at the memory.

"Next thing you know, there's cops everywhere. Swarming over the joint like giant, angry hornets." He snickered again, sending an unwelcome shiver down the length of the doctor's spine.

As the room fell silent, a dull crunch filled the air as the prisoner ground his teeth and studied his surroundings. Determined not to break the spell and allow his client to end the meeting as opposed to the clock on the wall, Dr. Griffin sat motionless—except for the finger that stroked a button beneath his desk that would activate an alarm and bring security bursting through the door within seconds should he need them.

"Ten bucks says I can guess what you're thinking," Billy said, suddenly jerking upright and sitting stiff in his chair, his body seemingly paralyzed by the venom flowing through his veins. "You're thinking I'm a twisted little asshole whose father couldn't possibly have deserved to die under such circumstances. I'm right, aren't I?" he pressed, not waiting for a response. "Well, double or nothing says I can change your mind about that quicker than it takes you to accept this bet."

Billy stretched out his cuffed hands, inviting him to acknowledge the bet, but the doctor didn't move as he silently urged him to continue. This was the moment he had been waiting for. Once a week for almost twenty years, the patient had sat in this office and refused point blank to utter more than a few words relating to that fateful night, as though he preferred the knowledge to slowly devour his mind like a malignant cancer.

"What have you got to lose?" Billy fidgeted impatiently in his seat.

The doctor's eyes travelled to his patient's outstretched hands. Slowly raising his own from beneath the table, he reached across and grabbed Billy's hand in an awkward grip and shook it.

"So, tell me, Billy. Why do *you* think your father deserved to die?"

"Midnight Massacre," he sneered, jabbing his restricted hands toward the newspaper article. "Bit extreme don't you think?" He directed a finger at the relevant segment. "I mean, there was only one victim and, while I can think of many words to describe our father, 'victim' definitely wouldn't be one of them."

"How would you describe your father?" The doctor held his breath in anticipation.

"The guy was a fraud. On the outside, to the rest of the world, he was honest, hard-working and law abiding

—a well-respected pillar of the community, if you like. He even attended church and organized fundraisers. People looked up to him, you know? They wanted to be more like him, but guess what?" He didn't wait for the doctor to respond. "Our *father*," he spat the word through clenched teeth, "also had a dirty little secret that he managed to keep from everyone for years."

"Go on," the doctor whispered.

"Jacob Jackson was a filthy little faggot who liked to fuck his own son." He paused a moment to allow his words to sink in. "That's twenty bucks you owe me."

SIN CITY

2019

"Such is the fate of those who are
greedy for financial gain.

In the end, it will rob them of life."

(Proverbs: 1:19)

CHAPTER TWO

Tuesday, August 20, 2019 (20:25)

BILLY

I USED TO WORRY ABOUT DEADLY SPIDERS, BUT THAT'S kinda crazy when you get to thinking about it. Home is in the tunnels beneath the "Entertainment Capital of the World." Las Vegas. The drains can stay dry for weeks—months sometimes—but they also fill with water real quick when it floods. Once I'd figured that out, getting bit by a black widow didn't seem like such a big deal after all.

Tonight, there's rain in the forecast. I can't risk my stuff being washed away so as I get ready to leave, I carefully place my things on the shelf I rigged up below a manhole. Snooze and you lose, that's my motto. I don't have much—a couple blankets, a cut of scabby old carpet, and a milk crate that doubles as a table when it's not crammed with junk from dumpsters that might come in handy—so it doesn't take long.

Once I'm done, I take one last glance to be sure I've

not forgotten anything and head down the tunnel, regularly checking over my shoulder to make sure nobody's following me. Can't be too careful. After a while, the tunnel straightens out and I hold my breath as I pass a mound of piss and shit.

Gotta clean this area up, man. Find myself a new shitter not so close to home.

The tunnel bends to the left and as I round the corner, a bright light shines in my face. *Metro?* I don't think so. It's too soon and the cops have to want you pretty bad to venture this deep into the system. Even so, I turn off my head lamp and slow my stride, the banging in my chest drowning out the echo of my footsteps.

"Who's that?" There's no response and the only sound is a repetitive click as a flashlight turns on and off in rapid succession. Squinting against the glare, I relax as I make out a silhouette in the distance and I turn my lamp back on as I approach. It's just "Dodgy Daryl," sitting in the middle of the passage, his grubby face half hidden by his even grubbier baseball cap.

"Quit with that light, will ya, Daryl?"

"Spare a dollar, bro? I'm thirsty."

"You ain't thirsty; you're a drunk." All the same, I stuff a dollar down his battered old boot as I step around him and continue toward a ceiling grate that casts grids of neon light onto the walls and floor ahead. I hear him scrabble to his feet and his footsteps approach from behind, but I can't be sidetracked by the likes of Daryl right now, so I speed up.

Pulling myself up onto the rungs, I climb out through a manhole and pause by a barbed-wire fence to watch a group of liquored-up tourists pose for selfies under the "Welcome to Fabulous Las Vegas" sign. I guess it's kinda funny when you stop and think about it: all that glitz and squalor sitting side by side like opponents on a checkerboard.

An airplane roars above my head as it takes off from the airport and as I turn to watch it, my eyes fix on the Strip, lit up in all its glory. In the day, it's hard to see what the fuss is about, but at night Vegas takes on a whole other meaning. The beam from the Luxor breaks the sky and stooping to pick up a couple of snipes, I pocket them to smoke later and head toward Mandalay Bay.

Last week alone, I hustled up almost five hundred dollars in left over credits from machines. People get careless. Spend your dough in the casino and the booze is free. It keeps people in their seats, but that's not the only reason the hotels do it. It's also because it clouds their judgment.

Tonight, I'm feeling lucky. I'm gonna play the twenty-five-cent slots and enjoy a beer—or two—courtesy of the Excalibur before trying my luck on the tables at the Lucky Plaza. I've got a good feeling about the next few hours, but first I need to get some new gear. It's not like I can just stroll into the Excalibur—or the Lucky Plaza, Bellagio, or anywhere else on the Strip—looking like I've crawled out the sewers and hope security won't notice, because as sure as God made little apples, they will.

Beware the spies in the sky that watch your every move.

I pause outside Liberace's and check out the selection through the glass window. Once the sales assistants are busy helping other customers, I enter, grab a few essentials—careful to rip off the security tags before stuffing the clothes into my backpack—and run. I'm in and out in less than a minute, and once I'm sure I'm not being followed I head for the nearest public bathroom to clean up. I know what you're thinking, but before you judge you should stop and think about it. Who's the real thief here? Me, with my five-finger discount, or Liberace's, with their hiked-up prices aimed at tourists with more money than sense?

As I head up the Strip, my eyes scan the shredded smutty handouts that litter the gutter; whores promising a good time to anyone lonely enough to fall for their tricks. Their decapitated heads smile sweetly up at me and remind me of Lorraine.

"I just wanna make an honest man of you, baby."
Shame she couldn't have been more honest.

Me and Lorrie got hitched in April of '97 at the Little White Chapel in the Tunnel of Love. We didn't even get out the truck. Drive-through weddings don't cost so much, and just so long as she married me, and Elvis married us, she didn't seem to care. I really loved her, you know. I thought she was different, but by April of the following year we'd already gotten divorced. Nobody tells you about that. They're quick to tell you there's a wedding every five minutes in Vegas but forget to mention there's a divorce every forty-five.

Looking back the signs were all there. When Elvis sang "Fools Rush In," I wanted to interrupt the clown and ask him what he was getting at, but as it happened he was right. Lorrie wasn't a one-man woman, and no sooner was I chucked in the slammer for something I didn't even do, she was shacked up with the scum who put me there. I don't see either of them no more, though I walk over the exact spot I buried 'em, every single day.

I spot a couple of quarters in the gutter and step forward to pick them up. Lady Luck is shining down on me tonight; I can feel it in my gut.

CHAPTER THREE

Tuesday, August 20, 2019 (20:25)

"I THOUGHT IT WAS A TOWEL OR PIECE OF CLOTHING AT first." The security officer was perched on the end of a sun lounger, his wet uniform clinging to him like a second skin. "The body wasn't floating, see? In the movies, they float, don't they? Facedown, arms and legs splayed out dramatically."

Bloated flesh soaking up the liquid like a sponge. Newly promoted Criminal Investigator Dennis Boyd finished the description in his head as he glanced one last time at the coroner making his final preparations to transfer the corpse to the coroner's office.

"You said some guests spotted it?" Detective Boyd asked, noting that according to the badge on his lapel, the security officer's name was Alfred.

"Them, over there." Alfred pointed to a young couple seated on loungers under a cabana at the far end of the pool complex. Half camouflaged by a jungle of lush palms that whistled in the dry, desert breeze and blocked out the artificial light above them, Detective

17

Boyd could only just make out his colleague Karl Andrews sitting with them.

"You know the hotel's hosting this murder mystery weekend?" Alfred continued, a mixture of shock, confusion, and something else the detective couldn't quite identify crumpling his otherwise youthful complexion. "Well, they seemed to think it had to do with that, but I knew that couldn't be right because it was agreed only yesterday that the pool area be closed off due to slippage risks… This was an accident, right?" His eyes begged for reassurance.

"Too early to tell, but we can't rule out intoxication," the detective replied solemnly. Some of the larger hotels on the Strip served more than a million free alcoholic beverages every day, meaning that alcohol-related incidents were common. If he was right in his suspicions about the identity of the victim, however, alcohol was unlikely to be a contributory factor. What he couldn't figure out was why Maddison Scott—a high-profile reporter with the *Vegas Observer*—would have been in the pool area of the Foo Dogs Resort when today's press conference upstairs had finished hours ago.

His preliminary discussions with the first paramedics on the scene had also seemed to suggest foul play and done nothing to prevent his suspicious mind from going into overdrive. "Bruising to the upper body would indicate some form of altercation," the older of the two paramedics had stated, reluctant to comment further until the medical examiner had assessed the body.

"So," Detective Dennis Boyd continued. "You came out and you saw what you thought was discarded clothing, and then what?" He was keen to glean all the facts from the man while they were fresh in his mind before shock set in and started to play havoc with his memory.

"Well, nothing at first. I stood looking, but all I could see was a dark shadow submerged at the bottom of the pool and even that was barely visible." As though determined to prove the point, Alfred stood up and stepped closer to the pool, leaning in as close to the edge as the crime-scene ribbon would permit. Dennis joined him and they both fell silent as they watched the water rippling and buckling the images underneath beyond recognition.

"It was there earlier. I'm sure it was. I just never gave it a second thought." Alfred looked at the detective, silently willing him to contradict him and tell him that this wasn't possible. "But that would mean they'd been swimming over it all day. Guests, I mean. Totally unaware, they splashed and laughed and fooled around over a dead body?" He shook his head in disbelief as Dennis guided him back to the lounger.

"They seemed so certain though," Alfred continued, gesturing once more in the direction of the couple being interviewed by Detective Andrews. "And what with all these drownings of late." Alfred's words hung heavily in the air and Dennis nodded somberly in acknowledgement. There was no plausible explanation why, but there had been an alarming increase in pool-related toddler deaths on the Strip over recent months.

"It's been so hot, hasn't it? Oppressively so, and in the end, I'm peering into the water asking myself, *"What if they're right and I don't do something?"* I'd lose my job, that's what, and the water's starting to look more inviting by the minute and so in the end, I figured, why not?" Alfred swiped at a trickle of sweat—or maybe water from his recent plunge, Dennis couldn't be sure— that weaved its course down his cheek toward his chin.

The detective tentatively glanced up at the vast expanse of glass that surrounded the complex from every angle. Strands of light spilled into the night from the myriad of bedroom windows, dancing on the water's surface and reflecting from the cool aquamarine walls of the pool beneath. There were no balconies, the hotel probably afraid that guests might jump to their deaths once they had been purged of their life savings in the casino.

The thirty-eight-acre property boasted more than four thousand guest rooms. If they were full tonight— and it had certainly seemed as though they might be when the two detectives had walked through the hotel foyer an hour previously—this equated to an impressive number of potential witnesses. Were any of them watching now? Lurking behind the glass window walls of their luxury suites, silently observing the goings on? Or were they all holed up in the dark, windowless arena below with no indication of time as they threw good money after bad in their desperate attempts to beat the casino?

At least four thousand guests—more likely, double that figure, Dennis thought to himself. Notwithstanding the huge influx of non-guests that a hotel such as Foo Dogs would attract. Dennis didn't care what kind of revolving-door policy the daily turnaround of guests created. Some-body must have seen something.

CHAPTER FOUR

Tuesday, August 20, 2019 (21:15)

BILLY

I'VE BEEN IN THE CASINO LESS THAN TWENTY MINUTES when I get lucky. Some guy needs to take a leak and rather than risk losing his machine, he asks me to guard it. Dumbass left over thirty dollar's credit and before he's even had a chance to unzip his fly, I've doubled it, cashed out, and am making my way across town.

The tables at the Lucky Plaza are busy, but I spot Mario a mile off. My eyes hurt just looking at him. Dressed in black leather pants and a leopard-skin shirt that's open at the neck to expose a thick gold chain, he looks more like an aging rock star than the deadly snake he is. Chunks of gold compete for attention on his tobacco-stained fingers and get close to him and you'll see your reflection in his designer shoes.

I sit down at a nearby table, close enough to watch the action but far enough to go unnoticed.

"Is this seat taken?" I glance over my shoulder to see Jabba the Hutt resting his king-sized gut on the back of the empty chair next to me. I want to tell him to park his fat ass someplace else, but I don't. I can't risk any trouble that might put me under the surveillance spotlight.

"I'm Nigel," he says, shrugging off his jacket and hooking it on the back of the seat.

"Billy," I mutter, ignoring the giant outstretched paw that screams at me for reciprocation.

The cocktail doll approaches our table and Nigel's eyes rake over her with obvious approval. She's hot, and her black leotard, fishnet stockings, and heels leave little to the imagination. It's kinda weird having to ignore what's staring me in the face, but the dolls are always the first to complain to their boss if they think you've overstepped the mark.

Nigel offers to buy me a drink, which I accept. I don't bother to tell him that while we're at the table, the liquor is free. It's better if he accepts responsibility for the doll's tip.

"You in?" He points at the roulette wheel, but I shake my head and hope my reluctance won't give me away. I don't know how long this is going to take and with only sixty bucks, I need to sit out as many rounds as I can without being moved on by security.

"Rookie, huh?" He grins, flashing a mouthful of snow-white ivories, which is curious. Between his meaty fingers, Nigel clutches a half-eaten candy bar that he's been stuffing into his piehole, so the weight thing can't bother him and yet his teeth are mint. This is a guy who once cared about his appearance, but then things change, I guess. People change.

Not all people change, the voice roars in my ears as I spot Mario reach across his table and place his chip on red fourteen. *One hundred freakin' bucks!* The maximum inside bet allowed and I know in that split second that Mario hasn't changed at all.

As I focus on him, Nigel doesn't come up for air. He tells me he's on vacation from Connecticut and that his wife recently left him for his best friend—a scenario that instantly puts Lorrie back in the forefront of my mind—and I'm struggling to zone out, but then the dealer at Mario's table spins the wheel and calls for no more bets. I catch my breath. This is the moment of truth.

I watch carefully as the little white ball spins around the edges of the wheel, bouncing from black to red, teasing its audience as it almost comes to a stop before ricocheting around the rim once more. Finally, it lands —as I knew it would—on red fourteen. Mario collects his chips and goes again, only this time he places his chip on black twenty-eight. Sure enough, as the dealer spins the wheel, the ball bounces back and forth from red to black before finally landing in place.

In less than ten minutes, Mario has managed to extract seven thousand bucks out the casino. Clean bucks. The dirty money from his strip joints in Reno no longer exists. I glance from the dealer to Mario, my eyes finally settling once more on the dealer, whose impassive face gives nothing away. My brother spent his whole damned life trying to figure out ways to cheat the casino and roulette must be the hardest game of all. Once that ball hits the wheel, there just ain't no guarantees. There are patterns, I grant you that, but any half-assed dealer would just alter their rhythm to push the odds back in favor of the casino. Which can mean only one thing…

My eyes flicker toward the ceiling, but it's him all right. Ethan—the Lucky Plaza's Director of Surveillance. I'd bet my last dollar on it. *Beware the spies in the sky that watch your every move.* Of course, if I'm right and the wheel's rigged, it's kind of sweet. They're screwing one of the most influential men in the city. Angelino Vitriano—the face of this casino and countless others on the Strip—won't think twice about their execution if he discovers he's been crossed. There's no way any of them would risk being caught, which means that this time tomorrow, tonight's recordings will cease to exist. There will be nothing to connect me to any of it.

The hot chick returns with the drinks, and I catch Nigel out the corner of my eye reach out to take his drink from her tray.

"You can't touch 'em!" I hiss, trying to grab his arm, but he swats my hand away like an irritating critter.

"I was just getting my beer," he whines. Crazy fool's been drooling like a two-dicked dog since he clapped eyes on her.

"Well, don't," I snap. The waitress catches my eye and smiles, and my cock instantly twitches at the unexpected attention. If things were different, I'd probably start hitting on her, but I've got to keep things professional and not draw attention to myself.

"You'll interrupt the balance and make her drop them all," I say, my eyes glued to her chest. I'm so distracted I almost miss Nigel slip a five-dollar bill onto her tray as she places our drinks on the table. Nobody tips five bucks for a round of drinks. It strikes me that this guy could be a useful ally and, as though reading my mind, he slides a small pile of chips toward me and tells me to spend them wisely.

"Can't take it with you." He smiles grimly as I eyeball him and silently question why he would help a complete stranger. It's clear he's seen right through me. He knows I'm a fraud. I can't afford to be at the table, but rather than create a scene he's decided to put me on a more even keel.

Of course, I've seen right through him too. Not everyone visits our city for the strippers, showbiz, or to win big. Some make the pilgrimage with the sole intention of ending their life, and one look at Nigel's face tells me everything I need to know. My brother had the same look about him before he ended his life, and suddenly the anger is roaring in my skull again, reminding me that it's time to right the wrongs.

My eyes swerve back to Mario's table just in time to see the dealer push a pile of chips toward him, my attention now glued to what sits underneath each chip. A pumpkin. Each and every one of them worth a cool thousand bucks. Scooping them up, Mario downs the remainder of his beer in one gulp and stands to leave.

I gaze sadly at the chips Nigel just gifted me. It's a shame to waste them, but I push them gently back across the table toward him. As he picks them up, he accepts my outstretched hand and gives it a firm shake, the pile of chips that now sits between our palms making the procedure almost impossible.

"Good luck, Billy," he says, and as he leans in for a brief hug, I pocket the chips that he forced back into my hand.

"Don't get angry, get even," I whisper in his ear before making my way across the floor, pausing only briefly by the cashier's cage while Mario cashes in his chips.

Then I follow him to the nearest exit and out onto the street.

CHAPTER FIVE

Tuesday, August 20, 2019 (21:15)

.

ANGELINO VITRIANO PUFFED GENTLY ON THE END OF A Swedish cigar and sank back against the cushions, the sumptuous leather of the couch swallowing his heavy bulk in an embrace. Pavarotti's dulcet tones filled the sky suite from the high-definition surround system, and Angelino closed his eyes to better appreciate the music —and the tart he had ordered via his personal concierge as she worked on relaxing the stresses and strains of the day, her blonde head bobbing up and down in his lap as she performed the most sensational bit of head he had received in a long time.

Emma, was it? The introductions had been a little thin and he couldn't remember. Not that it mattered. Tomorrow he would order a red head. He'd not had one of them for a while and they were always so very grateful. He let out a low, throaty chuckle of pleasure, the mere concept almost pushing him over the edge.

As the song reached a climax, so did he, and as the hooker sped up her pace, he pressed her head firmly into his groin and thrust his ample buttocks back and forth as he released himself deep into her throat.

"OK, pumpkin," he said. "Time's up." Roughly pushing her aside, he stubbed his cigar in the ashtray and relieved his wallet of a couple of fifties, which he pressed firmly into her palm. It was far more than agreed, but Angelino prided himself in looking after his hired personnel. It kept them wanting, but more than that, it kept them loyal, and a man in his position could ill afford dealing with loose-lipped women.

"Five minutes to make yourself beautiful, then time to perform a little magic trick." He slapped her on the ass as he stood up, snorting with amusement as she stuffed the paper notes greedily into the left cup of her bra before he could change his mind.

"Vamoose." He flapped his hand dismissively as he deftly zipped up his fly with the other when she made no effort to move.

"Can I see you again?" she asked. Angelino rolled his eyes and took a deep breath to keep his rising temper in check. What did she think this was? A scene from *Pretty Woman*? It was his place to request her presence again, not the other way around, and he didn't appreciate her overstepping the boundary. It was inevitable though, he supposed. After all, he had just doubled her going rate.

Determined to keep his cool, he ignored the question and clicked the remote to electronically open the blinds. Day or night, he never grew tired of looking over the Vegas skyline from the wall-to-wall windows, a tiny knot of pleasure twisting in his gut each time he considered how much of it now belonged to him. Approaching the minibar, he poured himself a healthy measure of Jack Daniel's, licking his lips in silent approval as the sound of the latch clicked into place and confirmed her exit. Taking a large swig from the tumbler, he flicked the remote to silence the music and began to step out of his clothes.

Twenty minutes of relaxation in the tub catching up with the latest news from the integrated LCD television, and then he would have a walk around the casino floor. Introduce himself to one or two of the more exclusive high rollers as he secretly kept a closer eye on his staff. Ever since the untenable situation all those years ago, when he had put his trust in certain individuals who had then crossed him and stolen vast amounts of money from under his nose, Angelino preferred to spend his evenings in one or other of his casinos. It kept the staff on their toes. Expecting him, yet not expecting him, because they never knew in advance whether he intended to grace a particular casino with his presence on any chosen night. Tonight, his casino of choice was the Lucky Plaza.

"You?" Angelino gasped, grinding to a halt as he strolled semi-naked through the open plan lounge of the sky suite toward the bathroom. He was so shocked at the nerve of the man—a mere employee—before him that he made no effort to retrieve his discarded clothes and make himself decent. What the hell did a member of his staff think they were doing barging into his personal space uninvited? And who had let him? The private housekeeper and concierge were both under very strict instructions, and if whoever was responsible for the indiscretion didn't have a damned good excuse, he'd fire them on the spot.

"You're needed over at Foo Dogs, Mr. Vitriano."

The young man shuffled awkwardly from foot to foot as he spoke.

"Why?" Angelino spoke over his shoulder as he slipped back into his shirt and pants.

"There's been a death. At the pool. It's the murder mystery weekend. The press conference was this afternoon."

"Slow down, man. You're making no sense." Angelino turned and studied him with suspicion. "Have you taken something?"

"We've done our best to contain the situation, but the area's now a crime scene and certain customers... well, they're refusing to accept it's not part of the murder mystery package they paid for."

"A crime scene?"

"Maddison Scott. The reporter..." He tailed off in the hope that his employer would fill in the blanks.

"What about her?" Angelino snapped, pacing toward the minibar to refresh his drink.

"She's dead." The young man shifted on his feet once more. "You need to get down there."

"Dead?" Angelino downed his drink in one slug and promptly refilled the glass. "Why the hell didn't someone call me?"

"Your cell's off."

"Shit!" he cussed, retrieving his cell from the pocket of his pants to see that it was out of charge.

"Mrs. Vitriano suggested we try you here, but I couldn't reach you on this line either." His eyes slid to the landline on the desk by the window, the handset clearly removed from the base.

"You called my wife?" Angelino felt the hackles rise on the back of his neck. *Great.* Not only did he now have irate customers to deal with, but also the firing squad when he got home and had to explain why he hadn't been where he had said he would be.

"I've been trying to track you down the best part of an hour, Mr. Vitriano. I didn't know what else to do." He couldn't believe he was being so ungrateful. If it wasn't for him, his boss would still be oblivious to what was going on.

"An hour?" Jesus Christ, this was going to take some explaining to Ronnie. "Has anyone managed to ascertain what happened?" He marched across the floor and placed the handset on the receiver.

"Only that she drowned," his employee said, shrugging uncertainly.

"What the hell was she doing in the pool?" Angelino could feel the tension building in his scalp as his blood pressure spiked.

"That's what the police are trying to figure out."

"Any witnesses?" Angelino swiped his keys and wallet from the coffee table as he spoke.

"Too early to say. The cops are still interviewing Alfred, but I suppose they'll want to speak to the rest of us."

"Alfred Turner?" Angelino felt the invisible band tighten around his skull as the young man nodded his confirmation and he pulled a strip of Aspirin from his pocket. "What's Alfred got to do with it?" Placing two pills on his tongue, he threw back his head and drained the glass of whiskey.

"He discovered the body. Well, a customer spotted it, but Alfred dove in and dredged her up."

"The press?" Angelino massaged his temples with

his forefingers in an attempt to relieve some of the pressure.

"They're everywhere," he said. "Security's doing their best to restrain them, but you know how pushy they can be."

Yes. Angelino grimaced. He knew exactly how determined they could be, and they were going to have an absolute field day unless he could persuade them to concentrate their efforts someplace else.

CHAPTER SIX

Tuesday, August 20, 2019 (22:00)

BILLY

As I follow Mario down the Strip, a clash of music and mechanical voices blares out from every joint we pass. Tourists dodge the smut peddlers who line the sidewalk, flapping cards plugging hookers in their faces as they pass, and I focus on Mario's vulgar shirt as I weave through the jam of bodies that push and shove from the opposite direction.

The buildings have soaked up the recent heat like a sponge and it now blazes from them like a raging inferno. Sweat snakes down my back and clings to my shirt and I'm asking myself if Mario's worth the effort when we reach the Bellagio. He stops to watch the dancing fountains, so I stop too. I've seen them plenty times but can't deny they're kind of cool. Tonight, they're dancing to Andrea Bocelli and Sarah Brightman's "Time to Say Goodbye," and I smirk at the irony.

Mario plucks his cell from his pocket and speed dials a number. I can't get close enough to listen; the music's cranked up and the crowd's going wild as the jets shoot enough water to supply a whole village, so I hold back and wait. I spot a group of tourists eyeballing a street magician and can't resist stepping closer to watch his antics.

"I'm going to deceive you," he announces to his audience, and I grin. *Everyone in Vegas is gonna deceive you. Get used to it.*

Keeping one eye on Mario, I watch as the magician floats a casino player's card mid-air, circling the audience as it hovers inches above their heads. Another fistful of coins clatters into his tray and our eyes lock briefly in amusement. These chumps are gonna piss their undies with excitement when they see what else he can do, but it takes more to hook me. Now Siegfried and Roy, they really were the masters of the impossible. Until that crazy incident with the tiger wiped out the best magic show I ever saw. Nobody ever did find out the truth about why the cat freaked out, but one thing's for sure: If a 400-pound tiger grabs you by the throat, there's no question it'd finish you off if it wanted to. The fact that it didn't tells me there's more to what happened that night than they let on.

When Mario finishes his call, we cross the street toward the Paris hotel. One of these days I'm going to go up that Eiffel Tower. The hotel was still under construction when I got locked up, so I never had chance, but I heard the views of Vegas are to die for.

I expected Mario to continue north, but he enters the Paris via the casino and I hang back. *Beware the spies in the sky that watch your every move.* This is not the time to get caught on film. As I try to figure out what Mario is up to, a waiter in the outdoor dining area of the adjoining restaurant catches my eye as he clears the final table and removes his apron.

"The parking garage?" I call out to him as a thought occurs to me.

"Casino brings you out on level three," he replies over his shoulder. "Your best bet is via Audrie Lane," he adds to my retreating back as I high-tail it around the back of the hotel.

As I reach the elevators, the indicator on the panel informs me that a cab is clattering its way to level three. *The casino.* It's a gamble. I could be about to lose Mario, but I'm sure he knows he's being followed; there's no other reason he'd choose the casino as his point of access if he's parked in the garage, so I decide to wait and see where it's headed. I don't have to wait long. *Level seven. Employee parking only.* Why would Mario be using the staff parking area? To keep away from the prying eyes of the desk clerks and valets, maybe?

There's only one way to find out, so I make a run for the stairs and as the elevator doors wrench open above me, I pull the fork from my jacket and tighten my grip on the handle.

"These stab deep into the dirt and lift out the roots with just one small twist of the wrist." The words of advice from the assistant at the garden center clang in my ears. I sure do hope he's right, and my guts clench in anticipation.

I'm in luck. As I exit the stairway, I spot Mario, so keeping a safe distance, I start to follow him through the garage. It's not easy. My sneakers keep squeaking on the floor—the sound amplified in the hollow space—and he keeps stopping to check over his shoulder like I've learned to do. I'm not about to give up, though. If prison taught me anything, it was the power of patience. Mario started this and now finally, I get to finish it.

As the metallic thud of a vehicle locking system disengages, I duck behind a pillar and try to contain the anger that Dr. Griffin warned me about. The doc couldn't help me—nobody could—but he was right about one thing. He said it wasn't healthy to bottle things up, that people should confront their problems. He said they should let their anger out and that's exactly what I'm about to do.

CHAPTER SEVEN

Tuesday, August 20, 2019 (23:55)

WHEN NIGEL BOOKED HIS ONE-WAY TICKET TO VEGAS, his plan was relatively straightforward. He would check in to his suite at Foo Dogs, take a stroll along the Strip to digest the sights and enjoy a few hours of reckless abandonment at the various gaming tables, and when he was good and ready, he would return to his hotel to check out. Permanently.

I can't even get that right, he thought to himself miserably as he glowered at the full-length windows that flanked the far wall of his hotel room.

Nothing could have prepared him for the distractions that lay ahead when he finally managed to get his key card to work and entered his room for the first time. The two king-sized beds dressed in crisp Egyptian linen even though he had reserved a single occupancy room. The state-of-the-art electronics and sunken living room, complete with fully stocked minibar and kitchenette. The remote-controlled curtains, behind which lay those stupid sealed glass units that overlooked the hotel pool, and a bathroom big enough to host a party. According to the card on the edge of the tub, his own personal butler was on hand via telephone (conveniently located beside the toilet) should he require him to draw his bath or pour some champagne.

Despite all this, Nigel had never felt as cheated as he did right now. His room had everything except the one thing he needed, but he had been so overwhelmed it hadn't even crossed his mind to check. He glanced at the digital clock on the bedside table. 23:55. Would the front desk even be manned at this time of night? *This is Vegas —the city that never sleeps,* he reminded himself as he stood and brushed at the creases in his shirt and pants before checking his reflection in the mirror. *Sober-ish,* he supposed, if you ignored the slightly glazed and blood-shot eyes, but what did the hotels expect when they continually thrust free drinks at you all night?

He had hung around in the casino at the Lucky Plaza far longer than intended. When his new companion, Billy, had rushed off in pursuit of the man at the adjoining table, Nigel had decided to have one last drink for the road. The lure of the overly attentive waitress, who had become more and more attentive with each hefty tip he placed on her tray, had, however, proven impossible to resist. As had the urge to prolong the inevitable.

Maybe he should wait until morning to register his concerns at the front desk? *No,* he frowned at his reflection in the mirror, barely recognizing the determined face staring back at him. Having finally built up the courage to see through his plan, he had to get it over and done with before he lost his nerve. Swiftly slipping on his shoes, he let himself out of the room and made his way back down to the lobby before he could talk himself out of it.

"We don't have any. I'm sorry." The clerk at the desk didn't even look up from the screen in front of her as he requested a room—preferably Strip facing—with windows that could be opened.

"A balcony then?" If it wasn't for the thick layer of makeup that looked as though it had been applied with a plastering trowel, she would be quite pretty. He flashed her the benefit of one of his smiles in the hope it might weaken her resolve. His wife always said that he could light up a whole city with his smile. *Until she ran off with your so-called best friend,* he reminded himself bitterly. *The whole reason you're now in this mess.*

"I'm sorry, no." The woman smiled apologetically, and as the frustration started to get the better of him, Nigel couldn't help but think that she wasn't sorry at all. She wasn't all that pretty either, he decided, and no amount of makeup could disguise the fact.

"I need *proper* windows," he moaned, the oppressive mix of anger and desperation building in his guts. "I can't sleep without fresh air."

"The windows have vents, sir," she answered, scribbling a note of his obvious anxiety and room number on the pad in front of her. She would have a word with the on-duty manager as soon as possible. *"What happens at Foo Dogs, stays at Foo Dogs,"* he would lecture at every available opportunity in that irritating singsong voice of his. *"Negative publicity reflects on future profits."* With one unexplained death already tonight on the hotel premises, he'd have a hernia if there was another.

"You just slide the little lever across." She turned her attention back to Nigel, moving her fingers from left to right as she mimicked the action. "And you're good to go."

"It's still too hot," he grumbled through gritted teeth, swiping irritably at the thin layer of perspiration that had formed on his upper lip.

"I could send maintenance up to your room to show you how to operate the air conditioner if you need further assistance," she suggested, more convinced than ever that the man standing in front of her was intent on taking his own life.

"What kind of establishment is this?" Nigel demanded, his chest swelling with irritation. Famed for its grandeur and world-class facilities, this was not what he had been expecting from such an illustrious venue. "What kind of hotel has windows you can't even open?"

"The kind that doesn't wish to destabilize the whole building," she replied politely, deliberately avoiding eye contact. The guest was clearly a little worse for wear and she had no desire to antagonize him. "Air pressure can be very dangerous for tall structures"… *and then, there's the jumpers,* the voice in her head wailed. There was no way on Earth she was going to be held accountable for upgrading him to one of the hospitality suites.

Nigel stamped his foot on the faux-marble floor in frustration. Even the hotel staff seemed to have antici-pated his intentions and were determined to thwart him at every turn. At a loss as to what to do next, but more alert than he had felt in weeks due to the sudden hit of adrenaline, he knew that he couldn't return to his room. Not yet. Following the signs toward the casino, he decided that it was about time his luck changed. Maybe if he took advantage of the free booze for a few more hours, he might even manage to drink himself to death?

CHAPTER EIGHT

Wednesday, August 21, 2019 (01:30)

MARIO LAY MOTIONLESS, HIS FACE PRESSED AGAINST THE asphalt as he listened to the sound of tires in the distance as they rumbled furiously down the freeway. A pungent odor of gasoline coated the air, and a muffled cacophony of music and computer-generated machines from a nearby casino echoed through the concrete walls.

Unable to bear the sensation of dirt and rubble digging into his cheek any longer, he slowly lifted his head, instantly regretting the action as a shot of pain seared through him. Defeated by his efforts, he allowed it to crash back down to the ground.

Breathe, he instructed himself as he tried to control the burgeoning sense of dread. *Calm the fuck down.* He sucked in a couple of deep breaths, but the overwhelming stink of bitumen and bitter taste of blood in his mouth made him retch. He lay still again and listened, quietly observing his surroundings as he waited for his heart rate to slow down to a more acceptable rhythm.

"Brilliant! You've done it again. Let's go bonus

round," a mechanical voice declared, accompanied by the distinctive, automated sound of coins clattering into the well of a slot machine. *The sound of rain.* He squeezed his eyes shut as the images of his late father crawled through his mind.

"Light and soft, hard and fast, there's just ain't no music like it," his father would chuckle as money showered into the tray. He would have turned in his grave at the introduction of coinless machines and their tinny recordings that were now part and parcel of every casino throughout the state. "About as much fun as sex with a condom," Mario could hear him grumble, his voice so defined that he may as well be right there with him on the floor of the deserted garage.

The sound of two car doors as they banged shut in tandem below interrupted his thoughts and, holding his breath to drown out the hammering in his chest, he focused on the retreating footsteps and muted voices as they approached the elevator.

Son-of-a-bitch! There had been only two options available to him: stay put by the car, or crawl to the elevator and attempt to hitch a ride. As he now listened to the creaking and groaning within the walls as it coursed its way through the building, Mario realized with absolute clarity that he had made the wrong choice.

He lifted his head again, determined to ignore the pounding in his skull as he strained his eyes toward the ramp that led to the level below. Maybe he could inch his way there instead? Make himself more visible to the next unsuspecting motorist to enter the lot? His shoulder blades burned in rebellion as he clenched at the floor with his fingers and slowly tugged himself forward.

"Help." Grit crunched between his teeth, and he

tentatively licked his lips to moisten them. "Help me," he tried again, but his mouth was so dry he managed only an incoherent groan in the back of his throat.

"Sssh!" Damian Adams placed his forearm across his girlfriend's chest to prevent her from stepping into the open doors of the elevator as it arrived at their floor. "You hear that?"

Wild Cherry's "Play That Funky Music" blared from a passing car on the street, and she wiggled her hips and sang along. "I hear it, baby," she giggled, making a playful grab for his crotch. "Whoops." Drunk on the atmosphere—and free booze, courtesy of their trip downtown to the Golden Nugget—she lost her balance and stumbled into his outstretched arms.

"My hero," she cooed, holding on to him firmly with one hand as she bent down and carefully placed the pitcher of margarita she had nursed back from down-town on the ground beside her. "Play your cards right" —she clung on to him as she straightened up—"and Melody's going to be a really bad girl tonight," she teased, her hot breath tickling his ear.

"Please, help me!" Pain punctured Mario's temples and raged through his ribcage.

"Now do you hear it?" Damian gently pushed her away from him and started to make his way up the ramp that led to the floor above. "Wait there," he whispered over his shoulder, frowning as he immediately heard the awkward clickety-clack of her heels reverberating on the asphalt as she made her wobbly ascent behind him.

Under normal circumstances, Damian would be stoked about how drunk she was. It tended to open up a whole heap of possibilities in the bedroom, but if he was about to walk into some kind of trap, the last thing he needed was her drunken antics putting them both in danger.

As he rounded the bend, the warnings from the online travel forum he'd read before leaving the UK bellowed in his ears. *Gangs rob tourists at gunpoint. Criminals claim to need assistance, then pounce.* He stared at the motionless body sprawled on the floor up ahead. Was this part of an elaborate scam? Damian glanced nervously around him, his eyes scanning the parking lot for places where an assailant could hide.

Should have left the passports and wallet in the room safe, he inwardly cussed. *Only brought out enough cash for the night.* There had been another post on the forum though. One that claimed carrying a passport in Vegas was mandatory if you intended to buy alcohol, use a bank card, or —and this was the one he had been hoping for—hit it big on the slots.

Damian cautiously stepped toward the lifeless figure. "You OK, mate?" He gently nudged Mario's shoulder with his foot.

"Ugh." Mario winced as Damian's boot made contact. *Don't fuckin' touch me.*

"Looks like somebody had too many freebies in the casino," his girlfriend muttered, crossing her arms and tapping her foot impatiently on the floor.

"No, it's more than that," Damian said. "I'm sure of it." He shook his head, at a loss for what to do next. *Send Melody to the hotel foyer to raise the alarm? But what if it's a trap? Anything could happen to her.*

"Money," Mario slurred, his breath catching in his throat as he tentatively reached down to feel the insides of his pockets.

"What's that?" Damian hesitantly lowered himself

on bended knee so he could get close enough to hear what he was trying to say.

"Think somebody wants his mummy," Melody snickered, stopping short as she observed Damian's hands and the look of horror on his face. "Is that blood?"

Damian nodded as he wiped his blood-smeared hands on the leg of his pants. "I think he's been stabbed with something," he said, his eyes glued to the metal spike poking out from the man's bloodstained shirt.

"Money," Mario groaned again as his fingers slowly explored his empty pockets.

"Stay still," Damian instructed as he caught sight of Mario fidgeting with his pockets. He pulled his iPhone from his pocket and touched the screen. No signal.

"That way," he hissed, thrusting the phone at Melody and pointing toward the ramp. "As soon as you get signal, call 911."

"I'm not leaving you." She shook her head defiantly, the fear instantly sobering her up.

"Just go!" he snapped. "I can't leave him but come straight back the second you're done." He turned his attention back to Mario, trying to figure out what the hell to do next, but the words of warning from another forum flooded his brain. This time about an innocent passerby who had moved the victim of a traffic accident to resuscitate her. The guy had later been sued by the family for supposedly worsening her injuries in the process.

Damian didn't like to sit back and do nothing, but the Yanks were renowned for their litigious ways, weren't they? He had the wedding to think about—only last night, they had agreed they would return next year to tie the knot—and then there was the honeymoon. Knowing Melody, that wouldn't come cheap. And what about the mortgage? He switched provider only a couple of months ago and the Bank of England was already threatening to increase their base rate. He'd come to Vegas to win big, not spend out, and there was no way he was prepared to lose everything on an unfair claim of negligence.

Damian wasn't proud of himself. He knew he should at least attempt to stem the blood, but as he waited for Melody to return he did nothing... except silently pray that the emergency services weren't as short-staffed and pressurized as they were in the UK. If this guy didn't get help soon, he didn't stand a chance.

CHAPTER NINE

Wednesday, August 21, 2019 (11:30)

DESIGNED DECADES PREVIOUSLY, THE CORONER'S OFFICE
was a modest facility housed in a remodeled church that
still featured some of the original stained-glass. The
interior of the building, however, bore little resemblance
to its past. Divided into cubicles, the space was now a
combination of autopsy suites, offices used by the inves-
tigators and medical examiners, and cold rooms that
served as fridges for the storage of bodies scheduled for
further examination or transfer to the mortuary.

Despite the building's ventilation and strictly
controlled temperatures, the acrid stench of chemicals
and the reek of mortality lingered heavily in the air.
Prior to his employment with the Las Vegas
Metropolitan Police Department, Detective Karl
Andrews worked as a death investigator for the Clark
County Coroner's Office. As such, he knew from experience that it would take several hours after he had left to
rid his mind and body of the smell.

At the specific request of his superiors, Karl was
accompanied by Detective Dennis Boyd, the newest

recruit to the homicide unit. Eager to learn and never complaining about the long days and even longer nights that were almost a prerequisite for the job, Dennis was fast proving to be a valuable asset to the team, and Karl couldn't deny the tiny swell of pride he had felt at being tasked to mentor the young detective.

Dressed from head to toe in surgical attire to prevent any cross-contamination, both men now walked side by side along the corridor toward the Chief Medical Examiner's office.

"Nice day for it," Karl commented, raising a hand to acknowledge a former work colleague as they passed. Temperatures were slightly fresher this morning and, although showers were forecast, the deep blue sky didn't seem to be in a hurry to disappear.

"Indeed," Dennis responded, focusing on the thought of a nice cold beer at the end of his shift as he tried to ignore the underlying smell of death that seemed to permeate from every nook and cranny of the building.

Pausing outside the first cooler, Karl pressed a button that opened the doors and revealed eight motionless bodies sprawled beneath plastic sheets on metal gurneys. As the combination of freezing air and the reek of decay hit them head on, Dennis held back and pulled the surgical mask closer to his face.

Karl, meanwhile, stepped forward and carefully lifted the synthetic material that covered the first of the bodies to reveal a clear plastic bag containing the deceased's organs. Leaning closer, he studied the attached toe-tag before replacing the fabric and moving on to the next. Slowly repeating the procedure, he checked the remaining corpses and correlating case numbers one by one.

"Looks like they started without us," he finally announced when he couldn't find what he was looking for, and he gestured at the doors to indicate that it was time to leave.

Still wrestling with his gag reflex, Dennis released an involuntary shiver despite the welcome blast of warm air as they exited the cooler. "How long do you suppose Maddison was there?"

"In the pool?" Karl asked as they walked toward the main autopsy suites. "Body hadn't risen to the surface, so not long," he continued. "Why?"

"Just something the security guy said about guests swimming over it," he said, wrinkling his nose in disgust. "He seemed to think it was there earlier in the day, but someone would have noticed, surely?"

"You'd like to think so," Karl agreed. "Seriously, Dennis," he added, noting his protégé's discomfort, "there's no chance on Earth anyone swam over and failed to notice the body."

"Why would Maddison have been at Foo Dogs prior to the press conference, though?"

"Why would Maddison have been in the pool area at all?" Karl stopped as he caught sight of a female forensic assistant through the small window as she removed rings from a corpse and bagged them to return to the next of kin. He tapped on the glass and, looking up, she waved and gestured with her hand for them to enter before returning her attention to cleaning and preparing the victim's hands for fingerprinting.

"Barbara." Karl smiled at his former colleague, wondering yet again why such a good-looking woman who could have had her choice of career would choose a morbid fascination with death as her priority. Last he'd heard, she was having marital problems, and his eyes wavered to her ring finger, but covered by a surgical glove, it was impossible to tell whether she still wore the ring. He hoped not. Karl had met the husband only briefly at a staff party, but it had been more than enough time for him to take an instant dislike to the man.

"Well, well, well, if it's not our very own Detective Andrews." Karl tensed as the voice that accompanied the footsteps approached from behind. He and George Harris had never seen eye to eye, but he also couldn't deny that he was one of the best pathologists the department had.

"I don't envy your job," George commented as he crossed the room and doused his hands in sanitizer from a bottle beside the sink.

"Meaning?" Karl bristled at the subtle criticism. George had been more than a little vocal when he had decided to hang up his medical gloves and cross over to join Metro as a criminal investigator, but it made no difference to Karl. They would both go home tonight with death on their hands and the stink of it on their body.

"It'd be easier to compile a list of names for those who *didn't* have it in for Maddison Scott," he quipped as he applied the obligatory gloves.

Karl had to concede that he had a point. Maddison wasn't exactly famed for her tactful reporting and, in her quest for promotion up the editorial ladder, she had made more than her fair share of enemies over the years.

"Foul play?" Karl asked, raising an eyebrow in Dennis' direction. Dennis had aired the same theory during the car ride to the morgue, but George was normally so tight-lipped pre-autopsy, it was a wonder he didn't squeak when he spoke. "Almost impossible to prove under the circumstances as well you know," he added, determined not to be undermined in front of his new disciple.

"We'll see about that," George answered evasively as he pulled a trolley loaded with surgical instruments closer to the corpse. "According to her husband, she was a strong swimmer," he mused, although Karl wasn't sure if this was for their benefit or whether he was just purely considering the facts aloud. "And the hotel pool's hardly a dangerous environment for a person proficient in the water."

Unable to tear his eyes from the scalpel as it carved a tidy laceration into the victim's throat, Dennis cleared his own. "Did the husband shed any light as to why she would have been there?"

"In the pool, no," George replied, without taking his eyes from the job in hand. "She was supposed to be attending the press conference on the third floor, and you both know as well as I do that given the chance, Maddison Scott would have been in the front row, vomiting difficult questions at anyone and everyone prepared to listen… especially your lot." He paused what he was doing and gave them a knowing look before pressing the blade firmly into the victim's flesh once more.

"She never showed," Dennis interjected, his eyes still glued to the victim's skin.

"Too busy taking a dip in the hotel pool by all

accounts." George gestured to Barbara, who, without words, passed the required implement to him. "Fully clothed," he added, his tone dripping with sarcasm.

"You don't think this happened in the hours preceding the press conference, then?" Dennis asked, keen to dismiss the security officer's suggestion that tourists had been using the pool with a dead body submerged at the bottom of it.

"Preliminary examinations will tell us more, but my gut instinct? The press conference was scheduled for four o'clock, yes?" It was more statement than question, but both men nodded. "And the body was found around eight that same evening?" Again, they both signaled their agreement. "Maddison's corpse is consistent with a body that had been submerged for no more than four hours, so no, I don't think this happened prior to the press conference."

"Would I be right in assuming the hotel's CCTV budget didn't stretch as far as the pool area?" George pressed on.

"Can't so much as fart in the casino without some-body witnessing it, but out there," Karl shook his head in frustration. "The customers don't seem to matter, just so long as the profits are protected."

"Gotcha!" George suddenly declared, carrying the foreign object that he had just removed from the victim's esophagus with a pair of long-bladed tweezers and placing it carefully on a thin piece of glass under the microscope.

"What is it?" Karl held his breath. He knew George well enough to know from his body language that he had found something crucial.

"Have a look yourself," he replied, stepping back

from the equipment, and inviting Karl to join him in front of the microscope.

As Karl positioned his eye for a closer look, he wasn't sure at first what he was seeing, but then he spotted it. Without taking his eye from the lens, he gratefully accepted the instrument that Barbara held out to him and gently began to pry the water-damaged material apart.

Finally, he spoke. "Is that what I think it is?"

CHAPTER TEN

Wednesday, August 21, 2019 (15:30)

Sergeant Burt Myers had a bad feeling in his guts. One homicide and an attempted homicide on the same evening within the same jurisdiction wasn't unheard of, but it was uncommon. Especially, given the unwelcome news that the two incidents were likely connected. As one of only four sergeants supervising a homicide squad of twenty detectives each, he could already feel the weight of the forthcoming workload pressing down on his shoulders.

"A playing card had been rammed down Maddison's throat?" he repeated, struggling to disguise his concern.

"Post-mortem, yes," Detective Karl Andrews confirmed, unscrewing the cap from a bottle of mineral water, and taking a large swig. "The jack of diamonds to be precise."

"The 'Laughing Boy.'" Burt was thoughtful as he leaned forward and rested his elbows on his desk. "Either of you gentlemen play poker?"

"No, but rumor has it you'd be the perfect opponent," Karl quipped, referring to Burt's reputation for being useless at the game.

Despite his best efforts, Burt's lip twitched in amusement. "In poker, the jack is known as the laughing boy because when a player draws the card they must chuckle. Everyone then knows who holds the card because they laughed when they picked up their hand."

"You think the killer is laughing at us?" Detective Dennis Boyd asked, scribbling the words "Laughing Boy" on the notepad in front of him.

"Perhaps," Burt shrugged. "Maddison was a reporter—a pretty ruthless one at that—so there's also a possibility the culprit feels mocked in some way."

"I don't think we can afford to disregard anything at this stage," Karl agreed.

"Tell me about Mario Brown," Burt continued. "You said the paramedics found a similar card on his person?"

"He had an eight of clubs in his jacket pocket," Karl replied. "But there's no way of knowing at this stage how it got there."

"Hand mucking?" Burt mused. In the 1980s, Mario had achieved dubious notoriety for his suspected involvement in an elaborate money-laundering scam involving several casinos throughout the state. Given his reputation, they couldn't ignore the possibility that he had been attempting to cheat the casino prior to the assault.

"Hand mucking?" Feeling completely out of his depth, Dennis made another note on his pad.

"The practice of removing a certain card from the table to insert back into the game at a more favorable moment," Karl explained. "It's possible," he pressed on, in response to Burt's question, "but not all that likely. There was no house identifier on the card, and Mario's a bit too sophisticated to risk detection using one of the oldest tricks in the book."

"Time moves on," Burt countered. "Have one of the team check the latest known methods involving card switching, especially any that might currently be in favor due to the likelihood of evading scrutiny."

"Mario didn't even stop to sample the casino hospitality, though," Dennis interjected. "He entered via the Strip and went straight to the parking garage."

"Where we lose him due to the lack of cameras," Karl added. "But where was he the rest of the night? A man like Mario's not going to be on the Strip without good reason."

"Needles and haystacks spring to mind. You got any idea how much manpower it would take to even attempt to establish such answers?" Burt closed his eyes and massaged the sockets with the balls of his fingers. His ophthalmologist had recently warned him against the habit, threatening acceleration of age-related deterioration to his vision, but he always found the action immensely soothing, and it never failed to halt impending headaches in their tracks.

"An appeal to the public for information about Mario's earlier whereabouts goes out later this afternoon," Karl commented. "And there's always Crime Stoppers if people want to remain anonymous," he added, observing Burt's skeptical look.

"Which will no doubt attract a ton of timewasters," Burt groaned. It never ceased to amaze him what lengths people would go to for their five minutes of fame. "Has anyone interviewed Mario yet?"

"He's still in the ICU." Karl shook his head. "Complications during surgery, but we've got on officer on-site who will call the second there's any change."

"Anything suspicious at all from the footage we do have of him?"

"Nothing yet," Dennis answered. "We've sent it for further analysis, but if anyone was following him, they were discreet. Maddison, on the other hand," he continued, "was running late according to her husband. She'd returned home for some papers and left with less than an hour to spare before the conference was due to start. We have her on camera at 16:18, taking the elevator at the north side of the casino."

"Interesting," Burt interrupted. "So, the press conference was already underway by the time she arrived at the resort?"

"Yes," Dennis confirmed. "And she seems edgy in the footage. Fidgeting and continually checking her watch."

"She wouldn't have taken kindly to missing anything," Burt answered. "I assume we lose her once she steps inside the elevator?" It was no secret that the security outside the main casino areas in most of the hotels left a lot to be desired.

"Officers are currently wading through all the available footage from that moment to when her body was discovered." Karl checked his iPhone to ensure he hadn't missed anything as he spoke. "They know to call me as a matter of urgency if they spot anything suspicious."

"OK, here's what we're going to do," Burt said, stepping out from behind his desk and approaching the small whiteboard at the far end of the room. Picking up the marker, he began to make bullet points on the board.

"We can't automatically assume a connection between the two victims, but we can't rule it out either. Given Mario's history, the only parallel between the two incidents—the presence of the playing cards—is weak, at best. It is, however, unlikely that a man of Mario's ilk would go anywhere without the ability to pay for goods and so the fact he had no wallet or money on him when he was found would point to robbery.

"As such," he continued, "we keep the playing cards under our belts, for now. Working the public into a frenzy, or encouraging our assailant, would be counter-productive. Our priorities are"—the marker squeaked its way across the surface as he frantically scribbled down various tasks on the board—"interview Mario at the first available opportunity. See if he can shed any light on the identity of his attacker. Let's also make talking to the couple who found him a priority. See if they mention anything we've missed. Obviously, we need to ascertain Mario's whereabouts in the hours preceding the assault and obtain any accompanying CCTV footage, and I also want someone to double-check the recordings from Foo Dogs. Pay particular attention to Maddison's arrival at the resort. Anyone suspicious hanging around in the vicinity, I want to be the first to know. Lastly, we hunt down any links between the two victims to include any grievances an individual could have against them."

"Any merit in checking out cold cases?" Dennis shifted in his seat. "Any unsolved murders where the M.O. included a playing card?"

"Good idea." Burt studied the newest addition to his

team appraisingly. "Can I leave that with you to delegate to an appropriate member of the team?"

"Sure." Dennis beamed with pride. It wasn't all that long ago that he would have been tasked with the job, and now here he was, being given permission to allocate the more menial role to someone else.

"Any other questions?" Burt asked, keen to draw the meeting to a close. "No?" he checked his watch and began to gather the papers on his desk. "In that case"— he looked pointedly at Karl and grinned—"you have a press conference to attend, and look what happened the last time someone turned up late."

CHAPTER ELEVEN

Wednesday, August 21, 2019 (16:30)

Nigel lay back against the pillows, one arm flung carelessly over his eyes to block out the late-afternoon sun that burned through the glass. His head was pounding and his mouth so dry it hurt to swallow. Some people were able to drink themselves into oblivion and forget everything that mattered, but not him. He had drunk enough to sink a ship the previous evening, and yet his marital problems had still bobbed buoyantly to the surface during the night.

He turned his face away from the window and squeezed his eyes shut, as though the action could permanently remove the memories as they came flooding back. It didn't work, his mind swamped with the images he'd worked hard to wipe out:

Sweaty limbs—one set, as familiar to him as his own— poking out from beneath sheets that moved in rhythm to muffled grunts of pleasure and left him in no doubt about what was happening. The split-second of agonizing silence before his presence had sunk in. The startled eyes—like deer caught in headlights—

that glared at him before the desperate scrabble for clothes from the foot of the bed had begun.

"What are you doing home?" The inference that his wife's indiscretion was somehow his fault had lingered heavily in the air.

"It's not how it looks," her lover had chipped in. "I was just…"

Just what? Keeping his side of the bed warm for him? He could have called ahead, but he had wanted to surprise her. Instead, it was him who got the surprise when he realized that he wouldn't be crawling into bed with his wife after the day from hell, because his so-called friend had beaten him to it. Unable to find the right words, he had said nothing as he slowly backed out of the room.

Nigel hadn't heard from either of them since his plane had touched down in Vegas, a fact that pleased and pained him in equal measure. He had no desire to hear their pitiful excuses and he certainly couldn't pretend to understand, but the idea that neither cared enough to check on his welfare cut deep. He briefly allowed himself to imagine their reaction to the news that he had jumped to his death from a hotel window, before he remembered that he couldn't even get that right. They were more likely to laugh at his ineptitude when they discovered the truth.

Rearranging the pillows behind him, he dragged himself up the bed and reached for the TV remote, not even caring about the time as the late-afternoon news anchor introduced herself.

"Police are appealing for witnesses," she announced, "to an incident that took place in the parking lot adjacent to the Paris Hotel, either late last night or during the early hours of this morning. In what they are describing as a vicious attack, the victim has now been transported to the ICU at Sunrise Hospital where his condition is said to be critical."

Nigel closed his eyes once more. A man had managed to cheat death while he couldn't even achieve it. Last night, having tried—and failed—to obtain a room upgrade, the owner of the hotel had later approached his gaming table and introduced himself. Wanting to know if he was enjoying his stay, he had asked whether there was anything he could do to make it more comfortable. Convinced that his luck was finally on the up, Nigel had seized the moment. A heated, drink-fueled discussion had followed about recycled odors, plug-in air fresheners, the stench of cleaning agents, and the overall health implications of stale air versus natural ventilation, but despite everything no upgrade had been forthcoming.

"With the recent tragic news of reporter Maddison Scott, whose deceased body was found last night at the Foo Dogs Resort," the anchor continued, "questions are being asked. Should the public be concerned? Can we consider the Strip to be a safe environment?"

Interest piqued, Nigel lazily opened one eye. Last night, he had also been approached by the resort manager who had explained that the police might want to speak with him about whether he had witnessed an altercation in the pool area earlier that evening from the very windows that were at the root of his current problems, which he couldn't deny, he had found somewhat distasteful.

"A body was found in the swimming pool this evening," he had admitted.

"Not exactly good for business," Nigel had blithely replied, still miffed by the hotel's refusal to offer him an alternate room with proper windows. Accepting his drink from the waitress, he had promptly raised the glass to his lips and downed the contents in one mouthful.

"Dead?" he had added, wheezing as the liquor burned a trail of fire down his throat and into his chest. It was a ridiculous question given the circumstances, but it was impossible not to envy yet another person who seemed to have succeeded where he had failed.

"Mario Brown," the anchor interrupted his thoughts, "better known for his suspected involvement in the Papa Smurf scandal of the '80s, was discovered by tourists at around 1:30 this morning, the remnants of a handheld gardening fork, similar to the one pictured, embedded in his torso."

Nigel stared at the screen, a ripple of unease travelling the length of his spine as his eyes flickered between the image of the weapon and another of the victim. *The man from the Lucky Plaza.* The one that his companion Billy had been showing an unhealthy interest in. *More than an interest,* Nigel reminded himself. *He followed him out of the casino.*

"Detectives would like to speak to anyone with information relating to the whereabouts of Mario Brown in the hours leading up to the attack." Was it his imagination, or was she addressing him personally as she eyed him suspiciously over the horn-rimmed spectacles perched precariously on the bridge of her nose?

What was it Billy had said as he left the casino? *Don't get angry, get even.* Yes, that was it. Nigel sat upright in the bed, reaching for the telephone as he scribbled down the number for Crime Stoppers that flashed across the screen.

He couldn't explain it if he tried, but as he spoke to

the kindly female voice on the end of the line, another voice—deep in the recesses of his mind—urged him to limit the information he shared. As such, having confirmed Mario's presence in the Lucky Plaza the previous evening, he replaced the handset and hoped there would be no repercussions for not mentioning Billy, or the fact that he had followed the man out of the casino.

CHAPTER TWELVE

The Beginning of the End (1997)

BILLY

MY BROTHER NATE WAS THE ELDEST. BY EXACTLY SEVEN minutes and thirty-two seconds. According to the medical profession we were identical, but that was insane. We might have looked alike, but the similarities ended there. Take math. While even the most basic sums evaded me, he was a mathematical whiz. After school, our mother would pull up outside the grocery store and we'd cruise the aisles, filling the trolley with mostly what we needed, but also the crates of beer for our father, Jacob. There wasn't a single occasion the cashier managed to tell Ma what she owed to the exact cent before Nate did. She placed him on a pedestal as a result—and of course, he was already "Daddy's Best Boy" for all the wrong reasons.

That day at the prison, the doctor didn't want to take my bet. I could tell from the look on his face, but in the end something deep inside him couldn't resist. Nate was the same, except he never needed asking twice. No matter the content or context, if there was a wager to be had, Nate was always first in line. Eventually, he got himself hooked on slots and was obsessed with mathematical probabilities, strategies, expected values, and all this other stuff that blew my brains. Casino rule number one: The house always wins. Nate's rule number one: If you want to beat the casino, first you gotta figure out how to cheat the casino.

Our father, meanwhile, loved *everything* electronic. He'd sometimes spend hours holed up in the dilapidated hut at the bottom of the garden, tinkering with some neighbor's ancient radio or television set. There wasn't much he couldn't fix and one day out the blue, he decided to open a repair shop.

"Can't survive fixing toasters alone," he argued when Ma tried to object.

Persuading people to use his services was never going to be a problem—he could have sold an air conditioner to the eskimos—but without Nate's technical expertise and wherewithal when it came to figures, the business wouldn't have stood a chance. Ma, on the other hand, had high hopes that Nate would attend college. He was too clever, she said, to waste his future in a backstreet electrical repair shop, although a backstreet shop was the last thing on our father's mind as it turned out. Within weeks, Spun had opened its doors at "Paradise Emporium," a recently renovated retail site full of units that promised to service every local's need.

"Got to spend to accumulate," he declared when Ma queried how we could afford it. "You want people to trust us enough to chuck their dough at us? First you got to give 'em a reason. Make 'em think everyone else is doing the same and they'll soon want a piece of the action."

As it happened, he probably had a point as within a month of moving in, he won his biggest contract to date: the maintenance and repair of all the slot machines under the ownership of the Midas Touch Empire. Midas was the brainchild of Vincent Vitriano, but when old age hijacked his brain and body, his son and only heir Angelino took over the day-to-day running of the family firm. The company owned four of the largest casinos in the city and was rumored to be buying one of its biggest competitors.

Nate and the old man were on a roll. Nobody could deny that in business they made a good team, but then a local cop by the name of Yorkie Fletcher paid them a visit. Yorkie had several business interests outside his daily remit, one of which was an allegiance with a guy named Mario Brown who ran an illegal money-lending operation.

"The bank's not an option for a guy like me, you know that honey," our father bleated like a flustered sheep when Ma learned about the level of his debt to Mario.

"Well, the cemetery clearly is," she snapped in retaliation. I'd never seen her so mad.

Yorkie's new rules were simple. The Federal Reserve had raised its key interest rate and it apparently followed that Mario would be increasing his terms accordingly. If they didn't pay on time, Yorkie was under instructions to *make* them pay, but, for what he described as a "minor fee," he promised to go easy on any punishment. Yorkie was basically offering them protection from himself.

Within a couple of months, the accrued debts to

both Mario and Yorkie had almost doubled. With the fees for late payment and protection spiraling out of control, it was going to take something drastic to get out the mess our idiot father had gotten them into.

"Nate's got an idea," he announced one night over dinner. Having been summoned there that evening, I should have known they were up to something.

"Well, don't just sit there," he pressed when Nate didn't speak. "Tell 'em."

Unable to ignore Nate's obvious discomfort and the blind determination written all over our father's face, my eyes wavered between the pair of them as I set aside my plate and listened. To this day, I wish that I hadn't.

CHAPTER THIRTEEN

1997

IF YORKIE HADN'T GOT DRUNK THAT NIGHT, IT wouldn't have happened…

The repetitive thud on the windshield as the wipers clunked back and forth in rhythm with the rain. The glare of approaching headlights blinding him. The blare of a horn followed by the squeal of rubber on wet asphalt seconds before the two vehicles collided—metal crunching against metal as they locked together in a mass of buckled steel.

The impact that forced his face to slam hard against the airbag before gravity pulled him back into his seat. A thin trickle of blood tickled his cheek as it weaved its way south. Elena, his wife, slumped motionless beside him, the ringing in his ears drowned out by her anguished groans. He couldn't bear to look at her, but equally knew that he must.

Crumpled, bloodied legs, trapped beneath the contorted sheet of metal—an image that will stay with him forever, alongside the guilt that sticks to him as fiercely as the injury does to her.

With vision blurred from alcohol, he stepped from the vehicle and staggered into the road, collapsing in a heap as his legs rebelled against him. He didn't try to get up. There was nothing left to get up for. Instead, he lay perfectly still and listened to the sound of approaching sirens that confirmed help was on its way.

If Yorkie hadn't got drunk that night, it wouldn't have happened. He would have been driving just like they had agreed. Instead, despite his promise—and the fact she hated driving after dark—Elena had taken the wheel.

The passengers in the other vehicle had escaped relatively unscathed, superficial injuries that would heal over time. It was a small mercy, but a blessing, nonetheless. Elena hadn't been so fortunate. Paralyzed from the waist down, her life would never be the same.

"With a bit of luck, the condition might be subject to some nerve improvement," the medics advised. A futile attempt to give hope to a hopeless situation and one that only served to bring the anger bubbling to the surface.

"With a bit of luck, the accident wouldn't have happened at all," she had snapped in retaliation.

Yorkie had tried his best to understand. Everyone had, but they couldn't. Not really. Adapting from an active lifestyle to one reliant on a wheelchair was something the able-bodied would never truly be able to comprehend.

It didn't matter how tough or willful Elena was; nothing could change the fact that she would never walk again. Or dance. Or reach for something from the top shelf. She would never be able to dash to the local grocery store or hop out of bed and run to the bathroom, nor would she be able to do something as simple as turn in bed at night unaided. The ability to perform so many everyday actions that most people took for granted were all now nothing more than a distant memory.

"If you hadn't got drunk, it wouldn't have happened." Over and over and over, she spat the words at him until eventually it became the truth. There had been no compensation to claim. Nobody to blame but herself. It was Elena who misread the lights at the junction and failed to stop but still she blamed Yorkie. Maybe she was right? If he hadn't been nodding off in the passenger seat, perhaps he might have seen the danger and warned her in time?

After the anger, came the overwhelming, all-consuming sense of loss and frustration as she grieved for the life she once had. She never seemed to realize that he'd lost his life as he knew it too. Nobody did. *"How's Elena? Poor Elena. How's Elena coping?"* Not once did anyone think to stop and ask how Yorkie was, or whether he was managing.

His once independent and successful wife—the breadwinner—was now dependent on him, a situation that was both emotionally and physically draining. Something had to give. Over time she would learn to adapt and prove that she needed him for very little, but until that time came, no end of reassurances would convince her otherwise.

"I'm a goddamned burden!" she had screamed one night as, careful not to trip on the catheter's tubing, Yorkie leaned over his wife and slowly eased her out of the bed and into the wheelchair. "I'd be better off dead."

During his darker moments, Yorkie had been inclined to agree. At least then, he would get his life back. He also sometimes wished that he could die instead so that he would be released from the misery and guilt that now surrounded their marriage, but who would look after Elena if he was gone?

Discovering that she hadn't qualified for Medicaid had been another blow. The state wasn't as generous as it liked to appear, always looking for ways to cut costs and their savings wouldn't last forever. They had relied on Elena's salary before the accident, and they certainly couldn't survive without it now. Suddenly, Yorkie had found himself trapped on a relentless merry-go-round. If he didn't employ help, he couldn't work. With no income coming in, there would be no food on the table and no way to pay the household bills. The physio, equipment, and round-the-clock care all came with a heavy price attached, and his monthly salary was soon greedily devoured by the costs involved looking after her.

And so, he had approached Mario Brown…

———

"Notorious businessman Mario Brown was found unconscious and severely injured during the early hours of this morning." The news anchor's voice broke Yorkie's thoughts and he reached for the remote to increase the volume. Elena was currently working with her physio; the punishing regime of assisted standing and hip, leg, ankle, and toe rotation enough to exhaust him just thinking about it.

"Mario, who reached dubious fame in the '80s for

his suspected involvement in Papa Smurf—the biggest and most elaborate money-laundering scam to hit the city since the days of Lefty Rosenthal—had been stabbed in the back with a handheld gardening fork similar to the one pictured. He is currently in hospital in a critical condition and detectives have confirmed they are treating the attack as attempted murder with a full investigation now underway."

Murder. The word bellowed in Yorkie's ears and swam before his eyes as the ticker scrolled across the bottom of the screen, causing a wave of nausea to sweep through his gut. If someone was upset enough about the loans to try to kill Mario, what hope did he have? He was the go-between. He was the one extracting money by whatever means. He was also the one who piled on extra pressure and blackmailed the victims for additional sums of money behind Mario's back.

And what about his job? It was only a matter of time before his colleagues connected him to Mario, and nobody liked a corrupt cop, least of all, other cops. His job was what made people respect him and without it he could wave goodbye to the protection money. He stood to lose everything he had worked so hard for. Yorkie wasn't proud of himself, but what choice had he had? The blackmail, the threats, the violence, and protection; all of it had been so his wife could live as comfortably and pain-free as possible.

At least, that had been the reason at first, but in truth Yorkie could have quit a long time ago. He *should* have quit a long time ago. Elena was more self-sufficient now than she had ever been. The anger and frustration she once carried around with her like an aggressive skin condition had long been replaced with a peace and solitude as she begrudgingly accepted her disability and the fact that life must go on.

Yorkie had squirrelled away more than enough over the years to fund Elena's care and retire if he wished, but the additional income had become a drug he was addicted to. The money had been something he could control for a change, but now at best he stood to lose it all. At worst he faced prison, or even death if the attempt on Mario's life had anything to do with the loans.

CHAPTER FOURTEEN

1997

BILLY

Ever wondered why the machines always pay out when you're near the entrance of a casino? Or when you're in line at the snack bar? It's no accident and it's all perfectly legal. Loose slots attract attention, they reel players in, and it's only once a target's been enticed into the lair that they discover the rest of them have been tightened. There will only ever be one winner and it's not going to be you or me.

Here's how it works: Operators aren't allowed to program a specific machine to win or lose. Those results are determined by the random number generator, but they can set average payout percentages and hit frequencies for their machines. A machine with a high payback percentage and a high hit frequency will gift lots of small payouts. A machine with a high payback percentage but a low hit frequency, on the other hand, means you have more chance of winning the jackpot.

It's complex, but trust me, loose machines are never what they seem. You'll win enough to get you hooked… and then you'll lose.

The day of my brother's "big idea," Angelino Vitriano had paid our father a visit with a proposition. It was the above tactic of programming the machines to behave in a certain way, and Angelino's plan to alter that behavior in his favor that first gave Nate the idea.

When I entered the factory, I spotted him straight away—the little beetles working overtime in his skull as he bent over the small worktop at the far end of the shop. I crossed the floor and stood behind him, quietly eyeballing him as he soldered components onto a computer motherboard, until he finally broke the silence.

"There's twenty-four in total, all needing attention before they're shipped out to the casinos in the morning."

I stepped forward and placed the bag of drinks and pastries I'd stolen from work beside him on the worktop. Technically speaking it wasn't theft, but my employers would have argued otherwise. Beverages were permitted only during a shift, an allowance I hadn't used that day, and I was supposed to sign out any food taken off the premises, even if it was only destined for the trash.

Eyes glued to the circuit board, my brother reached for a pastry. Mine stayed on him as he slowly and methodically soldered the pins.

"A few minutes alone with 'em is all it'll take," he

said, carefully cleaning the tip of the iron before moving to the next connection.

A few additional lines of code, that's all. His words from the previous night crashed through my brain. It was a dumb idea with lethal consequences if Angelino got wind of it.

I turned my attention to the cluster of slot machines lined up against the wall at the far side of the room. "They look mint. What's wrong with them?"

"Nothing," he shrugged. "Fell off the production line this morning, but Angelino wants the RNGs sorting before they're positioned on the floor."

The RNG—or the random number generator as it's more commonly known—is a complex piece of software: a device capable of generating thousands of random three-number combinations every second. The purpose of Angelino's visit had been to discuss the possibility of reprogramming the RNGs. He also wanted to cap the maximum payout of the machines within his care, and I'd have bet my bottom dollar he wouldn't be informing the Nevada Gaming Commission of his plan to override the manufacturer's pre-approved settings.

"Is that legal?" I asked. It definitely wasn't, but I needed to get through that thick skull of his. If Angelino was caught rigging his machines, he wouldn't confess, nor would our old man, which left Nate to shoulder any blame.

Nate placed the soldering iron carefully in its stand and turned to me. "Come on, bro. You ain't that stupid. They're all doing it. You only have to enter a casino in this town to see what's going on. The house always wins."

"And the only losers are the schmucks who think

they can beat the system," I gently reminded him. "Why can't the on-site techs do it?" I had a really bad feeling in my guts, but there was no talking him out of it.

"Angelino wants someone he can trust." He grinned and winked as he knifed me in the ribs with his elbow.

"Angelino will cut you up into little pieces and scatter you all over the desert if he finds out you stole from him," I warned, but I was wasting my breath.

"*If* he finds out, which he won't." He turned his attention back to the task in front of him. "How about you make yourself useful instead of just standing there?"

The risks rocked my skull, and I could feel the start of a headache brewing. My brother's modifications wouldn't be the only thing that would make these slots different. TITO—ticket in, ticket out—was a relatively new development, and it was of no real surprise that Angelino was one of the first in line to try the machines in his resorts. *When a customer spins, the casino wins.* By removing coins and the need to wait for attendants to pay out jackpots, the casino could speed up play. And by speeding up play, they stood to take more money. Especially if the machines had been rigged.

From my brother's perspective, there were other advantages. There would be no scrutiny from casino employees over winnings, no stream of coins tumbling into the hopper to alert them something was amiss. There would be nothing except a small printout showing a healthy credit to cash in on the way out. I licked my lips nervously, my mouth suddenly as arid as the desert outside. Reaching across the table, I grabbed my brother's coffee, instantly regretting it as the bitter fluid hit the back of my throat.

Would Angelino ever find out? Nate could still

tighten the slots as instructed so there was no reason he should.

A few additional lines of code, that's all. A code that could then be manipulated.

CHAPTER FIFTEEN

Wednesday, August 21, 2019 (22:30)

RECLINING HIS CHAIR TO MAKE HIMSELF MORE comfortable, Sergeant Burt Myers leaned back and rubbed his full belly appreciatively. Tonight was a rare evening off, one that he and his oldest friend Angelino Vitriano had been planning for weeks, but he was struggling to completely switch off.

"All work and no play makes for a very dull boy," Angelino had jokingly scolded when he'd tried to call the evening off. His friend had a point. He had some of the best detectives the LVMPD had to offer working tonight's shift and having enjoyed a meal fit for a king courtesy of Angelino's personal chef, he couldn't deny feeling thoroughly pampered.

The two men now sat on the terrace overlooking the swimming pool and landscaped grounds beyond. The women had retired upstairs to select a suitable outfit for Angelino's wife, Ronnie, to wear to a forthcoming function, and Angelino's daughter Alice, Burt's goddaughter, was currently in her room adding a few finishing touches to her dollhouse. The hand-crafted structure had been a gift from

Burt and his wife Nancy for Christmas, every minute detail specially designed to replicate Angelino and Ronnie's home. Having had several additional items custom-made, they had both delighted in her obvious pleasure when Burt revealed the contents of the small box he had kept hidden beneath the table until they had finished their food.

"She seems to like it." Burt smiled as he recalled her reaction. At just three years of age, Alice had been diagnosed with a degenerative disorder, her symptoms characterized by the physical appearance of premature old age. Five years down the line, Alice was still very much a child beneath the exterior and unable to have children of their own, Burt and Nancy doted on her.

"Like it? Thanks to you, I can't get the kid to concentrate on her homework," Angelino replied, grinning. "So, talk to me about Mario Brown," he switched topic, the ice cubes rattling in his glass as he picked it up and took a large slug.

"Not much to tell. He's still in ICU."

"Any truth to the rumors?" Angelino eyed Burt curiously as he spoke.

"What rumors?" Burt feigned ignorance and shifted in his seat to pet Angelino's dog as it placed a paw against his thigh and scrounged for tidbits.

"According to my sources, Mario was attacked by the same person who killed Maddison Scott."

"Your sources?" Burt shot him a quizzical look. It was inevitable, he supposed. A man of Angelino's ilk was bound to have powerful connections, but it still disturbed him to think that one of his own team might be supplying him with sensitive information.

"If I tell you, I'll have to kill you," Angelino chuckled. "You don't think I have a right to know?" he pressed. "This business with Maddison happened at one of my properties and the lead detective—my oldest chum—is holding back on me."

"There's strict protocols," Burt replied. "None of us are at liberty to discuss the case with members of the public," he added pointedly, concerned that he had a snitch within his department.

"Aw, c'mon, buddy. I won't squeal." He reached for the ice bucket in the hope that more alcohol might help loosen Burt's tongue. "You and me, we go way back. I get you need to weed out the nut jobs, but does our friendship count for nothing?"

"Spare me the guilt trip," Burt grimaced. The number of false confessions for no other reason than notoriety was one of the more frustrating aspects of the job. As he and his colleagues investigated alleged admissions of guilt, the real perpetrators walked the streets and continued to reoffend.

"It's a little ironic, don't you think?" Angelino continued. "Mario spends years stabbing people in the back, and now…"

"He's been found with part of a hand-held gardening fork embedded between his shoulder blades," Burt finished. He had been determined not to talk shop on his night off, but the alcohol, now well-rooted in his system, was making him more talkative.

"Could be a mugging gone wrong, I suppose." Angelino studied him carefully as he spoke. Burt's integrity was one of the many attributes that had enabled him to race up the ranks so quickly. He rarely discussed his work, but tonight—and he hoped that he was right—there was something about his manner that suggested he might make an exception.

"You don't believe that any more than I do," Burt said, picking up his glass and studying the contents.

"Perhaps not," Angelino conceded, "but concerns have been rife for months about the lack of security within that lot."

"We can't disregard it." Deep in thought, Burt rolled the glass between his palms before finally replacing it on the table untouched. He had said too much already but couldn't seem to help himself. "You already know about the playing cards, don't you?" he eventually countered.

Angelino didn't, so he picked his next words carefully. The last thing he needed was Burt clamming up before he had all the information he required. "Not the kind of detail you want to share with the press, huh?"

"Maddison *was* the press," Burt retaliated. "But they get wind that a playing card was rammed down her throat post-mortem and there'll be pandemonium." He reached for his glass again and downed the contents in one gulp. He'd regret it in the morning of course—the raging hangover, and the fact he had disclosed classified information that would completely obliterate any progress in the hunt for potential suspects if word got out.

"The card found on Mario could just be a coincidence?" Angelino suggested, reading between the lines. "He's renowned for his gambling exploits."

"No such thing," Burt replied. "You see coincidence, I see convenient."

"What then?" Angelino asked, pleased that his friend had finally decided to spill his guts.

"The killer's claiming responsibility, I'm sure of it."

"Except that Mario's not dead."

"Yet," Burt acknowledged. "But if he pulls through, he's one lucky son-of-a-bitch."

"We had a tip that Mario was in the Lucky Plaza earlier that evening," he continued when Angelino didn't respond.

"Not possible." Angelino slammed his glass down on the table between them. "He's blacklisted."

Mario had several dubious business interests, but the one that had always concerned Angelino the most was his suspected involvement in the infamous money laundering scandal of the '80s that the press had dubbed "Papa Smurf." It was alleged, although never proven, that Mario was the Papa—the father, leader, and chief of the Smurfs, who were employed by him to enter various casinos with money earned from illegal activities. The Smurfs would exchange the dirty cash for chips, gamble a while before then cashing in the chips and, bingo, they had proof of their winnings and the money had been cleaned. Every member of Angelino's security team was under very strict instructions that Mario, and any of his known associates, were not to cross the threshold of any of his resorts.

"If Mario was in my casino, I'd know about it," he insisted.

"I need to view last night's footage," Burt replied.

"That makes two of us," Angelino growled. "And, if I find that one of my staff let that crook into my casino, there'll be hell to pay." He stood up and grabbed his jacket. "I'll have my driver take us there now."

CHAPTER SIXTEEN

1997

BILLY

ANGELINO'S WAS THE OLD MAN'S BABY. IT WAS VINCENT Vitriano's first casino and he named it after his newborn son in a grand gesture of statement. It was *the* place to be and soon became synonymous with the father and son empire and everything they stood for. In later years though, popularity bombed as tourists jumped ship in favor of the slicker resorts that were surfacing out of nowhere.

Within twelve months, the Monte Carlo, New York, New York, and the Stratosphere—complete with puke-inducing gravity drop tower and revolving restaurant—had all opened their doors to the public. Construction on the Bellagio was underway, Bally had announced plans for a Paris-themed hotel, and both Sands and the Hacienda had been razed to make way for so-called megaresorts.

The more people itched, the more the developers scratched, and Vegas soon got itself a reputation as the

"Implosion Capital of the World." The older hotels didn't stand a chance, but the fact that Angelino's was quieter was the reason I liked it best. That, and because the security systems were ancient and with staffing levels at an all-time low, nobody paid me much attention or even seemed to care.

"Don't get greedy," Nate had warned. "Always hit for max $900, then move on. Next machine hit for less. $500 to $600, then move on again." He was really pig-headed about it and didn't even want me hanging out in any one casino for an extended length of time.

"Go over $1,200 and the machine will lock out," he had explained. "Then you'll have to wait for the attendant to issue a W2 with your winnings… tax," he added, when I pinned him a blank stare.

"One look at your ID and not only do we wave goodbye to the winnings, but you'll also wind up in jail for underage gaming." Once he started bitching, he couldn't seem to stop. "A dollar pays ten you won't resist the free liquor either, so best add that to your rap sheet if you get caught."

The crazy-assed politicians sure as hell had some dumb policies: I could drive, smoke, vote, marry, have kids of my own. I could—and later would—be tried in an adult court for murder. The puffed-up crooks could even ship me out to fight whatever Godforsaken country they happened to be bombing, but enjoy a swill of beer or spin on the slots on my return home? Not unless I wanted to be kidnapped by the cops, I couldn't.

"If you can't take the heat, it's time to step away from the stove." Nate eyeballed the doctored machines as they were loaded into the back of a delivery truck.

"You'd best pass me the salt," I said, giving him a

sharp, mocking salute. His scheme was bullshit and I wanted no part of it, but with Yorkie piling on pressure over the loans, we needed cash fast.

At first, things were good. Within a couple of weeks, we had accumulated more than half what we needed to pay off the debts, but then one night things started to go horribly wrong.

I'D BEEN ON EDGE ALL DAY. ME AND LORRIE HAD ONLY been married a couple minutes and she was already acting up, the latest fight because I was out every night. She said that I either let her come with me, which I couldn't do, or that she'd leave me, which I also couldn't let her do. There was only one thing left that I could do. I had to up the stakes and win enough to clear the debt once and for all.

Taking one last drag to settle my nerves, I stubbed out my joint and hoped I looked more measured than I felt as I passed through the revolving doors into the lobby of Angelino's. I paused like I always did to await the inevitable, but camouflaged by a couple trying to placate their screaming brat as they checked-in, the only staff member at the front desk was too occupied to notice me.

Careful to avoid unwanted eye contact, I strolled through the foyer toward the casino. *The house always wins.* Rule number one bounced around my skull like a pinball, but try as they might with their flashy marble statues and decorated ceilings, this house didn't look like a winner to me. Angelino's was a shithole and the only real surprise was that the old man hadn't made it disappear in a cloud of dust years ago, but maybe he couldn't? Maybe to do so would have been akin to killing his own son? Maybe he had decided to plug it instead for every last cent while spending as little as possible on the upkeep?

The mechanical tinkling of slots increased in volume the farther into the casino I got. My shoes stuck to the skanky, beat-up carpet, and I was breathing through my mouth to combat the toxic stench of cheap perfume and smoke. Rumor had it, the resorts pumped oxygen into the casinos to keep players awake, but the only vapor to enter Angelino's in recent months was ass gas, tobacco, and the overpowering trashy floral scent pumped in by management in their desperate attempts to perfume the pig. In truth, nobody would have missed Angelino's if they had injected some lethal flammable gas into the joint.

As I cruised the corridors, I gingerly touched the base of the well of every machine, cussing each time my fingers hit a piece of discarded gum, as I felt for the identifier that Nate had soldered to the machines. Eventually, I found what I was looking for. The fact that the machines had moved since my last visit should have been enough of a wake-up call, but I was blinded. I just grabbed a seat before anyone could beat me to it, the receptor gobbling up my note like a starving, rabid dog.

"Cash out." As the reels surged into action, the hot whisper of breath was so close it tickled my skin and I glanced over my shoulder at the uniform brushing against me. *Slot machine personnel.* The guys employed at ground level to keep an eye on customers and make sure everything went to plan for the casino.

"Huh?" According to the screen, I'd notched over

500 credits in one hit and I hadn't even used the special code.

"Cash out." He spoke kind of mellow, but one look at his face was enough to make me reach straight for the payout button. Turning away from me—arms stretched behind his back as he flicked his fingers in rapid succession—there was no room for misunderstanding, and I reluctantly pressed the ticket stub into his hand.

Having then made himself scarce, no one was more surprised than me when he came back a short while later with my percentage, the folded notes dropped by my feet in a move I almost missed as he passed. *Beware the spies in the sky that archive your every move.* Nate's rule number two slugged my ears, so I dragged the money under my boot but made no attempt to pick it up in case I was being watched.

Rule number three: *Keep the fires burning and the gears turning.* I inserted another dollar bill, determined to act normal like my brother had advised.

I was up almost a grand in credit when the wheels next settled and I shuffled uneasily in my seat, unsure about the protocol going forward. Nate hadn't explained what to do if the machine gave out before I'd even had the chance to enter the code.

"Shift your ass," the slot machine guy—Tobias, according to the badge on his chest—hissed as he hovered behind me. "I'm due a break."

The only sensible thing to do right then would have been to slow down so as not to draw attention and raise suspicion. Instead, I had an attendant breathing down my neck, threatening me to speed up.

"I'm going as quick as I can," I muttered, unsure where the allegiance would take me. Over-payers weren't all that common, but they weren't all that rare either. My brother's program could have developed a fault, but there was also a good chance that it was all just an innocent coincidence. Either way, Tobias seemed more interested in lining his pocket than protecting casino profit and having got in on the action there was no escaping him.

When he came back from his break, we picked up where we left off. Every fifteen minutes or so, I would signal to him as I pushed the cash out button. I'd then pass him the printout and he'd fold up the paperwork in the palm of his hand and head toward the cashier's cage, returning soon after with my share of the money. It wasn't an ideal arrangement, but we had ourselves an understanding and it was all going fine.

Until this other guy approached me. He wanted my machine and wouldn't take no for an answer. I told him I was losing and trying to get even, but he said he knew it was overpaying and if I didn't let him play, he'd have it shut down. Sure enough, within minutes, plain-clothed security had turned up and I was surrounded.

It was only after I'd been stripped of my winnings and steered from the building that I realized the real trouble had only just begun.

CHAPTER SEVENTEEN
Thursday, August 22, 2019 (00:55)

IT WAS ALMOST 1 A.M., BUT ONE GLANCE AT THE monitors that lined the walls and lit up the otherwise darkened surveillance room was enough to confirm that there was still plenty of activity going on in the casino below. Unopened food containers littered the desk in front of the three men, who sat hunched in their chairs over one monitor as they hunted for footage they were never going to find.

Sergeant Burt Myers had long gone—Angelino's driver had personally escorted him home—and the tension in the room was now palpable. Angelino hadn't uttered a single word since his friend had left, nor did he need to; his demeanor was more than enough to invoke answers as he paced back and forth, each heavy footstep reverberating from the floor and echoing the rhythmic beating in his employees' chests.

"Has anyone checked the player's card profiles?" Ethan Gardner's guilt infested eyes swerved from his employer to his subordinates. As director of surveillance at the Lucky Plaza, Ethan was one of the Vitriano family's longest-serving employees. He was also one of the least trustworthy and having personally deleted the profiles just hours previously, he was now eager to find a scapegoat before the shit hit the fan.

"Now, why didn't I think of that?" Angelino exploded. "It's not like we don't know who we're looking for, so why not? Why not find out exactly how much Mario stole from right under your goddamned nose?" He dragged a chair across the room and sat astride it behind Ethan as he tapped the request into the system.

"Well?" Angelino eyeballed Ethan with displeasure as he silently studied the spreadsheet on the screen in front of him. As soon as Burt had aired his suspicions about Mario's whereabouts in the hours leading up to the attack, Angelino had called in the request to view the profiles and already knew they were missing. What wasn't currently clear was why both the profiles and the all-important footage were missing. To make matters worse, one of his tables was down big time and if he hadn't been called away to deal with the stiff in the pool at Foo Dogs, he would have been on the floor witnessing Mario's antics first-hand.

"They're not here," Ethan said, shifting uneasily in his seat, a maneuver that wasn't lost on Angelino as his eyes burned small pinpricks of fury into the back of his employee's skull. He rested his chin on his crossed arms on the back of the chair and quietly studied the thin beads of perspiration that trickled down the back of Ethan's neck. It didn't take a genius to figure that one of his staff was somehow involved in the recent deception and, judging by the guilt screaming from Ethan's every pore, he was pretty sure he'd found his culprit.

"Make yourselves scarce," he purred menacingly to

the other men, the instant melody of chairs as they scraped against the floor testimony to their haste to extract themselves from their employer's wrath.

"First thing tomorrow, I want a breakdown from every camera that covers the entry and exit points," he added over his shoulder to their parting backs.

"So," Angelino said, returning his attention to Ethan. "Scum that's blacklisted from every casino in the state casually enters this casino and sits his ass down at a table to drink my free booze, and you don't even notice?" He kept his voice low, but inside he was struggling to contain the anger.

"One of my tables is down and the very cameras positioned to protect it are telling me zilch," he continued. "Why? Because *someone* wiped them, and I'm thinking that someone was you." By God, he was going to enjoy ripping Ethan apart limb from limb if he found out that he was in anyway involved.

"Without those recordings, you're my eyes and ears." He towered over Ethan now as his fury built. "So you're going to tell me what went on here last night if it's the last thing you ever do." Grabbing him by the scruff of his shirt, he twisted the cotton material in his fist so that it pressed firmly against Ethan's neck.

"I… I don't know." Ethan choked as Angelino tightened his grip. "I never saw him," he lied, his shirt now squeezed so tight he could barely breathe. "But there might be a way to retrieve the footage." He flopped back against the seat as Angelino released his grip.

"I'm all ears." Angelino reached for a cigar and carefully peeled away the cellophane without taking his eyes from Ethan's face.

"It's complex." Ethan readjusted his clothing in a

pathetic attempt to regain some composure. It wasn't actually complex at all, but he couldn't admit as much without implicating himself.

"Try me." Angelino studied his employee as he sucked hard on the end of the cigar. Ethan had been on his payroll for years, but could he trust him? All those years ago, when Billy Jackson was caught stealing from one of his casinos, those recordings had also gone missing. Coincidence? As his friend Burt had already pointed out, there was no such thing.

"Files aren't automatically erased from the system when they're deleted," Ethan said, scratching his scalp vigorously as he set about protesting his innocence. "They sit on the hard drive until they're overwritten."

"So, what are we waiting for?" Angelino felt a stab of excitement in his chest. Maybe he could trust Ethan after all?

"It's not that simple," Ethan warned. "These systems"—he waved his hands theatrically at the surveillance equipment that crowded the room—"use up a huge amount of space on the hard drive. There's a good chance they've already been overwritten." He omitted to mention that if someone had deliberately deleted the files, they would also have taken the trouble to overwrite them. Which was exactly what he had done after he had saved a backup to his memory stick.

It was a precaution he always took. Mario had far too many stooges planted within the casinos he targeted and everyone knew it only took one bad apple to spoil the bunch. Just as soon as he could, Ethan planned to determine exactly who had attacked Mario. Exactly *who* had stolen his share of the money.

"For your sake, you'd best hope they haven't,"

Angelino snarled as he stubbed the end of his cigar underfoot. "I need those recordings and if you know what's good for you, you'll make sure I get them."

CHAPTER EIGHTEEN

1997

BILLY

TRUE TO HER WORD, WHEN I GOT HOME THAT NIGHT from Angelino's, my wife had left me. Or to be exact, my bag had been packed and I had left my wife. We'd been living with her folks until we could scrape together enough cash to rent somewhere of our own, so it wasn't like I had any say in the matter.

With no money and no place to go, my pace was real slow as I zigzagged the back streets toward Fremont and tried to figure out what I was going to do. As I approached the main street, a manic cheer cracked the air and the false sky lit up my path as the Archie's "Sugar, Sugar" belted out from the sound system. The last of the nights "Experience" had kicked off, so I cut through a side street to duck the crowds. As I reached the intersection at East Ogden, Porky Pig jumped straight into my path.

"B-b-b-b-Billy," he chuckled, grabbing my shirt as I tried to push past. "Th-th-th-that you, Billy?" Finally, he removed the godawful mask and I relaxed. Theo and me went way back. He was one of the good guys.

"Well, well, well, if it ain't little Billy J," he grinned as he crushed me in a clumsy hug. "What's a no-good scaredy-cat like you doin' out after dark?"

And so, I told him about my troubles with Lorrie, though I glossed over the rest. The less people who knew about the scam, the better. Theo's landlady was a bit strict about overnight visitors, he said, so a couch for the night was out the question.

"Come with me, man. I know just the place you can rest in peace." He signaled me to follow as he set off down the street.

"Are you crazy?" I sniggered uneasily as I eyeballed the gaping hole to an underground tunnel that stretched out in front of me. Several hours later, as I ventured into the pitch-black passage and lay down to sleep in the shadow of some of the world's most valuable real estate, I figured it must be me who was crazy.

I barely slept that night, my brain firing bullets as it suckered up a catalogue of hidden threats inside the tunnel and my body ached from lying on the damp, hard floor. Using my bag as a pillow to protect my stuff, I lay still and listened to the sounds shifting through the hollow space: Tires rumbling on the highway overhead; water snaking down the walls and dripping to the floor; hushed voices racing down the tunnel and brushing over me like an invisible force. Even the buzz of mosquitos seemed loud as their eggs hatched on the stinking rain-water that settled in a wash of filth around me.

Eventually I nodded off, only to be woken by a voice so close I could hear the rattle of mucus in her lungs.

"Just a baby," she rasped, and my bones turned cold

as my groggy eyes wrestled with the decayed jungle of crooked teeth that loomed down at me like a hungry shark.

"Drink," she instructed, thrusting a scabby bottle of warm backwash into my hands. Dragging myself upright, I slowly unscrewed the cap and grudgingly placed my lips to the rim, my eyes all the while locked on the mountainous bulk watching closely behind her.

"You gonna find out what this trespassing piece of shit wants, or am I?" he grunted, shooting me evils out the corner of his eyes.

"Sssh." As she turned to silence him, I grabbed my bag and scrambled to my feet.

"Not so fast." The splinter of daylight that washed through the tunnel broke as he stepped forward and blocked my escape. "You might have managed to drag your skinny little ass into our home uninvited, but you sure as hell ain't leavin' 'til I say so."

"Please," I begged, struggling to control my bladder as he stuck a hand in his pocket and pulled out a set of brass knuckles. "Theo said it would be OK."

"What's your name, boy?" he asked, picking at his teeth with the edge of a razor blade.

"B-billy," I stuttered, vaguely aware that I was starting to sound like Theo doing his Porky Pig impression.

"Ha! Billy the whizz!" His full-on belly laugh filled the hollow space and vibrated from the walls, and I hung my head in shame as the stink of my piss-soaked pants bombed the air.

"Ya get it?" he cackled to his companion. "Billy the wh…"

"Come." The woman beckoned with her hand,

seemingly uninfected by his lousy humor as I reluctantly followed her through the tunnel. "You'll have to excuse the mess though, honey. Me and Kit wasn't expecting company." She pulled back a curtain and my eyes flitted between the cruddy carpet that covered the floor to a wooden pallet littered with canned food and pots and pans, before finally settling on a stained mattress jacked-up on grocery carts.

"We got all modern conveniences here," she chuck-led, ushering me into the tiny space. "Even running water." She pointed to a plastic container collecting rainwater that dripped from the ceiling.

"We got running rats an' all," Kit grumbled, as the sound of claws skittled across the floor. His initial aggression was just a front as it turned out. Act soft and people soon mistake your kindness for weakness.

"How about ya get yerself cleaned up while Nina here sorts somethin' to eat?" He handed me a pair of oversized sweatpants and pointed to a partitioned-off cubbyhole behind the bed.

"You listen up and you listen good," Nina told me a short while later as I sat on a crate and watched her warm a pot of soup with a propane torch. "You got nothin' to fear down here, not even this chump." She flashed Kit a toothy grin. "Only the water. You hear water, you get out fast cos if that don't kill you, the speeding debris will."

I ended up moving in with Nina and Kit and lived with them right up until the night of my father's murder. They taught me everything I needed to know about surviving in the tunnels and a whole lot more. They taught me about humanity. Respect. Each day spent with them was one less day I missed the outside world.

We got along good and everything was sweet until one day things took an unexpected turn. Waking early to raised voices at the entrance of the tunnel and construction work above my head, I grabbed my headlamp and went to see what was happening.

The street was busy, preparations for the New Year well underway. Workers set up barricades to protect the crowds from errant vehicles, and officials checked out vantage points from rooftops ready for the spotters to take up their slots. I walked a short distance unobserved, the workmen all too preoccupied to notice me, but then I skidded to a halt. Up ahead, laborers were welding down manholes as Metro searched the tunnels and moved the occupants on. I raced back down the street to alert Nina and Kit.

"Come with us," Nina cried, tugging at my sleeve, but my firmly rooted feet refused to budge. I'd heard all about the shelters where you couldn't even risk shutting your eyes for fear of being beaten, robbed, or worse. Maybe, if I'd known it would be the last I'd ever see of either of them, things might have been different, but instead I reluctantly made my way back to the old family home.

It was years later when I found out Nina hadn't acted on her own advice. Swallowed up by a storm that puked vehicles across the street like an upended Mikado board, she never stood a chance. Word had it Kit returned to Texas, but I can't see him leaving her behind and with no washed-up body, I'll never know for sure if he made it out alive.

CHAPTER NINETEEN

Thursday, August 22, 2019 (08:30)

"Don't get angry, get even." Nigel couldn't rid his mind of Billy's final words as he'd stalked out the Lucky Plaza in pursuit of the man the press was calling "Papa Smurf." He had been following the reports closely. According to the latest updates, the police were now hinting at a possible connection between the attack and that of the female reporter who was found dead in the hotel pool earlier that same evening.

He seared another shrimp with his fork and stared idly at it before placing it in his mouth and chewing thoughtfully. If he wasn't going to take the easy way out after all—even if it had been anything *but* easy as it turned out—he really was going to have to do something about his ever-expanding waistline. The idea that he could attempt to win back his wife in his current physical condition was frankly laughable, but it was so difficult. Everything in Vegas was big. The buildings, the people, the food portions. Even the restaurant where he was sat—one of five within the hotel complex—had enough seating for several hundred people.

His eyes settled on the breakfast buffet, where more than thirty separate serving stations stared tantalizingly back at him. Made-to-order omelets, wood-fired Neapolitan pizzas, prime Aberdeen Angus fillets, zesty fish tacos, oysters, mussels, peel-and-eat shrimps. New England Clam Chowder, Alaskan king crab legs, Chinese dim-sum, sushi, sashimi, caviar, and a sweet counter that was bursting at the seams with waffles, pancakes, donuts, and cakes. The list seemed endless, and he was only human. A bowl of cereal and a slice of toast would have sufficed, but he hadn't been able to resist. Once upon a time, his wife would have joked that he had eyes bigger than his belly as he filled his plate for the umpteenth time. *Not anymore,* he thought ruefully as he glared down in disgust at his protruding gut. The only saving grace was that even the plates were ridiculously large, which at least meant fewer walks of shame to and from the serving counter.

She'll soon tire of him, he attempted to reassure himself. He just had to hold firm and stand his ground until she came around. Which she would. Hopefully. Until such a time, he had no desire to return home where stifling reminders of her and how happy they had once been would threaten to suffocate him, so he had decided to extend his stay at Foo Dogs indefinitely.

"Don't get angry, get even." Billy's words filtered into his brain again. A murderer, though? However hard Nigel tried, he couldn't draw a parallel with the guy he had met at the roulette table and the one being depicted on every local news channel. This was a man who had inadvertently saved a life, not taken one. Billy might not know it yet, but he had given Nigel a reason to live. A purpose. Something to focus on other than his failed

marriage and impending suicide. Fixated on his wife's indiscretions, Nigel had allowed the business to slide over recent months, but Billy might be just the fix his ailing company needed. He closed his eyes a moment and allowed himself to picture the headlines:

INNOCENT
Highly Coveted Defense Attorney Forfeits Fee and Justice is Served

Nigel didn't normally focus on a client's potential guilt—that was the role of the jury. His job was to quietly plant a seed of doubt in their minds. *Beyond all reasonable doubt.* Those were the rules, and if he could create enough uncertainty to allow a client to walk free from court, his work was done. This client would be different, though. For starters, there was no saying Billy would even want his help and certainly no guarantee he would accept it. Always in high demand and used to cherry-picking his jobs, Nigel now found himself in unfamiliar territory. Which category would Billy fall into? Would he be the type of person who would do anything to avoid being caught, or would he secretly yearn detection so he could gain the recognition and notoriety he believed he deserved?

If he's even guilty, he reminded himself. Aware of the need to establish *who* Billy was, Nigel had spent much of the previous evening on his laptop in his room attempting to do just that. *Don't get angry, get even:* a statement that would be used against him if the courts got wind of his threat just seconds before he followed Mario out of the Lucky Plaza, and Nigel was determined to uncover the driving force behind the sentiment.

Mario Brown was, without doubt, a dubious character, but since the police hadn't managed to find anything on him that would stick, Nigel had decided to concentrate his efforts on the reporter instead. Maddison Scott was clearly an individual who didn't shy away from contention. Scathing articles boasting her name in the bylines flooded the internet and yet he couldn't find anything useful about Maddison herself. About to give up, he had then struck upon a website loaded with archived press releases dating back to the early 1990s. Rapidly creating an account and logging in, he then began to wade his way backwards from the date that Google was founded. It hadn't taken him long to find what he was looking for.

WHO'S LAUGHING NOW?
"Laughing Boy" to Serve a Minimum of Twenty Years

Adding his PayPal details to the new account, he had then downloaded every single article he could find relating to a case known as the "Midnight Massacre," and the boy that the dead reporter had branded the "Laughing Boy." *Billy Jackson.* Time might age the skin, but the eyes never changed and there was no doubt in Nigel's mind that he was looking at the same individual.

CHAPTER TWENTY

1997-1998

BILLY

NOTHING MUCH HAD CHANGED. IF ANYTHING, THE place was in worse shape and the only clue the house hadn't been abandoned was Ma's rickety old wicker chairs that sat proudly on the crumbled porch under a busted security light. Layers of flaking paint still held the building together and, as I yanked open the gate to the junk-filled yard, I stumbled backward as the rusted screws gave way. It didn't even look like anybody had mowed the grass since I'd been gone, so I figured the neighbors must have missed me.

Any hope that my father might have mellowed with time also soon evaporated.

"You... no... good... piece... of... shit." Each word he spat was shadowed by a strike of rawhide that tore through my flesh and added to the map of scars already tattooed across my skin.

"Five minutes, else I'm leavin' without you." Ma's

impatience scorched the air, saving me from further misery.

"We ain't finished," he hissed as he slowly and deliberately re-attached the belt to his pants. "Now get yerself cleaned up and over to the O'Haras as fast as those skinny little legs can carry ya. Your ma's already told half the neighborhood you're back and I won't have you make her look a fool."

"The boys are gonna meet us there, honey," he said as he joined her at the base of the stairs—the super-stoked assassin all smiles again as he readied himself to escort Cinderella to the ball.

I shouldn't have hung around and if I'd known what I know now I wouldn't have. Nate stayed too and with each beer he destroyed the more edgy he became.

"He's gonna kill you," he whispered as he rocked back and forth in the chair like a sick dopefiend who couldn't feed the greedy gorilla on his back.

"He won't kill no one. I just said that to freak you out." It was me who first put the idea into his mind that Angelino would bury us in the desert if he ever got wind that we crossed him.

"Not him. *FATHER!*" He leapt to his feet and furiously paced the floor. "We have to cut him loose else he'll beat us to it."

"Are you outta your tiny mind?" I wanted to believe it was the beer talking, but his face told a different story.

"Dead men can't tell no tales." He couldn't meet my eye, which was always a bad sign.

"No one's killing no one, so get your sorry little ass to bed and we'll talk once you've got your shit together." As I watched my brother climb the stairs, it occurred to me that I no longer recognized the person he'd become.

Sleep didn't come easy and the click of the latch as it snapped quietly into place was all it took to jolt me back to reality and alert me that Father was home. Alone. No hushed whispers or drunken giggles. No clatters of furniture or anguished squeals as Ma knocked into something.

I held my breath and listened to the whir of the refrigerator as the door opened and closed, followed by the telltale hiss and clunk as he opened a beer, downed the contents, and tossed the empty bottle in the garbage. Then, the rhythmic clumping of heavy boots on the wooden floor began as he slowly climbed the stairs, each step matching the thumping in my chest.

Clutching my switchblade firmly in the palm of my hand, I crept toward the door and backed myself behind the opening as far as the wall allowed. Crouched motionless, I silently watched his shadow form at the door, blocking out the light that entered the room through the crack underneath. I didn't know if he was coming for me or if Nate was his target, but as the floorboard outside my room creaked and the door slowly inched open, I had my answer.

The clock on my nightstand flashed 00:02 when the first bullet was fired, closely followed by a series of pellets as the shooter went all-out crazy. I didn't move— I couldn't—and my stupor was only busted when a door slammed, and footsteps heeled it on the path outside. Even then, I don't think I ever moved so sluggish my whole life as I peeled myself out from behind the door.

The first thing I noticed was the blood. It was everywhere—the walls, the floor, even the goddamned ceiling. Bits of Father's brain and flesh were added to the mix, shaking off any doubts I might have had. The king-sized heap of crap was dead. It was a time to celebrate; to laugh and joke and toast whoever had put us out our misery, but then I noticed something far more troubling. Right next to our father's body lay a hunting pistol, identical to his own. It could only mean a couple things: Either he'd intended to use it on me and it somehow backfired, but that wouldn't explain the other shots I heard, or someone else with access to the rifle had fired it.

We have to cut him loose. Nate's words wormed around my skull. "Nate?" I called out. "NATE!" I was talking to myself; my brother was long gone.

"What did you do?" I stepped over the body to retrieve the pistol.

"Hold it right there." My head jerked up and my eyes settled on the muzzle of the cop's gun, directed straight at me.

"It's not how it looks," I muttered, mindful how stupid I sounded, but Dutthie, the cop, knew me. He knew I wasn't capable of something so twisted.

"Why don't you put the gun down?" It was a request that stank of authority. Not really a request at all. For one split second, I considered blowing out his brains too and getting the hell out of there, but what then? If I cleared out, there would be nothing standing between my brother and prison. Nate had killed our father; I was sure of it and unfortunately he hadn't hung around long enough to convince me otherwise.

CHAPTER TWENTY-ONE

Thursday, August 22, 2019 (11:30)

"Where's the footage?" The heels of Angelino's Oxfords tapped on the hardwood floor as he pushed past Ethan and stalked into the apartment.

"I couldn't retrieve it," Ethan said, his fingers gently caressing the memory stick in his pocket as he followed his employer into the open-plan living space. He still hadn't decided what to do with the stick. Withholding information from the cops wouldn't end well if he was caught, but he couldn't figure out how to provide it without coming clean about his involvement with Mario.

"Why should I believe you?" Angelino's eyes swept suspiciously over the high-end fixtures and furnishings before finally settling on Ethan. Situated just one block from the Strip, the apartment boasted panoramic floor-to-ceiling views, a 24-hour concierge, private express elevator and a fitness center with heated pool and tennis courts. It was *not* the type of place that a Director of Surveillance could afford on wages alone.

"I only rent the pad," Ethan said, noting Angelino's distrust.

"Well, you might want to have a word with your landlord about the air conditioning," he sniped, fanning his shirt to cool himself down.

"I'm awaiting a call-back from maintenance," Ethan replied.

"Look after you well, does he?" Angelino mocked. "Scratch your back just so long as you scratch his?" Angelino had done his research and had been furious to discover that Ethan's apartment was owned by Mario Brown.

"Beer?" Ethan asked, briskly changing the subject as he crossed the room to relieve the fridge of a couple of cans. It was early even by his standards, but he sure could use something to settle his nerves. Having witnessed Billy Jackson on film closely watching Mario's every move in the casino, finally following him out just moments before he was attacked, he hadn't been able to sleep. How had he missed him? *Too busy watching Mario's antics, that's how.*

"Want to tell me how you came to be in cahoots with Mario?" Angelino inquired innocently as he accepted the beer and rolled the cold can against his cheeks and forehead.

"You have to trust me." Ethan cracked his can and took a large slug. "I never knew anything about his hustling."

Trust me. Angelino released an involuntary shudder as the all-familiar anger bubbled in his gut. Trust was some- thing to be earned and Ethan had done nothing of late to deserve the privilege. Also unable to sleep, Angelino had given the situation a lot of thought during the early hours and had reached two possible scenarios: Ethan was either complicit—in which case, he would see to it personally that he paid handsomely—or he had attacked Mario for the money and then deleted the footage to avoid being caught.

The more Angelino thought about it, the more the second option made sense. There was no way that Ethan's monthly wage would cover his rent, but maybe he knew his landlord was cheating the casino so decided to line his own pockets with the ill-gotten gains? He suppressed the urge to grin at the notion. Perhaps Ethan wasn't such a lost cause after all?

"You know how this looks?" Angelino asked. "Mario was stealing from me and next thing you know, he's laying in the gutter. They'll think I'm involved but it was you, wasn't it? You took the money to pay for all this." He directed an accusing finger at the ridiculously over-sized television as he spoke.

Ethan reached into his pocket and squeezed the memory stick between his clenched fist. He needed to let Angelino know that it was Billy who stole the money without implicating himself, but how?

"I don't care about Mario, and I don't care what the cops think," Angelino lied when he didn't respond. "I just want my money back," he nudged, determined to coax Ethan into admitting his guilt.

Don't we all, Ethan thought as he swiped at the sweat building on the back of his neck. He hadn't risked everything to walk away with nothing, but what choice did he have? He could tell his employer the truth or he could tell the cops. Either way, he wouldn't see the money again and would be forced to admit that he had deleted the footage… and why.

CHAPTER TWENTY-TWO

1998

BILLY

Everything went against me the moment we arrived at the Detention Center where I would be held until sentencing. The press—or to be exact, one hard-nosed low-life from the press—was waiting. Tipped off by the cops who came by the house to arrest me, Maddison Scott captured my arrival on film and produced what can only be described as a spiteful, misleading image that instantly convinced everyone of my guilt.

You'd think people would know better than to believe what they read in the tabloids, wouldn't you? Words that aren't worth the paper they're written on. Words created by low-grade novelists who make stuff up as they go along so their stories sound better and more interesting than they really are. Thanks to Maddison Scott and her relentless character assassinations, it didn't take long for people to jump to conclusions. The wrong conclusions.

The agitated gorilla leading the interview the night of my arrest was named Burt, though his sidekicks called him Fish which was curious. A nickname can tell you a lot about a person. Everything you need to know sometimes. It turned out he got his name playing poker which was kind of screwed up. He couldn't detect a liar during a simple game of cards but thought he could do better during a cop shop interrogation.

Fish did his best to finger me for the murder. So many loaded questions—fired as fast as the bullets that spread our father's brain about the joint that night—and it didn't matter how many times I told him he'd got the wrong guy, he wasn't listening.

"Tell me about the gun." His gut spilled from the waist of his pants as he leaned back in his chair and rested his legs on the interview table.

"Stupid chump was always leaving it lying around," I replied.

"So, you don't deny you had access to your father's gun?"

"Me and just about everyone else who came by the house." This wasn't strictly true but convinced of Nate's guilt, I had to make him think otherwise.

"And was there anyone else at the house tonight?"

"No." Afraid he'd see right through me I couldn't look him in the eye.

"Care to explain how your father wound up getting shot by someone other than you if nobody else crossed the threshold?" The argumentative ape had a comeback for everything. "Where was your brother tonight?" He glared at me bug-eyed, and I inwardly cussed my transparency.

"It's New Year's Eve," I shrugged. "I guess he had someplace else to be."

"But *you* didn't?" he pressed. "You know what I think? I think you planned it. *"He deserved it."* Those are the words you said to the arresting officer, are they not?" He made a scene of studying the notes on the table in front of him. "You didn't like your father much, did you?" he asked after a short delay. "I think you knew he'd return home solo and you seized your moment. Your parents often came home separately, didn't they?"

"No," I shook my head fiercely.

"No, you didn't plan it, or no, they didn't often come home separately?"

On, and on, and on. Twisting my words as only a cop can do and after a while, I gave up trying to convince him of my innocence.

Dutthie's written testimony didn't help. He swore he'd seen me fire the fatal shot that killed our father but that wasn't possible, so if he truly believed he'd seen me shoot, then it was Nate that he saw. And why would he lie? He was a neighbor. A friend. A cop.

Was it any wonder everyone was so quick to believe my guilt when I was just as quick to accept my brother's? It was only after—when I was locked up and had little else to do but think—that I realized Dutthie's story didn't stack up. If he had witnessed things like he said, he'd have also known that the shooter fled the scene. And another thing: they say every picture paints a story, so why did Dutthie look so pleased when he came by the house and found me like he did?

The public defender assigned to my case was Elizabeth Angel. I liked her. She had this way about her that made you trust her, and I suppose, I wanted to believe that she was an angel. It didn't take long for me to learn that she was anything but.

"They've agreed to a lesser sentence if you plead guilty," she told me one day.

"But I'm innocent," I replied.

"Billy," she shook her head and gave me the benefit of one of her reassuring smiles that I later discovered were worth jack shit. "Your prints were all over the weapon that a cop saw you fire, *and* by your own admission, your father deserved everything he got."

"A cop *says* he saw me fire the gun," I snarled between gritted teeth, pissed as hell that I'd somehow got myself a lawyer who was more interested in getting a plea deal than proving my innocence.

"Same thing," she shuffled the papers on her desk as she spoke. "They've got you between a rock and a hard place, sweetheart. Either you plead guilty and take the lesser sentence, or you're going down for life… or worse." She was talking about lethal injection and we both knew it.

"So, what's in it for them? If they're so sure I did it and can secure a conviction, why offer me a deal?"

"Trials cost big bucks, Billy. There's always the risk they could lose. Officer Dutthie's evidence and the prints are all they've got… ignoring your obvious delight about your father's demise. It's strong, very strong, but a jury *might* not agree that it's enough to prove your guilt beyond all reasonable doubt."

"Meaning I could win." I glared at her, trying to understand why she was so eager for me to plead guilty when I had the chance to walk out the courthouse a free man.

"And you could lose," she replied, cold as a grave.

"It's a gamble, Billy, but the odds are heavily stacked against you and I'm not sure you can afford to take the risk."

What would Nate do? The million-dollar question with no answer rocked my eardrums. What Nate *would* do, and what Nate *should* do weren't the same thing, and I was only in this situation because of him. The resentment started to eat away at me. I was saving his skin and he was doing fuck all to save mine. And what about Ma? How would she take the news that I'd supposedly shot Father? And what about my wife? You only had to mention my name to Lorrie these days and she'd look at you like she'd choked on citrus, so this was sure to send her over the edge. To everyone who mattered, I'd be guilty when I was no such thing.

"So, what kind of sentence are we talking if I agree?" I finally asked, licking my lips hesitantly as I waited for her answer.

"Twenty-five years or thereabouts." As she eyeballed me from her pulpit, I had no reason to doubt her. "The judge has the final say on the exact sentence once we agree on the deal. It's a good offer, Billy," she motored on when I didn't respond. "With parole you could be out sooner."

"How soon?" I asked as I tried to weigh the options.

"Ten years. Fifteen, if you're unlucky," she replied. "Take it to trial however, and you're looking at life without parole at best. It's your life—or lack of it—your choice," she shrugged, pushing her papers away from her nonchalantly.

It was blackmail, but eventually I nodded my consent. It was the only way to protect my brother and I owed him that. I never should have left him alone with that monster and moved in with Lorrie and if I hadn't, things might not have got so bad he'd done what he did. On October 16, 1998, I was sentenced to life in prison with the possibility of parole after twenty years. *Possibility*. I didn't like that word at all. Convinced my ears were deceiving me, I stared in horror at Elizabeth, and you know what? The bitch grinned back. I'd just traded the truth for my life and was going to wear my admission of guilt like a tattoo I couldn't laser off, and all she could do was fucking smile!

As the bailiffs led me away and my eyes zeroed in on her, I struggled to check the impulse to take a swing and split her skull with my cuffs, but one thing was for sure. One day, I was going to make her pay for what she'd done.

CHAPTER TWENTY-THREE

Thursday, August 22, 2019 (11:30)

ELIZABETH ANGEL WAS DOING HER BEST TO IGNORE THE haunted reflection that glared back at her from the mirrored interior of the elevator walls. The lack of air in the confined space was overwhelming and her skin glistened with sweat under the harsh lighting that bounced from the walls around her.

The hunger had died down hours ago, replaced instead with a dull ache and the occasional fit of nausea, but the thirst still raged in her throat and her tongue kept sticking to the roof of her mouth. She'd tried everything to relieve the sensation, even licking at her skin to pool enough moisture to enable her to swallow, but nothing seemed to work.

Cell phone clasped firmly in the palm of her hand, her fingers clamored at the screen as she attempted to light up the display, but it was useless. The battery had finally given out and she inwardly cursed her earlier impatience as she had repeatedly searched for a signal. Deep down she had known she should ration the use to conserve it but hadn't even considered that she could be trapped in this hellhole for days.

She sank to the ground in defeat, closing her eyes and focusing instead on the all-encompassing silence, the only audible sound, her own breathing. In, out. In, out. In, out. *You'll be out of here in no time,* the voice in her head assured her. *But how?* The other voice argued. *Nobody knows you're here.* At first, she had liked the voices—they had been strangely reassuring—but as time went on, the endless chatter as they continually bickered amongst themselves had started to grate on her already tattered nerves.

The second voice was right, of course. Who would miss her? Her soon to be ex-husband Isaac would, she supposed, but for all the wrong reasons. The recent breakup had seen to that, and he was no doubt currently luxuriating in their beautiful home as he pandered to his new lover's every whim. A home that Elizabeth had predominantly funded and paid for. She had assumed—wrongly, as it turned out—that he would know better than to pick a fight about assets with one of the most sought-after attorneys in the city, and the prospect of the embarrassing public wrangle that was sure to follow when she finally admitted to her colleagues that she needed their help didn't bear thinking about.

The anger began to well in the pit of her stomach again. If it wasn't for Isaac, she wouldn't be in this predicament. He should have been the one to move out, not her, and if she hadn't returned home early that night to find him in bed—their marital bed—with that slut, none of this would be happening. She wouldn't have felt so sickened that for the first time in years, she had been forced to take the annual leave entitlement she normally forfeited. How could her colleagues miss and report her absence if they weren't expecting her in the office? She wouldn't even be in this godforsaken elevator if it wasn't for him! She would be at home—her proper home—engaging in all the mundane tasks that normal married women did in an effort to juggle their career and family life.

Someone will report it out of action soon, the more positive of the two voices reminded her and for a moment she allowed herself to believe it. But then a small sliver of uncertainty coursed through her brain as she recalled the sales particulars. *Exclusive use of a private express elevator that transports clientele to and from the rooftop Penthouse Suite within seconds.*

She slammed her fist on the floor in frustration as she remembered the conversation with the agent that had followed, instantly regretting the action as a shock of pins and needles surged through her fingers.

"But surely, it's open to abuse?" she had asked. "Won't people use it anyway if there's no one there to police it?"

"Don't you worry your pretty little head about that ma'am," the salesman had smiled knowingly as he rocked back and forth on the soles of his shiny shoes. "They couldn't use it even if they wanted to. There are no openings on the other floors, see. Just a solid, concrete shaft."

A solid, concrete shaft. The agent's words reverberated in her ears and crouching to her knees, she placed her fingers as firmly as she could between the rubber seals that connected the doors as she tried yet again to wrench them open. Frozen in place, all she managed to achieve was two more broken fingernails and she nibbled irritably at them until they tore and made the delicate flesh beneath them bleed.

Transports clientele within seconds, the voice mocked. She'd only planned to grab her morning latte and a bucket of those irresistible bite-sized pretzels from the coffee shop around the corner, but according to her wristwatch, that was almost three days ago. Three days, captive inside this tiny box like a caged mouse with no food, no water, no damned bathroom and worse still, no indication whether anyone even knew she was trapped, let alone any hope of being released.

Elizabeth turned her attention back to the small emergency call box situated next to the panel beside the door, her fingers scrabbling in desperation around the empty container as though the handset could somehow have miraculously reappeared. Next, she stabbed at the alarm panel again but was met with further silence. Was it even working? She had no idea whether she could expect to hear the alarm sound from within her bullet-proof jail but if the lights were working, then why not the alarm?

"Help!" she tried to call out but no sound except for a racking cough escaped her lips. It was a waste of time and energy anyway, she knew that. If she couldn't hear anything outside, why would anyone be able to hear her on the inside?

As the fear threatened to explode in her chest, her bladder also chose that moment to rebel again. As it cried out at the unnecessary pressure being placed on it, her eyes scanned the ceiling, horrified at the prospect of CCTV, and being watched later by an unknown set of depraved eyes. It was all so degrading and undignified, but what choice did she have? Slowly pulling down her underwear, she lifted her skirt and crouched in the corner, her nose wrinkling in disgust at the stench as the liquid pooled around her feet.

Too exhausted to fight further, Elizabeth collapsed back to the floor and lay down in her own urine. It wasn't as though she could humiliate herself any more than she had already been forced to do, and what did it matter? There was no one to help her, no knight in shining armor to rescue her from the inevitable. She was going to die in this lousy elevator and there was absolutely nothing she could do to prevent it.

CHAPTER TWENTY-FOUR

2004

BILLY

YOU SHOULD NEVER SEPARATE TWINS. THE RESULT WILL always be messy. Kind of like trying to separate yolk from the white of an egg. It's not actually possible to carry out the procedure without leaving one part with the other.

A local rancher found Nate's body hanging from a rafter in his barn, his eyes bulging vacantly from his skull and a line of dried spit caked between his jaw and snapped neck. The words, *"he isn't guilty, he didn't do it,"* had been painted on the floor beneath him with a broken twig and some old paint that had been stored on a shelf in the barn.

I didn't grieve at first. I was too angry. I gave up my life so Nate could have his and it had all been for nothing. Nate could have confessed. He *should* have confessed. The truth could have set me free but instead, he'd left me to take the rap for his crime.

CHAPTER TWENTY-FIVE

Friday, August 23, 2019 (02:48)

ALFRED COULDN'T SLEEP BUT THIS WAS NOTHING NEW. IN prison, he hadn't been able to sleep either. Fear, and the overwhelming sense of dread had seen to that. The very same emotions that now kept him awake as he tossed and turned on an old mattress that sagged beneath his weight.

It wasn't so much the image of the bloated body he'd hauled from the pool at Foo Dogs that was invading his dreams. More, the parting threat from the detective as it echoed relentlessly around his skull. *We might need to speak with you again.* Any conversation with the cops would bring trouble, but it wasn't as though he had any choice in the matter.

He glanced at the time on the clock-radio he'd rescued from a dumpster outside the Hard Rock: 02:48. At least three more hours before the first sign of daylight snuck through the gaps in the paper-thin fabric he'd taped to the window in a futile attempt to block out the early morning sun.

"You've done nothing wrong," he tried to reassure

himself, instantly grimacing at the irony. He'd done plenty wrong and now it was all set to backfire.

THE STRIP HAD ALWAYS REMINDED HIM OF BASKETBALL. All that ducking and diving around the enemy to defend the ultimate goal. That August afternoon in '92, as the temperatures soared well above one hundred it was no different. Despite the sweltering heat, costumed impersonators lined the sidewalk, and the only remaining space was jammed with tourists clutching margaritas as tall as their eldest child as they paused to watch the action.

Alfred and Billy took the nearest escalator up and over the freeway, the bridge full of the usual suspects: Luciana, the Latino who sold knock off water for a dollar; Florian with his fake designer sunglasses; and homeless Harry, the Vietnam vet who danced for money. Each of them ready to pack up and run at the first sign of the cops. Harry had lost both his legs to a landmine but that never stopped him. Using his hands as supports on the floor and swinging his torso through them, he could still move faster on his stumps than the others when he had to.

As Billy stopped to watch Harry do somersaults across the bridge for his mesmerized audience, Alfred— determined to catch up with the others—went on ahead.

"Escalator's broken down," Billy called out moments later, his knuckles turning white as he gripped the stair rail with enough force to snap it.

"C'mon buddy, we ain't got all day!" Alfred yelled

back, the threat of what would happen if they were late burning his brain.

"Can't," Billy shouted, his feet firmly rooted to the spot at the top of the stairs. "It's bad luck."

Superstitious little freak. "Either you quit this shit, or I go without you," he warned, but as the never-ending procession of feet filtered up the steps in the opposite direction, Billy refused to budge.

Whose stupid idea was it to invite him along? The kid was a liability. *Whose stupid idea was the dumbass initiation cere-mony?* He inwardly cussed the mess he'd got himself into. Everything about Sin City Boyz was dumb; the name, the members, not least the crazy stuff they did and if Billy didn't get a grip sometime soon, the pair of them would be laughing stocks.

"Bock, bock, bock, bock, bock, bock, bo-ooock." Right on cue, he turned to see their leader flapping his arms as he impersonated a chicken and rounded the bend, the rest of the gang hot on his tail.

"Come on," he begged through gritted teeth as Billy made no attempt to move. "They'll rip us both new assholes if you don't step on it!"

Finally, Billy made a run for it, slamming into people in his haste to get to the bottom of the stairs and Alfred sighed with relief as they cornered the bend in pursuit of the others… and then he froze.

"What's up lil' girl? You scared of a stuffed doll?" The gang leader's hot breath tickled the back of Alfred's neck as he stood and eyeballed the mannequin on the sidewalk in front of him, the robotic eyes of a perfectly preserved corpse burning deep into his flesh.

Six years old again; huddled beneath the blankets and studying shadows bouncing across the wall in the moonlight—his baby sister curled up to him, her icy cold hand clutched in rigor to his own.

"It blinked," he mumbled, unable to tear his eyes from the living statue's penetrating glare. Ever since his sister died in his arms that night, Alfred had struggled with an irrational fear of the living dead.

"You bet it did, you creep," Billy drawled.

"What did you say?" He spun to face Billy, fighting the urge to smash his ugly mug into the asphalt. He'd stood by this jerk only seconds before and this was how he repaid him?

"Look around you, what d'ya see?" Billy grabbed the bucket of tips from the floor and waved the pitcher under the living statue's nose, but he didn't react. Not so much as a wink or blink. Disappointed by the lack of reaction and determined to goad him, Billy took a handful of coins from the bucket and pocketed them, but Mannequin Man still didn't flicker.

"It ain't real," the gang leader joined in. "See?" Stepping forward, he slapped the man across the face, a deep red welt instantly forming on his heavily made-up cheek but still, he remained rigid, his blank expression giving nothing away.

"Nothing to see here except a dummy," he pressed on, kicking the tub from Billy's hands, and sending the remaining coins scattering across the street.

"Why not settle it once and for all?" Blade—silent until that point—chuckled menacingly as he reached into the pocket of his pants and withdrew his namesake.

The rest of it happened quick. Too quick to make sense of what was about to happen before it was too late. The flick of the switchblade as it was released from its catch, the blinding glint of metal, the tear of flesh as the steel grated against bone, and the gurgling sound of a blocked drain as blood flooded the living statue's lungs and suffocated him. All of it over in less than a minute.

Four lousy years serving a prison sentence for a crime he didn't commit before the Supreme Court threw out the conviction due to a lack of evidence. Four lousy years to think, but Alfred still lacked answers. Why didn't Mannequin Man do something to prove Billy right instead of just standing there? And why didn't the others speak up and clear his name when they had the chance?

Finding somewhere to work when he was released had been nigh on impossible. Nobody wanted to employ a convicted felon, least of all, one with no qualifications or experience, who had escaped his sentence on a technicality. The question was pretty much standard on every application form: *Have you ever been convicted of a crime?* It was pointless trying to deny it. It wasn't as though they wouldn't run checks on him. It might have been nice though, if they'd left enough space on the form for applicants to explain the full nature of their alleged crime and whether they had in fact been wrongly convicted.

Mud sticks, his ma would say, when he complained. And it did. Just like the paste he used to seal the glitter to the greeting cards he made in the prison's art class to send home, the mess of his past was almost impossible to rid from his skin. While prospective employers couldn't legally discriminate, they always found a way.

The answer to his problems had eventually come

from his ma; the only person to remain firm in the belief that he was innocent.

"There's a security job available at Foo Dogs," she announced one evening over dinner.

"The new casino?" he asked, his belly cramping with excitement before reality kicked in. "Nobody's going to employ the likes of me, Ma."

"You need to get creative, that's all." She gave him a cheeky wink as she rose from the table and approached him. "Be a bit loose with the truth and you'll have 'em eating out your hand."

He scowled as she kissed his cheek affectionately. "You're asking me to lie?"

"Do you want a place to call your own, or not?" she asked. He did. He craved it.

"Well, that settles it then," she said when he didn't answer. "What your pa don't know can't hurt him," she added, as though reading his mind as she carried the empty plates to the sink and plugged and filled it with soapy water. "It can be our little secret."

Forging his identity and documents hadn't been that difficult as it turned out. He'd made some useful contacts in prison and within days, he was booted and suited and patrolling the grounds of the new Foo Dogs, Resort and Casino. *Alfred Turner.* The name had a nice ring to it, and it no longer mattered what people thought of the 'old him'. That person was now buried in the past.

Pretending to be someone he wasn't hadn't been so easy. Physically, he was up to the role. There had been little else to do behind bars except visit the prison gym, but mentally, he struggled. Every moment at work seemed to involve a more extravagant performance than the nightly shows laid on by management for the customers, and *trust* was a word he'd long since forgotten. Sometimes, he thought prison had been easier. Granted, he'd still had to watch his back, but at least he knew what people wanted from him. Now, he couldn't even talk for fear of giving something away, and friendships were out the question. How was he supposed to build relationships when everything he said and did was the product of a lie?

He needn't have worried. His employer managed to uncover the truth anyway, and in return for his silence and continued employment, issued him an impossible ultimatum that would change all their lives forever.

CHAPTER TWENTY-SIX

2006

BILLY

I DIDN'T GET MANY VISITORS IN PRISON, BUT SOMETIME after Nate's death, I had a request from a dude named Bo Purdy. I can't deny being curious. I mean, I didn't know anyone by that name, but maybe my brother had? Besides, like I said, I didn't get many visitors and it got kind of lonely, so I figured why not?

Bo sat across the table sucking air like a beached fish. "Do I know you?" I eventually asked. It felt stupid having to ask, but there was something familiar about him I couldn't place and he sure as hell hadn't ever served me at the local drive-thru or behind the counter at Walmart's.

"I have reason to believe you were acquainted with my dad." He picked nervously at an invisible fleck of lint on the leg of his pants. "Tobias?"

"Nope." I shook my head, struggling to hide my disappointment that the visit was about to end before it even started. "I'm sorry buddy, but I think you wasted a trip."

"About the time your troubles started, I think you met him at Angelino's. It's a casino on the…"

"I know what it is," I interrupted, "but I don't recall ever meeting your father." And yet, I couldn't rid my gut of the uneasy feeling of familiarity when I first clapped eyes on Bo.

"I understand that you entered into an agreement with him?" He tried to pull his chair closer to the table, but it was fixed to the floor. "He was a slot attendant."

I froze as the memory maggots crawled around my skull. *Cash out… Shift your ass… I'm due a break.*

"What of it?" I asked, eyeing Bo with disgust as he spat out his gum and stuck it on the underside of the table. One of my jobs was to remove that shit.

"He never came home that night. He never came home any night since. The night you got yourself evicted from Angelino's, my dad vanished."

"Maybe, he found himself a fancy piece to spend his ill-gotten gains on?" I suggested.

"No," he shook his head in denial. "He had him killed."

"Who?" I whispered, not wanting to draw the guard's attention. "Angelino Vitriano? No offense, dude, but murder's a big leap from your old man taking off."

"He wouldn't have just left, he loved us."

"People cheat all the time and trust me, Bo, your father *was* a cheat." My remark blew over his head like tumbleweed.

"He didn't even take his passport or a change of clothes, and his bank cards were never used."

"What did the cops say?" I wasn't buying his story

but talking to Bo sure beat sitting bored out my skull in my cell.

"Same old story," he replied, struggling to disguise his anger. "No evidence of foul-play, blah, blah, blah. After a while, when it was clear they weren't taking me seriously, I took matters into my own hands."

"Go on," I encouraged.

"Same name kept cropping up."

"Which was?" Being bored out my skull in my cell was becoming more appealing by the minute.

"Alfred Turner."

"Never heard of him. Look Bo, it's been fun meeting you but I'm kinda wondering what any of this has to do with me?"

"Don't you see?" He leaned forward and rested his elbows on the table, his eyes flashing with excitement. "The same person who killed my dad also killed yours."

"How d'ya work that out?" I side-eyed the guard, wondering what he made of the nutjob sitting opposite me.

"Why did your brother kill himself?"

My jaw clamped tight at the mention of Nate.

"He isn't guilty, he didn't do it, were his words on the note he left, yes?" he carried on, oblivious to my discomfort. "Your brother knew."

"Of course, he knew." I wrestled my shackles under the table, fighting to keep my hands under control. "Because *he* killed our father."

"No, he didn't," he replied, "but he knew who did."

"What are you talking about?" I lifted my cuffed hands and brushed away a stray tear with the back of my wrist. "Why are you fucking with my head?"

"Does the name Alan Dutthie mean anything to you?"

"What's that scrawny little crybaby got to do with anything?" I hissed.

"He's built like a brick shit house now."

"What about him?" I spat through clenched teeth.

"He killed your father."

"Make up your mind," I lowered my voice as the guard eyeballed me across the room. "Just now you said some guy named Alfred Turner did it, now it's Alan Dutthie?"

"Like puzzles did he, your brother?"

"You're nuts." I shifted uncomfortably in my seat and tried to get the guard's attention, but it was like he was suddenly, deliberately, ignoring me. "I want you to go now."

"He isn't guilty, he didn't do it," he cut me off as he repeated my brother's final words. "It's an anagram, Billy. Rearrange the letters and see what you have."

I didn't speak. No way could I figure it out without pen and paper.

"How does, 'Dutthie lying, the son did it,' grab you?"

"Alan Dutthie killed my father?" I repeated numbly.

"No matter how deep I dig, the same name crops up," he nodded. "Alan Dutthie—aka Alfred Turner—works for Angelino. He has for years."

"His father fingered me for the murder?" My brain crushed my skull as everything slotted into place.

"To protect his son from prison," he nodded again.

If it wasn't so crazy, it could almost have been funny. Angelino only had to ask, and I'd have been happy to do the job. Instead, I got the luxury of jailtime for someone else's crime. I wanted to shout and scream about what Bo had told me; demand the scum guarding and watching my every move release me and carry that filthy, lying son-of-a-bitch Dutthie to the cells.

As the bell rang to signal the end of the visit, Bo stood and attempted to shake my hand, but I swatted him away. The guards would have been all over us like a case of scabies if he got that close.

"You got an address?" I whistled through my teeth as he turned to leave.

"Check your mailbox," he winked. "Be sure to look me up if you ever get out this shithole."

I didn't know how to feel as I watched him walk away. I finally had answers and yet, trapped in prison, there was nothing I could do with the knowledge I'd been gifted.

CHAPTER TWENTY-SEVEN

Saturday, August 24, 2019 (15:45)

Elizabeth Angel's corpse had been removed from the elevator by the time Sergeant Burt Myers arrived at the scene, but the stench of stale urine and excrement lingered. As did the officers stationed at the entrance to keep the rapidly growing number of reporters and rubberneckers at bay.

Maddison Scott would have loved all this, he thought to himself as he ducked under the crime-scene ribbon that flapped in the tepid breeze. Crossing the foyer toward the "Closed for Maintenance" sign that was still positioned strategically outside the elevator, Burt was pleased to see that Detective Karl Andrews was still present. Karl had been the first detective on the scene, and his previous experience within the coroner's office made him one of the more accomplished criminologists that his unit had to offer.

"Looks like rain's coming," Burt commented, slapping Karl gently on the shoulder in greeting.

"We can but hope," he replied, swiping the back of

his wrist against the thin layer of perspiration that had formed on his forehead.

"First impressions?" Burt asked, observing a Crime Scene Investigator he didn't recognize studying a kaleidoscope of scratch marks that lined the interior of the elevator walls.

"Crime Scene Destruction Team were as helpful as ever," Karl quipped in response. Focused on saving lives, the paramedics were never as rigorous when it came to protecting crime scenes.

"How long was she trapped?" Burt asked.

"Up to a week," Karl replied, his eyes scanning the small prison as he spoke.

"A week?" An involuntary shudder rattled Burt's bones.

"Concierge found her. Dennis is interviewing him now but from what I could glean, he left to visit family in North Carolina last weekend and today was his first day back. He noticed the 'Closed for Maintenance' sign, reckoned there'd been no instructions left for him about any servicing works, and so he called the office only to discover that his replacement hadn't turned in."

"And they didn't think to send anyone else?" Burt asked, his tone riddled with contempt.

"Something about a computer glitch and the system not registering the pre-authorized leave," Karl replied.

"So, nobody was even aware that the building was unmanned for a whole week?" Burt shook his head in disbelief.

"Seemingly not," Karl said. "Although, we'll need to speak with them. If nothing else, to rule out the possibility that a member of their staff could have deliberately tampered with the system."

"I'm smelling a strong case of negligence against the homeowners' association."

"Different circumstances, and Elizabeth Angel would have been just the lawyer to take it on," Karl agreed before continuing. "With no work scheduled, the concierge decides to check out the elevator and that's when he realizes the power's been tripped. The electrics are all in that closet over there," he said, pointing to a small door behind the main desk. "Flicks the fuse and bingo, he can now open the doors, although I bet he wishes he hadn't."

"Emergency call box?" Burt eyed his colleague, struggling to comprehend how a person could find themselves trapped in an elevator without anyone knowing for any duration of time, let alone a week.

"Had been removed, and the circuit to the alarm had also been tripped but not the lights for some reason."

"Whoever did this deliberately wanted her to witness her own suffering?" Burt suggested.

"It's possible," Karl answered, disgust clouding his features.

"Do we have an estimated time of death?"

Karl scrolled through the litany of photographs on his iPhone before pausing at one of the victim's bloated body. "See those impressions?" Burt's eyes followed the direction of Karl's finger to some dark purple discolorations on the victim's chest. "Blood settled at least twelve hours prior to this photo, which was taken," he pressed a button as he spoke, "at exactly 11:48 this morning."

"Meaning?" Burt waited patiently for him to elaborate.

"Assuming the perpetrator didn't return to move the body, she was found in the position she took her last breath. According to this photo, she did that at least twelve hours before it was taken."

"At least? Surely, we can narrow it down better than that?"

"Considering her height, age, build and outside influences such as the temperature of her environment, our victim would have lasted about three days. Lab will be able to tell us more and, if we can ascertain when she was last seen alive, that will help narrow it down, but I'd say she'd been dead a couple of days before the concierge found her."

"Go on," Burt encouraged.

"Check this out." Karl enlarged the screen to its full capacity and Burt found himself viewing a short video of the deceased. In the video, a hand protected by a latex glove (that Burt assumed was Karl's) gingerly lifted one of the victim's arms. Holding it slightly elevated from the ground, the gloved hand then rapidly released it, an audible thud resonating from the device as the limb hit the floor. The procedure was then repeated, except this time, the gloved hand shook and wobbled the victim's hand around a little before once again allowing it to collapse to the ground.

"I'm thinking this goes against protocol?" Burt commented as he assessed the younger man quizzically. "What's your point, Karl, because while anyone who gets ahold of your cell in the interim might think you're a creepy little asshole, I know you'll have one?"

"Look again." As Karl dutifully reset the video at the relevant point and pressed the play icon on the screen,

Burt willed his tired and offended eyes to concentrate. "Hand's floppy at the wrist."

"Meaning that rigor mortis had come and gone," Burt stated as a matter of fact as the relevance sank in.

"Exactly," Karl pushed on. "Meaning we're talking some forty-eight hours after her heart caved for the body to be discovered."

"Out there," Burt sighed with exasperation as he pointed in the general direction of the Strip, "those rollercoasters and thrill rides installed to put the fear of God into tourists are death traps waiting to happen, but a trivial ride in an elevator?"

"She put up a good fight." Karl returned his attention to his cell, this time producing a close-up of the victim's mangled hands. "Wouldn't have done her any good, mind you," he grimaced. "Even if she had managed to wrench the doors open, the elevator only served the penthouse."

"You hinted earlier that you thought this was the work of our card killer?" Burt glanced over his shoulder as he spoke, checking to make sure that no one could overhear. The presence of the playing cards still hadn't been disclosed to the press and the name was very much an informal moniker being used solely within the department.

"We've got another one." Karl held up the tiny evidence bag that contained the card between his thumb and forefinger. "Wedged inside one of the rubber seals of the elevator doors."

CHAPTER TWENTY-EIGHT

Sunday, August 25, 2019 (11:40)

ETHAN RODE HIS TRIUMPH DAYTONA AROUND THE LAS Vegas Metropolitan Police Department parking lot several times before he finally settled on a slot that he liked the look of. It might be old, but the bike was his pride and joy and there was no way he was risking it being damaged or stolen if he could help it.

His bay of choice was between a white Mercedes with vanity plates and a black Lexus that was so clean, it could have been driven directly from the showroom. The perfect combo in his book. Neither driver would risk damaging their own vehicle if they returned before him, and any potential thief wouldn't look twice at his Triumph given what it was parked next to.

As he walked across the lot, his boots stuck to the asphalt where vehicle tires had melted in the heat and left behind a thin layer of silica and rubber. Pausing briefly under the shade of a large tree, he shielded his eyes against the Mojave glare that glinted from the windows of the concrete jungle up ahead. Maybe he should abort the whole stupid mission while he still had the chance?

Keep quiet and you'll be their number one suspect if it gets out, he reminded himself as he wrestled with his conscience. *You deleted crucial evidence.* He'd gone over and over it in his head the past couple of days. Not only had Billy watched Mario's every move that night, he also definitely followed him out of the Lucky Plaza. The punk had stolen his money, he was sure of it. If he didn't disclose the footage though, he was going to look guilty as hell if the cops caught on and there was no way he was taking the blame now that they were connecting the attack on Mario to the deaths of the news reporter and lawyer.

Mind seemingly made up, Ethan strode purposefully toward the building before he could change it again. He would be glad to step out the furnace for a while, if not glad about what he had to do.

The station was quieter than he'd expected, given the volume of vehicles parked outside and within seconds, he had been issued a number and directed to the waiting room. *No going back now,* he thought a short while later as he nervously waited to be buzzed through the door when his number was called.

"Want to tell me what this is about?" Detective Karl Andrews asked as he escorted him through the maze of corridors and offices beyond. The man hadn't uttered more than two words since he'd clapped eyes on him.

"You told the clerk you had information about the attack on Mario Brown?" he nudged as he showed Ethan into the allocated interview room, but still he didn't respond.

"Look, buddy," Karl struggled to hide his frustration

as Ethan sat down and began to silently pick at the label on his bottle of water, "I'm kind of pushed for time so you need to start talking or else I'm calling an end to this meeting."

"M-Mario Brown," Ethan finally stuttered, his eyes not budging from the bottle as he methodically scratched at the adhesive behind the label.

"What about him?" Karl leaned forward and snatched the container from Ethan's fingers. Having made a couple of calls before collecting him from reception, he had managed to ascertain that Ethan Gardner was Director of Surveillance at the Lucky Plaza.

"He was in the resort the other night." Ethan wiped the sweat from his face with his T-shirt as he spoke.

"We know." Karl slanted his head and studied him quizzically. The appeal for witnesses to call Crime Stoppers anonymously had been an instant success, and the man on the recording had been adamant that it was Mario he had seen playing the tables in the Lucky Plaza prior to his assault.

"What we don't know is how—or even why—the footage came to be missing," he pressed, as Ethan licked his lips and coughed, as though to clear his throat but didn't speak.

"Another drink?" Karl waggled the empty bottle at him before firing it at the trash container in the corner of the room. Having observed Ethan's body language at the mention of the missing footage, he was going to have to tread gently to coax whatever information out of him that he was struggling to convey.

"Please," Ethan nodded.

Excusing himself from the room, Karl took his time approaching the water cooler. It was just along the corridor, but he needed to think. Up until now, he had mildly toyed with the idea that Angelino might have deleted the footage, but he was now 99 percent sure. Why else would Ethan be so uncomfortable? Snitching on his boss could carry huge ramifications if Angelino found out.

Filling two styrofoam cups to the rim with the tepid water, Karl walked carefully back down the corridor to avoid spilling the contents. "How they can call that thing a water cooler, I'll never know," he joked in an effort to put Ethan at ease as he placed both cups on the table. "I've tasted colder cappuccino."

"Everything you tell me in here is off the record," he cajoled softly when Ethan didn't react. "It's just me and you. No witnesses, no recorder running, absolutely nothing that can incriminate you."

"Except the word of a cop," Ethan suddenly snapped, the vehemence in his voice taking Karl by surprise. What did this guy have against the force? Nothing had cropped up when he'd carried out his checks.

"Whoa," he held up his hands in mock surrender. "I'm the good guy, remember?"

"Like Yorkie Fletcher, I suppose?" Ethan retaliated bitterly.

"*State Trooper* Fletcher?" Karl didn't know the man personally, but he knew the name. He had a bit of a reputation, and not the type a self-respecting police officer would be proud of. "What's he got to do with any of this?" His brow creased in confusion as his brain tried and failed to make a connection between the two men.

"Mario and Yorkie are business partners," Ethan sighed. "The greedy lend to the needy," he hinted when Karl gazed at him nonplussed.

"They're loan sharks?" Karl leaned forward in his seat and rested his elbows on the table as he waited for Ethan to elaborate.

"Mario lends the money, Yorkie collects. By whatever means, but you can pay extra for him to go easy."

"Son-of-a-bitch," Karl muttered under his breath. It wasn't the first rumor he'd heard about Yorkie accepting incentives to finance his wife's care and he doubted it would be the last. It didn't explain though, why Mario had been in the Lucky Plaza or why he had been attacked. He leaned back in his seat and waited patiently for Ethan to continue.

"Stealing was never part of the deal." Ethan's leg jigged rhythmically under the table and reverberated against the floor as he spoke.

"What deal?" Karl was struggling to make sense of Ethan's involvement with a notorious crook like Mario Brown.

"I was supposed to overlook certain…"—he struggled to find the appropriate word—"activities. It was a trade for a debt," he added, unable to look the detective in the eye as he blatantly lied to save his own skin.

"So, you deleted the footage?" Karl suggested as the missing pieces of the puzzle slotted awkwardly into place.

"What? No!" Ethan reached for his water to try and keep his trembling hands occupied. It didn't work and, as the liquid sloshed all over the table, he quickly put the cup back down. No way was he admitting something like that. Given what he'd just disclosed, they were sure to think he attacked Mario for the money, if they knew it was him who deleted the evidence.

"So, who?" Karl asked.

"I dunno, Angelino maybe?" He needed to make them see that he wasn't the only one who could have a motive for deleting the recordings. "I figured he knew what Mario was up to and decided to challenge him, but then…"

"Then, what?"

"There was someone else interested in Mario that night."

"Who?"

"You need to watch it."

"Well, I would Ethan, except that it's missing," Karl replied, struggling to disguise his irritation.

"Files aren't automatically erased from the system when they're deleted," Ethan mumbled, repeating the line he'd already fed his boss, only this time he wouldn't claim that they'd already been overwritten. Just so long as Angelino's hot shot detective friend didn't get wind of it, his nose was clean.

"You managed to retrieve the footage?" Karl asked, a sliver of hope flooding his veins.

"Angelino must never know," Ethan replied.

"Right now, you're a suspect," Karl threatened, itching to get his hands on the evidence that might give them the breakthrough they so badly needed.

"I never touched him!"

"Prove it! Mario would have been carrying a substantial amount of money that night, and yet when he was found—close to death—his pockets were bare. You, the pit boss, the dealer… you're all up to your necks, so if you can demonstrate otherwise, now would be a good time."

Ethan reached into his rucksack and retrieved the USB memory stick, slipping it across the table towards him. "If it *was* Angelino that deleted it and he hears I've gone behind his back, I'm done for."

"Want to give me a clue what's on here?" Karl tried to pick up the thumb drive from the table, but Ethan's fingers were pressed down firmly on top of it.

"Promise me he won't find out," he persisted, his fingers still holding it in place.

"What's on the USB, Ethan?" He wasn't giving any assurances until he knew what was on it, although he was more convinced than ever right now that Angelino was involved.

"Just watch it and form your own opinion." Ethan finally relinquished his grip on the data drive. "But if Angelino finds out, I'm a dead man walking."

CHAPTER TWENTY-NINE

Sunday, August 25, 2019 (19:00)

ONCE AN ILLEGAL DRINKING DEN CONTROLLED BY THE mob, Willie's Bar was now, ironically, a favored haunt for many serving officers of the Las Vegas Metropolitan Police Department. Situated half a mile from the Strip, the place was never particularly busy. It was too far off the beaten track for the average tourist and most locals weren't comfortable drinking under the watchful eye of the law.

This evening was no exception, and the only other patron was an elderly drifter whose calloused hands vigorously swirled the liquid in his glass as though he might find a solution at the bottom of it. Detective Karl Andrews was also pensive as he sat at the bar nursing a Jack D on the rocks. He couldn't rid his mind of the fear and desperation that Elizabeth Angel must have felt trapped in the elevator without food or water until death had finally claimed her. The discovery of another playing card wedged inside the seals of the cab doors had only aggravated his concerns.

Awkward questions were being asked and even

without the knowledge of the cards, the local press was hinting about a localized serial killer. The resulting hysteria that such an accusation would create didn't bear thinking about, but Karl didn't think this was the work of a serial killer. These were spree killings and whoever had committed the attacks was motivated. Hasty. They were reacting to a specific situation and trying to tell them something through the cards, but what? Understanding the motive would be key to identifying them.

If the recording that Ethan Gardner had finally relinquished this morning was anything to go by, there was little doubt in his mind that Billy Jackson was responsible for the attack on Mario Brown. The evidence was also mounting up that the assault on Mario was connected to the murders of Maddison Scott and Elizabeth Angel, and the fact that Billy might have an accomplice—the man who sat with him at the roulette table in the Lucky Plaza that night—was also of interest. Locating Billy's whereabouts—and better still, his companion that evening—was now their priority, but with a population of more than two million—not accounting for illegals and the homeless —it would be nothing short of impossible. Especially since they had been instructed to tone down any publicity to avoid alerting Billy and his partner in crime of their suspicions. At what cost, though? How many more needless deaths before they caught up with them?

The allegations that Ethan had made against Yorkie Fletcher also plagued his mind. If they turned out to be true, Karl had some difficult decisions ahead. The invisible wall of silence was in fact so visible it might as well have been etched above the entrance to the Police

Training Academy. The rules were simple: Challenge the establishment; prepare to be hung out to dry.

But what if safeguarding the thin blue line also meant treading a fine line between protecting a serving officer from disciplinary action or protecting them from harm? If Mario's money lending operation was the root cause of the trouble, there was a risk that Yorkie would be next. Karl needed to ascertain the level of his involvement, and fast. Otherwise, it might be too late.

He glanced at his watch. Xavier was almost thirty minutes late. Would he even show up? They had studied together at the Academy—working the same department before they went their separate ways—but it wasn't as though they ever mixed socially in the same circles. Who knew what kind of worms would be released by digging into a mutual colleague's past?

"No ice," Karl mouthed to the barman as he ordered another drink. Determined not to get drunk, he had taken his time and his Jack D was now more water than rock.

"And whatever he's having," he added, spotting Xavier making an entrance through the concealed doors at the rear of the building.

"What's up?" Xavier shook Karl's outstretched hand as he stood to greet him. "Bottle of Bud," he confirmed, grinning at the barman who already knew his drink of choice by heart.

"You said it was urgent," he said, turning his attention back to Karl.

"Which is why you were in such a hurry to get here, I suppose," Karl gently mocked.

"Ten minutes before the end of my shift, a motorist jumps the sidewalk and strikes a pedestrian. You know the score." He thanked the barman and took a healthy slug of his drink.

"Back in 2008," Karl decided to get straight to the point before he could talk himself out of it, "after the Dankworth debacle, you were partnered with Yorkie Fletcher?" He extracted the last bits of ice from his now watered-down whiskey and added them to his fresh glass as he spoke.

"The guy should have got the death penalty for making my life hell, never mind Dankworth's murder," Xavier responded bitterly.

On the night of July 18, 2008, Deputy Dankworth pulled into a gas station in downtown Vegas. As he filled up his car, a black male approached from behind and shot him in the back of the head. The following week, there were two other ambushes of LVMPD officers, which resulted in the Clark County Sheriff ordering all officers to partner up and ride together on patrol. The two-officer-per-vehicle deployment was only temporary; there weren't the finances or the officers to cover the jurisdiction unless they rode solo, but given the choice Xavier would have preferred to take the risk rather than partner with the likes of Yorkie Fletcher.

"Whatever your gripe, Karl," Xavier continued, "you'd better watch your back. Yorkie's a mean bastard. Meaner still if you cross him."

"An allegation's been made." Karl picked his words carefully, unsure how to proceed when he hadn't even informed his own colleagues about Ethan Gardner's recent accusations. "You ever hear him talk about a Mario Brown?"

"The guy who was attacked?" It was more statement

than question. "This one day, Yorkie pulls over a motorist." Xavier spoke quietly, but his anger was evident. "Claimed he was tailgating the vehicle in front, but I never saw that. Next thing you know, he starts kicking the guy's ass. I was worried at first. I mean, Metro didn't have cameras in the vehicles, but we were on patrol that day. I figured the guy must have said or done something real bad for Yorkie to be so pissed. Didn't want him getting into trouble over some no-good piece of shit, so I intervened and reminded him he was on film." He pressed the bottle of lager to his lips and drained the contents.

"He yelled at me to get back in the car, so I did. When he was done, once the driver was face down on the asphalt, unconscious and bleeding out, Yorkie calmly walked back to the patrol car, climbed in, and thanked me. The son-of-a-bitch thanked me and told me I needn't have worried. Reckoned the dash-cams were fixed in one position and just so long as he wasn't near the front during an altercation, it would be his word against theirs." Xavier thanked the bartender as he placed a refill in front of him.

"They didn't always get a beating," he continued. "Most of them paid up. Then, bold as brass, dash cam or not, Yorkie would accept the payment, slide back into the driving seat and we'd leave. At first, I thought he was accepting bribes in exchange for citations, but then…" he frowned, pausing mid-sentence as though deliberating how much detail to impart.

"Then what?" Karl leaned in and rested his elbows on his thighs. He had a fair idea what was coming, but he still needed to hear it.

"Nothing," Xavier replied, as it dawned on him that

he might be considered guilty by association. "It's been a long day, man. Don't pay no attention to me."

"If a Nevada State Police officer is involved in illegal dealings with Mario Brown," Karl hissed, "I need the heads up. Press gets wind of it first and they'll blow any case out the water before we've even had the chance to build one."

"OK," Xavier raised his palms to calm him. "Mario and Yorkie are up to their necks in it, but you didn't hear it from me. Yorkie's the go-between. He collects the money, but he adds his own interest and it's not like his victims can go running to Mario, can they?"

Despite having only confirmed what he already knew, Karl stared at him in shock. "It's all so fucked up," he finally groaned, sinking his head into his hands. "Report him and I'm screwed, but whoever attacked Mario meant to kill him and if the culprit is who I think it is, there's a good chance Yorkie's next."

"You can't seriously be considering protecting him?" Xavier leaned forward so that he could keep his voice down. "If the roles were reversed, Yorkie wouldn't give a damn about no code of silence, and I suggest you do the same. No one would blame you," he added, "but if he winds up dead and they find out you kept stuff back, you're finished."

"Physio, rehab, 24-hour care, it all costs money," Karl moaned. "You think no one will blame me when he can't cater to his wife's needs?"

"A state trooper's salary wouldn't even scratch the surface. You know it and I know it, so there's no reason anyone else will fail to miss the fact that Yorkie hasn't been funding his wife's care through his employment with NSP." Xavier knocked back the last of his lager.

"Maybe," Karl shrugged. "Report him though, and all they'll see is a snitch with a grudge. I'll be shit on their shoe—the kind of cop who puts promotion over a fellow officer and the needs of his handicapped wife."

"I saw Elena the other day, as it goes," Xavier replied. "Out for a walk with her physio, although she obviously wasn't actually *walking*." He flexed his fingers and made virtual quotation marks to emphasize the word. "I got the impression she was doing OK, so stop beating yourself up and do the right thing."

"Like you did, you mean?" Karl snapped, instantly regretting it. Xavier wasn't the bad guy here. He owed him nothing, but he'd still come clean and told him all he needed to know.

"Hardly the same thing and you know it."

"I'm sorry." Karl massaged his temples wearily with the tips of his fingers. "I'm just so worked up right now, but that was out of line."

"Which is why you're going to pick up the tab," Xavier grinned, so he knew there were no hard feelings as he stood to leave. "Look, I gotta run. I promised Rach I wouldn't be late, but one piece of advice: Overlook what he's done because of some stupid code, and it'll be your funeral when it backfires."

"Oh," he turned and added as an afterthought, "and this meeting never happened. You so much as hint to anyone I spoke to you about any of this, and I'll deny every word."

CHAPTER THIRTY

Monday, August 26, 2019 (09:45)

"What I'm struggling to accept," Burt's toes curled as Karl slammed his foot on the brake and narrowly avoided hitting the car in front, "is that Angelino would deliberately keep the footage of Billy following Mario out the Lucky Plaza from us."

"I'm not convinced he even knows about it." Karl hit the accelerator and shot past the offending vehicle. "At first, I thought he was responsible for the missing footage and Ethan sure as hell did his best to implicate him, but now I'm not so sure. Ethan's clearly up to his eyeballs whereas if Angelino knew but failed to disclose it, he'd know only too well how it would look when the truth came to light."

"Any more thoughts on the guy that sat at the table with Billy that night?"

"I've asked Dennis to take a further look but since he stays there most the night doing his best to hook up with the waitress, I think it's likely innocent, which is more than we can say for Angelino's Director of Surveillance."

"Stealing from Angelino either makes him incredibly brave, or stupid," Burt mused, shaking his head in disbelief.

"Quite possibly both," Karl agreed.

"Any chance he came forward with the footage to take the heat off himself?"

"You think he attacked Mario?" Karl risked a glance at Burt before returning his eyes to the road.

"You don't find it strange that Mario cleaned out the casino but when he was found, his pockets were bare?"

"Except for the playing card," Karl reminded him, mulling over the suggestion. "I don't think so," he eventually continued. "By bringing it to our attention, he's all but admitted culpability in a major case of fraud against the casino… not to mention facing the wrath of his employer if he were to find out."

"So, why speak up at all?" Burt wondered aloud, the highway making him giddy as it rapidly swept beneath them. "If things don't work out with Metro, you could always take up motor racing," he added sarcastically as Karl pressed his hand firmly on the horn and cut through a red light.

"You're the one who said we needed to get to Yorkie as soon as," Karl bit back, his eyes never wavering from the interstate as he concentrated on the traffic ahead. Having ascertained that Yorkie hadn't shown up for work since the news of Mario's attack had broken, Burt had suggested paying him a surprise visit at home. Which was where they were now headed, the windshield wipers of the unmarked Buick clunking furiously back and forth as they fought the onslaught of rain.

"You reckon he'll talk?" From what he had learned over the past few hours, Karl wasn't convinced. Yorkie had avoided any backlash from his actions for years, so it was highly unlikely he would give up anything now without a fight.

"We have to make him believe we intend to keep quiet about his indiscretions in exchange for answers," Burt advised. "Only once we've got what we need do we break the news of his imminent suspension."

"You did the right thing telling me," he added as the car fell silent except for the sound of the wipers as they fought the rain tapping on the glass.

"Let's hope everyone else agrees when Yorkie can no longer afford his wife's care," Karl replied grimly. It didn't matter how mixed up in all this Yorkie was, it hadn't made snitching on a colleague any easier. *Thou shalt not speak out against a fellow officer;* the unwritten commandment that was silently drummed into every applicant from the moment they entered the gates of the Academy.

"Even if Yorkie does confirm that the Jacksons borrowed money," he continued when Burt didn't respond, "I still don't see where Maddison Scott or Elizabeth Angel fit into all of this."

"Billy could bear a grudge against everyone he believes crossed him in the past," Burt suggested. "Maddison wasn't exactly renowned for her empathy and from what I remember, she wrote some pretty damning character assassinations of him at the time."

"She was vicious," Karl agreed. Unable to sleep after his meeting with Xavier, Karl had spent the rest of the evening on his computer, scrolling the deep web for articles relating to the Midnight Massacre case that ordinary search engines might have failed to index. "Check out some of these," he added, passing Burt a printout of some of Maddison's more scathing headlines:

**CRACKPOT KILLER CLAIMS FATHER
DESERVED IT
DELINQUENT DESERVES DEATH PENALTY
SAVAGE, SICK & SADISTIC
DERANGED DEVIL
WHO'S LAUGHING NOW?
BILLY THE BEAST
IS HE A PSYCHOPATH?
BRAIN-SICK BILLY
COLD HEARTED & CRAZY...**

"Billy still entered a guilty verdict though?" he pressed, chewing his lower lip thoughtfully as Burt fell silent and quietly studied the list. "The case never even went to trial."

"No jury in the land would have found him innocent," Burt sighed resignedly. "Not with Maddison's intervention and the testimony of a police officer against him."

"You think he pled guilty to secure a lighter sentence?"

"I don't doubt it," Burt replied. "A guilty plea isn't automatically an admission of guilt."

"I suppose it would explain any gripe against Elizabeth Angel if he blamed her for the length of sentence he ultimately received."

"Exactly," Burt echoed his agreement. "Although, he should probably consider himself lucky he avoided the death penalty."

"Not that anyone's actually been executed in the last decade," Karl pointed out.

"Costs to go to trial, costs to keep them in solitary confinement, the list is endless," Burt countered. "Any death sentence would automatically be appealed to the Supreme Court, meaning more costs, more delays, and yet more costs as the lawyers go round, and round, and round in the vicious circle the system creates."

"Did Billy's parole officer call back?" Karl changed the subject as he steered the Buick into the private road that led to the gated community where Yorkie lived.

"Billy apparently fell off the radar a couple of weeks ago."

"Did she report it?" He glanced briefly at Burt before focusing his attention back on the road.

"Apparently Billy wasn't expecting her so there was nothing to report. Latest initiatives," he added by way of explanation. "If they aren't expecting a visit, they can't hide anything. The downside being, they also can't be brought to task for failing to attend a meeting they weren't aware of."

"Meaning what? She tried once and didn't bother to follow up?"

"Usual excuses," Burt shook his head. "Overworked, understaffed, not paid enough to babysit offenders. She classed him as low-risk and said that the mother wasn't unduly concerned."

"She was hardly likely to draw attention to any problems, was she?" Karl scoffed as he pulled up in front of a large set of metal gates and opened the driver's window when the security guard stepped out from behind his post and approached the vehicle.

"Anyone would think he was the law, not us," Burt

muttered when the guard finally finished his checks and returned to his station to grant them access.

Accelerating through the gates before there could be any change of heart, Karl pulled into the curb as close to Yorkie's residence as he could without alerting him to their presence. The rain had eased off, but the sky still looked thick with it, and he wanted to avoid getting wet if possible. As he cut the engine, his cell rang out and inspecting the screen, he swiped to answer it.

"Dennis," he mouthed to Burt, who eyed him curiously before relaxing back against the passenger seat.

"Uh-huh," Karl murmured as he listened to the young detective. "Yup, he's sitting right next to me. OK," he continued after a short pause, "secure the scene—no press access—and we'll be there as soon as we can." Ending the call, he turned his attention back to his sergeant.

"We need to keep this brief," he warned, sliding from behind the wheel.

"Spit it out." Burt studied the windows of Yorkie's townhome as he extracted himself from the vehicle. The downstairs curtains were drawn, which was strange. There was currently no sun to block out, and he hadn't imagined the twitch of the material as their vehicle had approached. He wondered if the security officer at the gate had called ahead to warn the occupants of their imminent arrival. Looking forward to taking Yorkie by surprise, he certainly hoped not.

"Contractors have unearthed remains within the in-house sewage plant at the Old Citadel Hotel. Two bodies, both dismembered and…" Karl paused, raking his hands through his hair, and massaging his scalp as the horror of his words sank in.

"Go on," Burt squirmed in his seat. He could have predicted what was coming, but still needed to hear it first-hand.

"They also found a couple of playing cards in the pit."

CHAPTER THIRTY-ONE

Monday, August 26, 2019 (14:30)

Alice Vitriano wandered aimlessly through the large community park, her school satchel swinging haphazardly by her side. The rain had finally stopped, replaced by a strong wind that was forcing the petals on the pretty tree-lined trails to fall to the ground in a blizzard of brightly colored snowflakes. Glancing at the sky, she studied the threatening clouds—indication there was more rain to come—and was about to retreat in the direction she had come when she noticed a homeless man slouched on a bench watching her.

"Hey, Billy," she said, giving him a wave and increasing her pace as she approached him. He had been hanging around the park a lot of late—no place else to go, she supposed—but he was always real friendly, and she sure could do with a friend right now.

"Shouldn't you be in class?" He glanced sideways and nudged her playfully with his shoulder as she sat down.

"Not like anyone will miss me." The damp cotton of

his shirt felt cold and uncomfortable against her skin, so she shuffled sideways a bit to get away from him.

"Hungry?" she asked, opening the container filled with snacks that her father's personal chef had placed in her satchel that morning. Her dad would kill her if he knew, and the teachers were always preaching about the vagrants who hung out opposite the school gates—mustn't look at them, mustn't talk to them, mustn't feed them—but what did it matter if she had no appetite, and it would be wasted?

"Always," he grinned, grabbing the lunchbox gratefully.

"Want to talk about it?" he asked, his mouth full as he bit into a pastry.

"Not really," she replied sullenly. "Jennifer Smart's got a big fat bum, but they don't treat her differently," she carried on regardless. "And Donna Taylor's got a yucky, spotty face, but no one seems to care. They'll both 'grow out' of it apparently." Her curled fingers twitched like a rabbit's ears as she spoke. "But I won't, will I?" She glared at Billy, daring him to contradict her.

He didn't. From a distance, Alice seemed pretty normal. Dressed in a pleated skirt and navy-blue polo shirt, she looked the same as all the other kids who boarded the bus in the morning and filtered into the playground during break. It was only when you got up close that you realized she wasn't like the other kids at all, and her haggard features and wrinkled skin kind of reminded him of Benjamin Button.

He diverted his gaze back to the lunchbox. "I used to skip school too." He sank his teeth into a juicy apple. "My brother was clever—a genius, even—unlike me." He chewed rapidly, part of him desperate to impart the information now the floodgates had opened. "You want to know the most important thing I ever did when everyone else was in class? Distract the shopkeeper," he pressed on, without waiting for her to answer. "While someone lifted the stock, I'd sidetrack 'em and look at me now. Don't make the same mistakes I made Alice."

"Is your brother like really rich and famous now?" she asked, giggling nervously.

"He's dead," he snapped bitterly. Instantly regretting it, he reached for her hand and squeezed it affectionately. It wasn't Alice's fault. She never chose to be fathered by that evil son-of-a-bitch.

"How did he die?" Alice whispered, plucking a couple of grapes from his lap, and popping them into her mouth as the silence ballooned.

"He got ill," Billy mumbled, unable to find the words to explain that her father might as well have killed him with his bare hands.

"Buddy got ill and died too," she replied sadly.

"Buddy?" he asked, looking at her curiously. If she was going to trust him, he needed to know everything about her.

"My doggy, but Daddy got me another one," she answered, her eyes suddenly glistening with excitement. "He's called Murphy."

If only it could have been that simple to replace Nate. Billy shredded the uneaten bread and threw it on the walkway for the birds.

"Murphy likes me for who I am," she gushed. "He's my bestest friend in the whole wide world. You're next," she added, patting his hand with her own.

Billy smiled wistfully. Abducting Alice was going to

be unbelievably easy and yet, it was also going to be the hardest thing he'd ever had to do.

"Do you like books?" She changed the subject as she observed his mood change. Billy told her once that he suffered with nightmares even though he wasn't actually sleeping. It didn't sound very nice but when she had a bad dream, she found it really helped to talk about nice things afterwards until the memory went away.

"I guess," he shrugged, trying to think of a time he'd ever read one.

"Come with me." She grabbed his hand and tugged him away from the bench.

"Where are we going?" he asked, laughing as she pulled him toward the path.

"There's this really cool place I want to show you. It looks like an old church but inside, it's full of books."

"I don't have money to chuck away on books." He stopped in his tracks and shook his head dismissively. Entering a bookstore, or any other shop with Alice, was too big a risk. When the time came to take her, the less people who could ID him, the better.

"You don't have to buy them, silly." As she yanked at his hand again, he allowed himself to be dragged away from the peace and tranquility of the park. He'd figure out how to let her down on the way.

"Mary-Anne says that reading's good for you. She works at the book church," she added before he even had the opportunity to wonder who Mary-Anne was. "She says that reading makes you live longer, although I can't see how, but if you promise to bring them back, she'll even let you take some home. Look," she said, removing her backpack and showing him the contents. "This one's really good," she declared, thrusting it into his hands. "It's all about a dog who saves its master's life."

They had paused in front of a large set of wrought-iron gates that separated the park from the highway, beyond which lay what was left of the old Citadel Hotel. With a history that read like a "Who's Who" of the criminal underworld, the hotel's implosion had been one of Vegas' most extravagant shows. Billy and his fellow inmates had crowded around the small television in the prison common room to watch, cheering and whistling and clapping like frenzied supporters at a baseball match as the dynamite took hold and folded the building in on itself like structural origami.

He was in no mood for celebrating now however, as he stood and stared at the rhythmic strobes of light pulsating from the emergency vehicles up ahead. He scraped his boot on the ground in frustration. If they had found what was left of Lorrie and that son-of-a-bitch she shacked up with already, kidnapping Alice wasn't going to be so easy after all.

"Billy?" Concern clouded Alice's face as she studied his sickly complexion and the thin layer of perspiration that had appeared on his skin. "You don't look so good."

"It's fine," he mumbled. "I'm fine." He sucked in a large mouthful of tepid air as he warily stepped forward. He couldn't walk away now. He needed to know the reason for the police activity.

He didn't have to wait long, his bowels almost giving way at the number of cops crawling the site like maggots on a corpse. *Lorrie's corpse,* the thought drilled holes in his skull.

"We need to go back." He pointed at the uniformed officers dotted all over the site.

"The police?" Her eyes widened in terror. "Are they looking for me?"

"You?" He cocked his head in amusement despite his fears. The kid sure could be melodramatic sometimes.

"Ms. Miller once threatened Jennifer Smart that she'd call the cops if she missed class again," she said, her eyes scanning Billy's for further instruction. "And my uncle—although he's not my *real* uncle—is a police-man," she pressed on, her lip quivering as she fought back the tears.

Alice's godfather. The detective who couldn't detect fact from fiction if his life depended on it.

"He's going to kill me," she whispered theatrically.

"We can't have that, can we?" Billy smiled kindly as an idea occurred to him. It wasn't quite what he'd had in mind. He'd have preferred more time to prepare, but still felt excited as she placed her small hand in his own and allowed him to lead her back into the park.

"Let's get you somewhere safe. Somewhere nobody will find you."

CHAPTER THIRTY-TWO

Monday, August 26, 2019 (18:15)

ANGELINO SCOWLED AT HIS WIFE'S REFLECTION IN THE mirror as she sat in front of the antique dresser and applied yet more mascara and another layer of lipstick.

"I swear to you, honey, I was bang on time, but you know how kids are." She began the finishing touches to her hair, coughing as she generously doused her head with the asphyxiating lacquer. *Good.* Lying bitch could choke to death for all he cared. If his daughter wasn't missing due to his wife's tardiness, the idea that Ronnie might have been on time for anything would have been laughable. His wife would be late to her own burial, which was going to be a whole lot sooner than she imagined if his daughter didn't turn up safe and well.

"Alice isn't like other kids though, is she?" he snarled, the unwelcome mix of fear and fury gaining momentum in his gut.

"Of course, she is," Ronnie scoffed in retaliation. "And if you stopped treating her like a fragile piece of china for five minutes, you might just realize how alike other children our daughter really is. Just because she *looks* different, Angelino, it doesn't make her different, and it's time you accepted that fact before you completely ruin her."

"How late were you?" he growled, the urge to grab her immaculately coiffed head and smash it into the pile of cosmetics on the table in front of her growing by the second. Unless she started to tell the truth, he had no hope of narrowing down the exact timescale that his daughter had been... been, what? Snatched? His insides lurched at the prospect.

"Ten minutes. Twenty tops," she sighed, sliding from the stool, and making her way across the room to the window. "Must you really make such mountains out of molehills? Any minute now she'll come skipping up that path as though nothing's happened."

"And if she doesn't?" His fists curled with rage as he struggled to suppress the desire to throttle her. Ronnie had never cared, not really. The second his wife realized their daughter was different—that she wouldn't blossom into a young woman interested in makeup, dresses, shopping excursions, and all the other girly things she had planned for their daughter before she had been born—she had totally lost interest.

"Then we contact Burt."

"Over my dead body!" He blocked his wife's exit as she made to push past him. "I'm warning you, no cops," he snarled. Involve Fish, and Alice's disappearance would be the least of his problems.

"Burt's not *'cops'* though, is he? Not really." She pressed the palms of her hands against his chest and attempted to maneuver past him. "He's her godfather—your best friend—and if anyone can find her, it's him. Not that I think she needs finding," she added, pushing against her husband in a further failed attempt to persuade him to let her past.

"If anything's happened to her, I'm holding you personally responsible," he threatened, his breath warm on her skin as he hissed the words into the crease of her neck. "And the fact you could even think about a night out when she's missing makes me sick," he added, taking an exaggerated step back to let her pass.

"She's hardly *missing*," she groaned, making a beeline for the door before he could change his mind. "Besides, we've had this evening planned for ages and I can't let Bella down."

"But you don't mind letting Alice down!" he roared at her departing back, struggling to contain his temper as, seemingly unconcerned, she made her hasty descent down the stairs. Did she know more about all this than she was letting on? He eyed her warily as she retreated. It was all a bit too convenient for his liking. Not only did Alice vanish on her watch, the fact she couldn't care less was making him more suspicious by the minute. About to follow and continue the argument, his cell vibrated in his pocket and distracted him.

It was a video from a random number not stored in his list of contacts. *Curious.* As he sat himself down on the edge of the bed and clicked the button to open the accompanying link, a sickening scream pierced the silence.

Angelino stared in horror at the screen, his eyes fixed on the water that gushed like open taps down the walls behind his daughter into a fast-flowing stream which raged past her and almost knocked her from her feet. Alice couldn't swim, but as she wrestled with the torrents of water that surged toward her, she was at least managing to keep upright. It was a small consolation and did nothing to placate him as she frantically thrashed around and choked on mouthfuls of rancid water as she cried for help.

Where are you, Alice? In the background, he could hear rain lashing against something metal that vibrated around the hollow space like a steel pan. Adjusting the brightness of his screen as much as the device would allow, he restarted the video and concentrated on her surroundings.

Above his daughter's head, torches had been crudely strapped to a low ceiling, the little light they provided reflecting from the walls to the murky water beneath her feet. His eyes settled next on a mass of interlocking letters that were engraved into the stone walls behind her and, pausing the recording, he zoomed in to study them more closely.

"Dammit," he grumbled, as he glared hopelessly at the distorted image that was now too blurred to decipher anything, let alone the etchings. Someone must be able to identify her prison, but who? Fish? *No cops,* he reminded himself. The last thing his daughter needed was Metro swarming in and forcing her kidnapper into an action that couldn't be reversed. Besides, how would he explain the motive? It was Billy Jackson who had taken her, he was sure of it, and what use would he be to Alice holed up on death row if he had to admit the truth?

"Should have dealt with the boy properly when I had the chance," he cursed under his breath. *Seen to it personally that the paltry contents of his brain were also left decorating the hovel they called home.*

He wondered if Ethan could help. He was still

denying it, but Angelino was certain that it was him who had broken into the state-of-the-art security system and remotely deleted the recordings. If he was right, the man had the technological expertise to pick apart this film and figure out when and where it was taken. Better still, he might even be able to trace the current location of the cellphone and the scumbag using it.

Frustration shredded his insides as he speed-dialed Ethan's number and it went directly to voicemail. "Call me back," he instructed.

As he paced back and forth, he stabbed urgently at the keypad again, this time dialing the number that had sent the short film. "Pick up, you asshole," he snarled, seconds before the call diverted to an automated voice that instructed him to try again later.

About to hurl the cell against the adjacent wall, it pinged with an incoming text. He stood motionless as he read it, every nerve on high alert before he finally smashed out a reply and hit send.

CHAPTER THIRTY-THREE

Monday, August 26, 2019 (18:15)

"Still here then?"

Yorkie turned at the sound of his wife's voice and watched as she wheeled herself into the room and deftly maneuvered herself out of her chair and onto the couch. In many ways, Elena was fitter and more able than most people he knew. She didn't need him. He doubted she ever had.

"In case it escaped your notice, I'm suspended." Her skirt had slipped, and his eyes settled on the scars, the permanent, sobering reminder of why he had started the allegiance with Mario in the first place. Not that he needed any further reminder since his wife hadn't been able to talk about anything else since the two detectives had left.

"Not yet, you're not," she replied. "You were advised to report to your sergeant and that you *probably* faced suspension."

"Same thing," Yorkie grumbled. "We might as well face facts, I'm finished." He sank onto the couch next to her and buried his head in his hands.

"You'll be lucky to escape prison." She smacked her lips with disapproval as she deliberately goaded him. According to the detectives, her husband had been intimidating and traumatizing the vulnerable for years, and yet he had the nerve to sit here and act as though he was the one being wronged.

"At least I'd get some peace and quiet from you," he snapped in retaliation. In truth, the prospect had haunted his every waking hour since he'd heard the news of Mario's attack.

"I wonder what your victims would make of you now, hmmm?" she asked, warming to her theme. "Yorkie Fletcher, the big 'I am'—threatening and tormenting *innocent, desperate* people—afraid to face the consequences of his own actions. You're pathetic." Scorn and derision dripped from her every word.

"I walk in there of my own free will and I turn myself in. You ever stop to think how you'd cope without me Elena, because I have? You wouldn't last five minutes." All these years, he had supported her. Was it too much to expect a little loyalty in return?

"I'd survive," she scoffed, picking up the remote from the arm of the couch and selecting the news channel in the hope there would be more speculation connecting the recent murders to the assault on Mario. It would be rewarding to see a little of that misery Yorkie had inflicted on others all these years, finally reflected on his own face.

"From what I'm hearing, you've built up quite the little nest egg," she added spitefully.

"Which they'll confiscate if I'm charged," he reminded her, shocked by her blatant contempt. "My salary was hardly going to pay for all of this, was it?" He waved his hand defensively at the exercise equipment and mobility aids. "I didn't have a choice."

"Oh yes, of course," she sneered. "I forgot you did it all for *me*. Standing there all high and mighty, telling them it was for my benefit. *My* benefit?" Her voice rose a decibel with every word. "Well, fuck you, Yorkie. I didn't need you then, and I certainly don't need you now." She turned up the volume on the set and hoped he would get the hint that, as far as she was concerned, the conversation was over.

"For years, you've pointed the finger," he said, his face flushing red at the injustice. "Blamed me, but you know what? You've got nobody to blame but yourself for the hole we're in." He stood and crossed the floor, the proximity of her making him claustrophobic.

"We?" she stuttered incredulously. "Don't you *dare* drag me into any of this."

"You were driving Elena, not me." Yorkie turned his back on his wife and stared out the large glass doors that overlooked the backyard and valley beyond. He could lose himself for hours some days admiring the view and despite what his wife said now, it had *not* all been for nothing. Without Mario and their partnership, they could never have dreamed of living in a home such as this.

"I didn't have a choice," he repeated.

"I didn't have a choice," she mimicked bitterly. "Well guess what? Neither did I, or did you conveniently forget that you were so inebriated, I had to drive?" Her voice trembled with anger as she spoke. "I have a choice now though, don't I?"

"Meaning?" He swung on his heels to face her.

"I'm leaving you," she sighed, the fight draining from her body as soon as she uttered the words.

"You're… leaving… me?" He released a hollow laugh. "Well, go on then. *Walk* out. Let's see how far you get on your own two feet without me to support you." No sooner had he spoken, he regretted it, but it was too late. It was *all* too late.

"You make me sick." Elena spoke quietly as she checked the brake on the chair and levered herself back into it.

"All of it was for you," he cried out as she wheeled herself to the door. "All I ever wanted to do was make it better, you remember that." He took a couple of deep breaths and tried to calm the rising panic in his gut. She couldn't leave him. Not now. Without her, there was absolutely nothing standing between him and prison.

"Make it *better*?" she spat, her tone dripping with sarcasm as she paused in the doorway. "You scared the living hell out of people who couldn't afford your demands even if they wanted to."

"I'm sorry, OK?" He sank back onto the couch and rubbed his palms wearily across his face. "Please Elena, I'm sorry."

"You're not sorry," she replied, carefully negotiating the chair through the gap so that the wheels didn't catch on the frame. "Only that you were caught and that's not the same thing."

Yorkie quietly watched his wife leave the room. She was right, of course. They hadn't needed the additional income for a long time, but the lure had been too big a temptation. Even now, if it wasn't for the attack on Mario, it would be business as usual. He sat still, deep in thought until the buzz of an incoming message on his cell phone distracted him. Retrieving it from his pocket, he flipped open the cover and scanned the contents before rising to his feet and hurrying from the room.

Located in the basement, Yorkie's study was cloaked in darkness and his fingers fumbled a moment before settling on the light switch. Crossing the room, he retrieved his gym bag from behind the desk and approached the storage unit that lined the far wall. Crouched on bended knee, he swept his hand across the interior of the one he needed to access, sending the contents placed to make it look like any other closet crashing to the floor. He then stretched his arm to the back and felt for the small nail that acted as a handle so he could extract the false wall and reveal the secret safe housed behind it.

His breathing was rapid as he entered the code that he had never shared with anyone, not even his wife. *Access denied,* the small screen flashed back at him, and he swiped irritably at the thin film of sweat on his upper lip.

"I think I know my mother's birthday, don't you?" he cursed. *Two more failed attempts and you're screwed.* The system was designed to lock out permanently after three.

Kneeling on the floor, he leaned into the closet for a closer look before reaching for the dial again. *Easy does it. One... slow... digit... at... a... time.* His hand trembled as he carefully, but precisely re-entered the code. He sat back and waited until finally, he heard the grinding of the inner bolts as they were released from their bindings.

The handgun was heavy, but the cool steel felt remarkably soothing against his skin, and he held it a moment longer than was necessary before dropping it in the bag with the silencer and bullets. Conscious of his wife silently stewing somewhere above, her senses on full alert as she waited for his next wrong move, he then crept from the room and let himself out of the house through the back door.

CHAPTER THIRTY-FOUR

Monday, August 26, 2019 (19:00)

BILLY

Even Daryl's cleared out and he'd normally be off his face by now, pissing and shitting in the same spot he sleeps.

"Have it your way dude," he mumbled as he packed up, "but they forecast enough water to fill every backyard pool in the city."

As I watch the water belching from the pipes into a stream of flowing garbage, his words spill into my brain. I can see the start of a tidemark appearing on the tunnel wall though—a sure sign that the water levels are starting to fade and as I lean in closer to inspect it, a disgruntled voice cracks the air.

"Hungry!" I've been so caught up with the situation, I'd almost forgot I've got company. Alice sits upright, cross-legged on a bunk stowed on top of an overturned shopping cart that bobs about like the wasted containers beneath it, and her knuckles have turned white from clinging to the sides.

"Hungry!" she grumbles again, and my eyes shift from the shackles that secure the cart to the roof as they tug against the rungs and threaten to snap free, to her face. If looks could kill, I'd be dead meat.

"Soon." Climbing down from my own bunk, I break off a slab of candy and slosh through the muck to pass it to her.

"I need *real* food." The spoiled brat swipes my hand away, and I fight the urge to slap her. This whole situation is getting to me now and I'm seriously pissed with Bo. When I got out of prison, I looked him up as agreed. He had all these ideas for getting revenge on Angelino. Taking Alice was one of them, so how come I got stuck babysitting her? *"Cops will be out looking for you, man. It's best you keep a low profile."* He has a point, I guess, but right now, it seems like he only wants a part of the good stuff.

"I want to go home," Alice whines and any remaining patience I had gets shredded. Granted, this isn't her fault, but she'd do well to remember it's not mine either.

"Zip it!" I snap as the wave of anger smacks my skull like a bat against a baseball. "Not long now and we can eat," I add more gently as she starts to cry. At least I hope we can, but Bo's been gone ages now and I'm starting to think he's never coming back.

At least my outburst has silenced the kid so I can study the tiny beads of moisture in peace as they weave their way through the maze of inscriptions carved into the tunnel walls. *"Enough water to fill every backyard pool in the city,"* Daryl said, which means there's more rain to come. Maybe we should make a run for it before it's too late? I turn my attention to the main artery that separates our camp from the exit, but however hard I try, I can't think of a better place to stash a kid—especially, one who's getting more vocal by the second.

Right on cue, Alice starts up again. "I need to go bathroom," she moans, but she's got no chance. Our crapper is located about half a mile downstream and right now, it's getting one God Almighty flush, the force behind the water enough to wipe a child off their feet and carry them all the way to Lake Mead.

The sound of approaching footsteps splashing through sludge interrupts my thoughts. *Bo?*

"Honey, I'm home," he calls out jokingly.

"Where the fuck have you been?" I watch him as he struggles to hold his flashlight and two heavy shopping bags above the water as he wades back to our camp.

"Calm down man." He ditches his haul on the bunk beside Alice. "It's kinda rough out there. I did message you," he adds as he offloads his inside pockets of the remaining contraband he acquired while he was out.

"You left because you couldn't get a signal down here, but you messaged me," I repeat, struggling to keep my temper in check. "Well, guess what, Bo? I never got your stupid message."

"The stage is set," he replies, deliberately swerving my mood. Bo had this crazy idea to engineer a meet between Angelino and Yorkie. *"He'll lose his cool when Yorkie won't tell him where Alice is… because he can't."* His laughter was uncontrollable and after a while, it became contagious.

"They fell for it?" I'm still not convinced we can pull this off.

"Hook, line, and sinker," he grins.

"And the cell?" It's bugged me from the start that the cops might track the activity on Mario's cell phone, so he better have disposed of it like we agreed.

"Just this little baby to go." He pulls the tiny SIM card from his pocket and flicks it between his fingers before discarding it in the crud beneath our feet.

"And if it goes wrong?" I jerk my head sideways at Alice. "What if Yorkie overpowers him? Or they figure it out and involve the cops?"

"We ditch her." Bo shrugs, like this would be the easiest thing in the world but it's not him the cops would come looking for. Snatching Alice has complicated everything, and she knows too much about me to ever let her go.

"Billy?" My chest tightens at the sound of her voice, my reminder that finally free from a lifetime behind bars, I'm now trapped by a kid.

"What?"

"Can we play another game?" Alice should be freaking out, but I'm more bothered than she is. The kid trusts me, which is not good news for her. My passion to punish Angelino means I'm not thinking straight right now.

I steal another look at the wall, the rodents in my brain busy fighting over the possible consequences if the rain picks up again, but the tidemark is definitely telling a different story.

"What did you have in mind?" I ask. *Please, nothing too dangerous this time,* I almost add as I catch sight of the determined look on her face. In truth, we've already got more than enough to bait Angelino, but I need something to distract me and as Bo sets about refilling the gas canister to the portable stove, it's clear it's going to be a while before we get any food.

"Want to drown again," she declares, and I flinch. Her clothes are still damp from our last efforts and unless we can light a fire and sort her a change of clothes sometime soon, she's going to get sick.

CHAPTER THIRTY-FIVE

Monday, August 26, 2019 (19:55)

THE SECLUDED MEMBERS-ONLY LOUNGE AT THE PARAGON Resort was the one place that Yorkie felt truly relaxed, and it was no surprise that Mario would suggest meeting here. What was surprising however, was that Mario was in any fit state to meet with him at all since all the news reports indicated that he was still in hospital, fighting for his life. The hard-assed bastard was crazy enough to discharge himself as soon as he was capable, he supposed, but Yorkie wasn't taking any chances. Hence the gun; his one piece of insurance should he need it.

The lounge was quiet—just one group of four men he vaguely recognized sitting around a small table at the far end of the room. Neither them nor the bartender seemed to notice him as he entered the room and quietly slipped back out moments later.

He crossed the corridor and entered the adjacent restroom, handing the attendant a ten-dollar bill to make himself scarce. He needed his wits about him— something that wouldn't be possible with an overly attentive attendant breathing down his neck trying to douse him in moisturizer or sickly smelling aftershave.

Floor-to-ceiling mirrors flanked the restroom walls and reflected the neon light from the street below, except for one; a dramatic picture window that overlooked the famous Fremont Street and mountains beyond. Yorkie approached the window and stood awhile, soaking up his favorite view of the city that had both made and broken him in one fell swoop.

Designed for the sole use of the patrons using the lounge, the restroom was surprisingly large—similar in size, in fact, to the footprint of his marital home. *More peaceful though*, he reflected. *Nobody hell-bent on giving you earache, here.* He had visited the Paragon a lot during the weeks succeeding Elena's accident but in recent months, he had neglected his own personal sanctuary. Something he now regretted as he felt the overwhelming sense of calm wash over him.

Retrieving the gun from his pocket, he walked over to the wash basin and set it down on the marble countertop, Elena's words all the while bombing his brain. *"Yorkie Fletcher, the big 'I am'—afraid to face the consequences of his own actions."* He eyed the pistol nervously as he considered the text he'd received.

I KNOW WHO ATTACKED ME & WHY.
MEET ME 8PM—PARAGON.

It could be from Mario, but Yorkie couldn't rid the nagging doubt from his mind. *"Pockets were bare,"* the news reports had all said. Meaning that whoever attacked Mario and stole the money also took his cell. *Billy Jackson?* Ever since the police confirmed they were connecting the attack on Mario to the other deaths, Yorkie had convinced himself that Billy was responsible. Billy was also one of the few people beside Mario who knew that the Paragon was his preferred meeting spot.

"Fuck you Elena," he spat, plugging the sink, and filling it to the brim. There was nothing cowardly about what he was about to do.

He held his breath and submerged his face in the ice-cold water. Only briefly at first—he just wanted to stay alert—but it felt good cleansing his brain of all the clutter that was preventing him from thinking straight, so he did it again. For longer this time, and then longer again, each time testing his lungs as they tightened and threatened to implode in his chest.

122… 123… 124, he counted the seconds in his head. *Go for 200,* the thought flashed through his mind. Should he? He wasn't in any pain, so it suddenly made sense. *132… 133… 134,* he continued to count. *150… 151… keep going, you can do this. Can't. Need air. "I didn't need you then and I certainly don't need you now,"* Elena's words thundered through his brain. *177… 178… Gonna die. Need to breathe. "You make me sick"… 192.*

Yorkie yanked his head from the water, his head spinning uncontrollably as he clung to the edge of the counter and gasped greedily at the air. In, out, in, out, in, out. Gulping gratefully until finally his breathing returned to a more regular rhythm. What the hell had he been thinking? He had come here to put an end to his troubles, not his life. Grabbing a couple of towels from beneath the unit, he dropped one to the floor to soak up the water under his feet while he began to dry himself down with the other.

And then he froze, his eyes glued to the mirror and

what stood behind him, the muzzle of his own gun aimed directly at the back of his skull.

"You?" he squeaked, struggling to hold his body upright as his legs threatened to cave beneath his weight.

"Who else?" Angelino growled, his fury toward the man who stood in front of him knowing no bounds. "Where is my daughter?" He stepped forward and roughly stabbed the tip of the gun against the back of Yorkie's scalp.

"I don't understand," Yorkie whimpered. "I don't know anything about your daughter."

"Enough!" Angelino roared, smashing the pistol against the back of Yorkie's skull. "You think I'm stupid? You send me a video of her close to death followed by a text to meet you and you think I won't connect the dots?"

"M-Mario," Yorkie stuttered, his eyes watering in pain. "That's who I'm here to meet. You must believe me; I never sent any texts."

"Escape your notice that Mario's currently holed up in ICU, did it?" Angelino seethed.

"I thought he discharged himself."

"If you thought that, you didn't think at all," Angelino snapped, grinding the tip of the gun into Yorkie's head again. "I won't ask again. WHERE IS SHE?" he demanded as the red mist rapidly descended and obscured any rationale.

"I don't know," Yorkie squealed as his head connected with the faucet. "I'm telling you; I had a text from Mario, only it wasn't Mario, was it? Here, check my cell." He scrabbled in his pocket to retrieve it but lost his balance as Angelino's knee smashed into the back of his own.

"Not so fast," Angelino warned. He didn't trust him not to pull a knife and he could check the phone when he was good and ready.

"We've been set up," he begged. "Billy Jackson has your daughter, not me."

"What do you know about Billy?" Convinced of his involvement from the start, Angelino wanted to hear Yorkie's take on it before he silenced him for good.

"He attacked Mario!"

"And you came here to claim your share of *MY* money from him?" Angelino spat. "You always were a greedy son-of-a-bitch!"

"Jesus, NO! It wasn't like that," he cried as Angelino slammed his head against the porcelain. *Shit!* How had he got it so wrong? It must have been Angelino who attacked Mario. He'd caught on to the con and was now out for revenge.

"You know what? I think I believe you," Angelino dunked his head in the water as he spoke. "You aren't clever enough to mastermind a meet like this, let alone a child's abduction.

"I always knew you were stupid," he continued. "I just didn't have you down as suicidal!" The force behind the hand as it shoved his face into the water took Yorkie by surprise and he spluttered, gratitude enveloping him seconds later as a firm grip took hold of his hair and pulled him back out.

"Now, where were you before I so rudely interrupted?" Angelino asked innocently. "Ah, yes, that's right, but let's start at the beginning again, shall we? On the count of three... one... two... three."

As Yorkie's face smashed the surface once more, he knew there would be no reprieve. He started to count in his head again but couldn't concentrate and soon lost count. *Mustn't panic.* Panic spelled death.

"102," the voice was muffled, but still audible. "103… I tell you what, I'm feeling generous tonight." Angelino ripped his head from the water and Yorkie's lungs clutched desperately for oxygen before he was plunged below the surface again. On, and on, and on, until eventually, he was inwardly begging him to hurry up and put him out of his misery.

Burying the keys to his father's rental car in the sand on their first trip to England, the past began to spool through his brain. *Losing his footing as he climbed the stage to collect his graduation honors and spending the evening in the hospital being treated for an inflamed Achilles… the first time he clapped eyes on Elena in the grocery store, instantly knowing he was looking at his future wife… the wedding… the honeymoon… the accident… if you hadn't got drunk, it wouldn't have happened…*

"I could find your daughter," he tried—failing—to convince Angelino as his lungs filled with water. "I could help you." Close to blacking out, a thought came out of nowhere. *"I didn't have you down as suicidal."* Angelino was going to make it look like he'd killed himself. It shouldn't matter, but it did. Elena already thought he was a coward and now she would be proved right. Suicide had never been part of his plan, but now that was exactly how she would remember him.

Placing as much weight as he could on the countertop in front of him, Yorkie curled his right leg around Angelino's and tugged forcefully, determined to unbalance him, but it didn't work. His opponent was too strong, and the remaining fight drained from him as he slumped forward and accepted the inevitable.

CHAPTER THIRTY-SIX

Monday, August 26, 2019 (20:00)

THE BLINDS WERE DRAWN, AND THE ROOM WAS DARK except for a soft glow from the computer screen which illuminated Detective Dennis Boyd's face. His shift had finished hours ago but the discovery of the two mutilated bodies at the old Citadel Hotel had left his brain too wired to relax.

He tapped at the keypad with the rhythmic precision of a concert pianist, a montage of faces floating across the monitor in front of him. Morgue photographs, artist sketches, forensic reconstructions; hundreds, upon hundreds of eyes staring out at him, begging for recognition. *Name us,* their ghosts silently cried out.

NamUs (The National Missing and Unidentified Persons System) was open to anyone who cared to look at it, a fact that had initially appalled and fascinated him in equal measure. The thought that the authorities were uploading photographs of dead bodies on the internet for everyone to see seemed incomprehensible. The deeper he delved however, the more he realized that for many anxious relatives, a body was preferable to no body at all.

"I need closure," one such contributor had commented on an online forum that Dennis had visited. "Ask yourself this. If you lost a loved one and it meant the difference between finding out what happened to them or never knowing, what would you prefer? The not knowing... that's the real killer." Words that now haunted him as he scrolled through the reams of faces pleading to be identified so they could finally rest in peace.

"Grub's up." Becca's voice travelled up the stairs, reminding him that time was no longer his friend.

"Five minutes," he called back, his eyes urgently scanning the supporting evidence for every unidentified corpse that was currently tagged in a morgue or buried in an unmarked grave across the country. It was the unrecovered bodies he was interested in; the families and friends who had posted as much information about their loved ones as they could in the hope of matching them with an unidentified John or Jane Doe.

"I'm starving," she moaned, the irritation in her tone palpable as he waited for the data to load. There were enough cadavers in the system to populate a small city and yet, as the database returned the latest set of possible percentages, he knew he was onto something.

"Almost finished," he replied far too quietly for her to hear as engrossed in his task, his fingers deftly scrolled over the keys as he tweaked some of his search criteria.

"Come on, come on," he urged, his eyes glued to the screen as it slowly loaded the information.

"Den?" Her voice was closer now as she climbed the stairs to fetch him.

"Just five more minutes," he begged, his eyes never leaving the monitor in front of him. The database was downloading the information rapidly now and if the accompanying chart was to be believed, he was finally getting somewhere.

"You said that ages ago," she complained, studying him from the doorway. "I thought we had a deal?"

"We did… Do," he instantly corrected himself. He had promised they would spend the evening together, but he couldn't quit now. His hand pressed the small box in his breast pocket that held the ring. Tonight, he'd intended to finally pluck up the courage to ask her to be his wife, but it might have to wait.

You're going to lose her, the voice in his head taunted him, but as the system finally finished updating, it no longer seemed to matter.

"Yes!" He punched the air with his fist. "We've got a match." He swung around on his chair to face her. "I can't stop now, you know that, right?"

"I'll carry on without you," she grumbled, loosening her grip on the doorframe as she left him to it.

"I'll make it up to you, I swear," he whispered as he focused on the information in front of him.

"Edward Dutthie," he breathed as he returned his attention to the screen. The officer who witnessed Billy murder his father and helped secure his conviction. Dennis hadn't been convinced that Billy was their man, but now? This was huge! Forensics would have to be involved, of course. They'd have information outside his remit to prove it definitively, but he was now 99.9 percent certain that one of the partially mutilated bodies belonged to none other than Edward Dutthie… which could mean only one thing. He duly entered the relevant information into the system as quickly as he could.

Minutes later, he was reaching for his cell phone. "Burt?" His eyes shone with excitement as he spoke. "I've got a match for our John and Jane Doe."

CHAPTER THIRTY-SEVEN

Monday, August 26, 2019 (21:30)

IT WAS SURPRISINGLY EASY TO TRACK SOMEONE'S movements if you knew what you were doing. They were called "Smart Phones" for a reason and the average person was blissfully unaware they were carrying around one of the most sophisticated tracking devices ever invented. GPS, Wi-Fi, IP addresses, Twitter, Instagram, Facebook; all of them stashed away enough personal data to build a detailed map of the user's activity over time.

The software that Ethan had developed was equally high-tech. Just one anonymous call to a target device was enough to generate a unique code that was needed to link it with his own. The whole process had taken less than a minute, and he was now able to sit back and access everything that occurred on the other appliances.

Catching sight of his employer's Dodge Durango entering the parking lot on the display in the right-hand corner of his computer screen, Ethan dialed the concierge on the internal line and instructed him to make Angelino wait a few minutes before granting him access. He chuckled quietly to himself. The casino mogul seemed to think he was invincible, that he could bark out orders and everyone would instantly comply. It felt good to claw back some control.

Ethan didn't plan on telling his boss about the hacking software. Now that he knew it worked, he intended to put it to good use. Angelino had been acting odd of late, and his determination not to involve the cops over Alice's recent disappearance was making him more suspicious, so he had already put a trace on Angelino's cell phone to see what dirt he could dig up.

He hadn't recognized the number that sent the video of Alice to Angelino at first. His landlord was stored in his list of contacts so there was no need to pay attention to the physical digits. Thanks to his program though, he now also had access to all the activity on the device, which had already produced some interesting results.

Earlier this evening, Mario's cell phone had been used to send both Angelino and another number—which Ethan now knew belonged to Yorkie Fletcher—a text scheduling a meeting between the two of them at the Paragon Resort. A quick glance at his wristwatch confirmed that Angelino had probably made his way here straight from that meeting, but since Mario was stuck in hospital and didn't have a cell on him when he was found, the odds were that they had been sent from Mario's attacker. Billy Jackson. Ethan was sure of it.

A short while later, something even more curious happened. Another message had been sent from Mario's cell to a different number:

ETA, 15 MINS.

It could only mean that Billy had an accomplice. The text was still sitting in the inbox undelivered and when Ethan had tried the number, he'd reached an automated voicemail. It hadn't stopped him from hooking the device up to his own but so far, it had given him very little to go on.

"Well?" The door struck the adjoining wall as Angelino barged into the apartment and Ethan deftly switched the screen to the video that had been forwarded to him. Ethan's neighbor meanwhile—an elderly, serial complainer—began to repeatedly bang her walking stick against the wall in an obvious act of defiance.

"She'll stop eventually," Ethan said, glancing from the computer to his employer as he spoke. The guy looked like shit. Dressed in a T-shirt drenched with water or sweat, and grubby running pants and sneakers, he could easily be mistaken for a homeless person instead of one of the city's most successful businessmen. What *exactly* had gone on at the Paragon this evening?

"She's got one minute, else I'll personally make her," Angelino snarled, the stress of the past hour and his daughter's abduction playing havoc with his patience.

"Grab a seat," Ethan instructed, eyeing him warily. He brought to mind a coiled snake that was about to crush its prey and sink in its fangs and he had no intention of being at the receiving end of the venom.

"You got my message?" He had decided to give Angelino enough ammunition to protect his own ass, but not a single bullet more.

"That the video was sent from Mario's cell?" Angelino nodded. "Proper little Sherlock Holmes aren't you, but if you know what's good for you there'd better be more."

"There is." He clicked open an image and adjusted the monitor slightly so that his employer could see from the angle where he was now seated.

"What's this?" Angelino struggled to control his temper as he glared at the screen, his eyes glued to a graffiti mural he recognized from the video he had been sent of Alice. "I asked you to locate her, not enhance the video."

"This isn't from the video," he replied. The cell being used by Billy—or his accomplice—was pretty new, the only recorded location within the vicinity of the Tropicana. Even more interesting was that they—or at least the device—hadn't moved for several hours. That section of street was closed off to pedestrians so Ethan had done a quick search of the internet to check for any incidents that could explain the time-lapse, but the freeway had been clear of collisions all day. Which, had given him another idea...

"Does the name Matthew O'Brien mean anything to you?" he asked.

"Should it?" Angelino snarled.

"He's a writer."

"And?" Angelino was struggling to breathe as the frustration built in his chest and threatened to explode. What part of *Alice is missing, and her life is at risk* did Ethan not understand? The last thing he had time for right now was a lesson about Vegas' literary talent.

"Are you going to shut her up, or am I?" he snapped, as the continual banging from next door increased in volume.

"O'Brien goes that extra mile. He goes places

others won't, can't, or simply don't dare." Ethan ignored the jibe about his neighbor, hoping for her sake that she shut up soon. "A few years back, he discovered this whole urban netherworld going on beneath the Strip. *Beneath the Neon,* it's a good book, you should read it."

"Go on." Angelino shifted his seat closer to the screen as the relevance started to sink in.

"There's this maze of pipes and washes underground that work like bathtubs, collecting the rainwater and draining it to Lake Mead."

"And you think that's where Alice is?"

"The photo you're looking at is downloaded from the internet, but according to my software it's definitely the same as in the video."

"So, where is she?" Angelino leaned forward, his face animated. Finally, they were getting somewhere.

Just enough ammunition and no more, Ethan reminded himself, struggling to suppress a smile. "There's at least 300 miles of these underground channels, she could be anywhere." He carefully watched his employer's reaction in the reflection of his screen, curious to see how far he would go at the expense of his child.

"So, call the writer and ask," he hissed.

"And tell him what? Your daughter's been abducted, but you'd rather deal with it yourself than involve the cops? Get real, Angelino."

"Tell him she's missing, but scrub over the rest." If there was any chance that this O'Brien could identify Alice's whereabouts, it had to be worth a try.

"He'll still want to know why we haven't involved the cops," Ethan stood his ground. "The tunnels are no place for a child… the residents are likely dangerous," he added, doing his best to sound concerned as he secretly taunted him.

"There are people living down there?" Angelino felt the all-familiar bile rise in his throat. What *type* of person currently had access to his daughter? Rapists? Drug addicts?

"Jesus Christ, Ethan," he seethed. "We had him. Right there, in my casino, and you let him go. You *gave* him my daughter."

Ethan stiffened, his skin tingling as the hairs stood to attention on the back of his neck. So, Angelino did know about Billy. Did this mean he also knew about his recent visit to the police station? That it was him who deleted the footage?

"We need to involve the cops," he bluffed. If Angelino knew he'd already done exactly that, he would surely have let on by now.

"No cops!" Angelino stood abruptly, almost knocking over the chair in his haste. "You'd best find her Ethan, and you'd best find her fast," he said, deliberately slamming the door against the wall again on his way out.

CHAPTER THIRTY-EIGHT

Tuesday, August 27, 2019 (05:35)

CAREFUL NOT TO DISTURB HIS WIFE, SERGEANT BURT Myers gently eased the sheets from his body and swung his legs over the side of the bed. Picking up his iPhone from the bedside table, he scanned the latest updates from Detective Andrews before tapping out a quick response.

SUICIDE OR FOUL PLAY?

Within seconds, his phone vibrated with a reply.

THE LATTER, NO PLAYING CARD THOUGH.

Burt was pensive as he fixed his hair and went to work on his teeth. No matter how Yorkie had died, he couldn't help but think that he and Karl had played a part in it. Their priority should have been safeguarding him from harm but instead, through threats and intimi-dation, they had propelled him directly toward it.

"The cab's booked for seven, try not to be late," his

wife mumbled groggily as he selected a clean shirt from the dresser.

"Hmm?" He was squinting in the dark as he tried to check his pants for creases and turned on the bedside lamp for a better inspection.

"The restaurant." She stretched and pulled the covers over her head to protect her eyes from the harsh light.

Their anniversary. He'd completely forgotten. Thankfully, he'd had the foresight to organize his gift with the local jewelers weeks ago—a necklace that Nancy had been hankering after for months. Now all he had to do was remember to pick it up.

"Would I be late?" he joked innocently as he sidled up to the bed to kiss her, but one quick glance at his shoes made him hesitate. Reaching for a discarded sock from beside the bed, he spat on the linen and began to carefully polish each toe. Finally satisfied, he reached over and planted a kiss on the back of his wife's head, promising to be home in record time for their restaurant reservation.

His journey across town was slower than it should have been, the leftover debris from yesterday's storm creating havoc on the highway and almost an hour had passed by the time he stepped over the threshold into the restroom where Yorkie had taken his final breath.

"CCTV?" Dressed in protective gloves, coverall, and footwear, he moved from stall to stall, gently pushing each door against its hinges as he surveyed the scene before moving on to the next. All of them were empty— not so much as a discarded paper towel in a trash can that might carry traces that would lead them to their killer.

"Same old story." Detective Karl Andrews stepped aside to allow a member of the forensics unit to squeeze past with a large UV lamp. "No profit, no need to protect."

"Any cameras at all between here and the casino?" Burt was studying a handprint on the mirrored wall behind one of the urinals. It could belong to anyone, but he still wanted it checked. He wanted every fingerprint from every surface throughout the whole damned restroom lifted and compared against their records. Eventually, their killer would get careless, and a hotel restroom was as good a place as any.

"Nope," Karl shook his head. "I've got Dennis wading through what we've got from the casino exits, but it's going to take time."

"That we don't have," Burt snapped. "Any sign of Billy Jackson?"

Retrieving his cell phone from his jacket, Karl swiftly checked the screen before responding. He had instructed Dennis to contact him immediately if he caught so much as a glimpse of their target. "Nothing yet."

"I thought the restroom was manned 24-7. Where the hell was the attendant?"

"On a break, apparently," Karl replied, raising his eyes to the ceiling. "Clearly, we can't arrest the guy for taking time out from the most boring job in the world, but until we speak to him, we can't write off any involvement either. He agreed to accompany Noah to the station for questioning," he added, predicting Burt's next question.

"On a scale of one to ten, how likely would you say it was that the killer struck lucky and disposed of his target while the attendant was on his break?" Burt paused briefly, before pressing on. "Exactly. Either, our attendant is a creature of habit, or…"

"He received a substantial tip to make himself scarce," Karl finished, his eyes scanning the selection of fragrances and lotions that were neatly laid out on the man's table. He picked up a tube of hand cream and studied the label. "You're only as old as the body you feel," he read aloud. "Silky smooth skin for you and your loved one in just one application… who the heck designs this shit?"

"The same kind of idiot who tampers with evidence before it's been properly processed." Burt threw him a disapproving look and signaled for him to put the lotion back where he had found it before any of the techni-cians noticed. "I think it's time to pay Elena a visit," he continued, ushering Karl out of the restroom.

"Can't see us being that welcome."

"I'm not asking her to bake a cake and invite the neighbors, am I?" Burt replied, pressing the button to call the elevator. "It's just good manners, that's all. A courtesy. Yorkie was one of us, and while we're there, we can see if she can shed any light on his final movements and who he might have been planning to meet."

"I still can't see her greeting us with open arms at this time of the morning." He glanced at his wristwatch to reiterate the point.

As the elevator clattered its course to the ground floor, Karl's cell pinged with an incoming message. Voicemail. Stepping into the fresh air moments later, he paused on the sidewalk to listen to it.

Glancing behind him to see what had caused the hold-up, Burt stopped walking and turned to address Karl. "Well?"

"No sign of Billy Jackson." Karl tucked his cell back into his pocket as he approached Burt.

"There must be. Have him check again."

"He's checked twice already. The only way in—or out—is via the casino. All exits were covered. No discrepancies, no missing footage, no Billy."

"He's definitely our man, I'm sure of it." Burt chewed his bottom lip, thoughtfully.

"There was no playing card though," Karl lowered his voice and leaned in, conscious that anyone passing might overhear.

"Means nothing," Burt automatically rejected the comment. "He could just have been disturbed, that's all."

"Or the obvious answer isn't necessarily the right one," Karl retaliated.

"That maybe, but I still want that footage checked again. Fresh eyes, fresh perspective. Dennis must have missed something important," Burt replied stubbornly.

"OK," Karl reluctantly agreed. "If it makes you feel better, I'll go through it myself after we've seen Elena, but I guarantee we won't find anything. Dennis is one of the most thorough on the team and you know it. He doesn't make rookie errors."

"Just humor me," Burt replied, grateful it wasn't him who was going to have to pore over hours and hours of footage just to prove a point. "Hop in," he added, pressing the button on his key fob to unlock his vehicle, and slipping behind the wheel. "We'll pick up breakfast on the way."

CHAPTER THIRTY-NINE

Tuesday, August 27, 2019 (17:15)

THE DAY HAD PRODUCED NOTHING BUT DEAD ENDS. Yorkie's wife hadn't even heard her husband leave the house the previous evening and claimed to have no knowledge of who he planned to meet. She had openly revealed that they had a big argument earlier that evening, so Burt was inclined to believe her.

The trace on Yorkie's missing cell phone had come back blank—the killer presumably disposing of it at the first available opportunity, and Karl Andrews had called a short while ago to confirm that there was no CCTV evidence of Billy Jackson at the Paragon in the lead up to Yorkie's murder.

Burt was now seated on a rickety wicker chair, studying Billy Jackson's mother as she finished her cigarette and promptly lit another. Face devoid of makeup, Marlene's once-porcelain complexion was now scarred with age and the mischievous sparkle in her eyes had been replaced by defeated, sunken craters. Bones jutted furiously through the thin fabric that covered her flaccid shoulders, which were only mildly camouflaged by the curtain of greasy silver hair that hung limply to them. A mere shadow of her former self, she was barely recognizable. Burt found the transformation unsettling.

Aware that he was staring, Burt turned his attention to his surroundings instead. Clearly neglected, it was still hard to imagine that the house had once been the scene of a brutal murder. Mismatched furniture coated in a thick film of dust littered the room and did nothing to conceal the worn, threadbare carpets that lay underneath. Atop the furniture sat an array of tarnished frames, all filled with old family photos: Billy and Nate as children, carefree and happy as they ran giggling and open-armed toward the photographer; Billy and Nate on either side of their mother, clutched under each arm like a mother hen protecting her chicks; Marlene and Jacob on their wedding day, the obvious devotion as they looked into one another's eyes, impossible to ignore. Not a single picture of the children with their father though, he noted.

From where he sat, Burt also had a bird's eye view of the kitchen. Dirty dishes filled the sink and garbage spilled onto the floor from the refuse container. The worktop, mostly camouflaged by opened packets of food and discarded containers, contained a small television in the corner, which currently displayed images of the once-thriving Citadel Hotel. Despite the lack of volume, it wasn't difficult to follow the story. Recently reduced to rubble, work on the proposed new multi-billion-dollar luxury hotel had now been delayed due to yesterday's grisly discovery.

"No prizes for guessing why I'm here, Marlene." Burt picked up his cup, but one glimpse of the thin layer of skin that had formed on his drink was enough to make him put it straight back down.

"Why can't you leave him alone?" Marlene wrung her hands anxiously as she spoke.

"Billy's parole officer hasn't seen him for weeks," he pressed.

"It's not been easy, you know. My boy waited years to get his life back and when he did, it wasn't the life he remembered." She stubbed her cigarette and lit another with shaking hands.

"The address given to the board was yours, Marlene," he nudged gently.

"Everything had changed, even the people."

"He's in breach of his conditions."

"The neighbors didn't take kindly to his presence," she admitted, although this was no surprise given all the painted threats on the outside of the house.

"If you know where he is, you need to come clean."

"So you can lock him up again?" Marlene inhaled deeply on her cigarette and began to cough as the smoke hit her lungs.

And throw away the key, Burt thought as he stood and walked into the kitchen to increase the volume on the television. "We just need to talk to him," he replied, jabbing a finger at the television as he spoke.

"What the hell has that got to do with my boy?" she squeaked, clearly taken aback.

"I was hoping he could tell us that," Burt retaliated. "You see, we have reason to believe that the bodies are your son's wife and her lover." It went against all protocol to disclose such information until formal identification had taken place, but he had to get her attention.

"*Ex*-wife," she snapped, reaching for a tissue, and

dabbing at the film of sweat that had formed on her razored cheekbones.

"They weren't formally divorced though, were they?"

"I hope they rot in hell!"

Momentarily stunned into silence by her hostility, Burt's mind struggled to keep up with the questions thundering through it, mainly... why she hadn't registered any surprise about the identity of the victims? Did she already know?

"Failing to disclose Billy's whereabouts makes you an accomplice," he threatened, sickened by her disregard for the victims and her son's potential involvement.

"Is it not enough for you that he already spent years locked up for a crime he didn't commit?" she spat, unable to disguise her anger.

"If he's innocent, he's got nothing to worry about," he replied, deliberately ignoring the suggestion that Billy had previously been wrongly convicted. Burt had been confident of Billy's guilt then and he was just as confident of it now.

"Like last time," she sighed bitterly.

"Billy was caught red-handed," he reminded her.

"Is that so?" Marlene eyed him with disdain.

"It's a matter of public record," Burt replied. "Officer Dutthie's testimony was key to your son's conviction."

"Edward Dutthie was a *liar*!" she hissed. "He framed my son to protect his own."

Was, Burt's ears pricked on high alert at the use of the past tense. "And your evidence to corroborate such a claim?" he asked, his tone dripping with sarcasm.

"Do you recall Nate's suicide note, Sergeant Myers?"

"I recall the note, but not the exact content," he replied solemnly, wrong-footed by the sudden change of subject.

"He isn't guilty, he didn't do it," she said, the words instantly triggering a memory. At the time of Nate's suicide, there had been some debate over the meaning of the note, some of his colleagues believing that it was an attempt at a confession; that Officer Dutthie might have identified the wrong twin. Of course, since it wasn't possible to ask Nate what he had meant, the suggestion had been overruled as mere speculation.

"Nate was confirming Billy's innocence," Marlene continued when Burt didn't respond.

"Not really concrete though, is it?"

"You'll be laughing the other side of your face once you see the truth's been staring at you all this time," she snapped.

"Enlighten me." He leaned back and did his best to look comfortable in what he suspected was quite possibly the world's most uncomfortable chair.

"Nate was wasted in that repair shop." She pulled another cigarette from the packet as she spoke. "He was too clever, and that's why his suicide note didn't make any sense to me at first."

"In what way?"

"It wasn't exactly profound, was it? Your last chance on Earth to have your say; to make people listen and that's it?"

"So, what changed?"

"The knowledge he was telling us the identity of the real killer."

"Come again?" Burt shook his head nonplussed.

"It's an anagram," she replied. "Rearrange the

letters and they reveal who killed my Jacob." She deliberately omitted mentioning that it was Billy's new friend,
Bo, who had first alerted them to the fact. She couldn't
be sure, but she suspected that her son was currently
staying with Bo and the last thing she wanted to do was
lead them to him.

"What name came up?" Burt asked, unconvinced.
Contrary to public opinion, police perjury was
extremely rare.

"Alan Dutthie," she answered, puffing hard on the
end of her cigarette as she watched him closely to gauge
his reaction to the news. "Edward's son!"

"OK, let's just rewind a second." Burt stood up and
paced the floor as he tried to think. Edward Dutthie had
taken the stand and sworn to tell the truth, the whole
truth, and nothing but the truth. Was it really feasible
that he had in fact stretched that truth to portray a
sequence of events that never happened?

"You ever stop and ask yourself how Nate could
have known this?" he finally asked.

"He was there that night," she shot back without
hesitation.

"He wasn't though, was he? Billy even confirmed as
much."

"Because he was trying to protect him," she replied
vehemently. "He thought Nate did it."

"So why didn't Nate speak up to clear his name
when he had the chance?"

"Now that, Sergeant Myers, is a good question, but
it's not like I can ask him now, can I?"

"Let me put it another way then. Why would Alan
Dutthie have shot your husband?"

"You think I don't ask God the same question every

night before I go to bed and every morning when I wake? He's not answering though, is he? Maybe you'll have more luck," she responded.

"We'll speak to Dutthie," he promised, glancing at his wristwatch, keen to bring the meeting to an end so he could get home in time to wash and change before the cab arrived.

"You'll have your work cut out," she scoffed. "He no longer exists. Goes by the name of Alfred Turner these days."

Alfred Turner? Why was that name so familiar? As Marlene closed the door behind him, he stood a moment on the path, lost in thought as the name raced through his brain.

CHAPTER FORTY

Tuesday, August 27, 2019 (22:45)

Burt sat in his favorite armchair, nursing a tumbler of bourbon in silence, and staring absently at the half-empty bottle on the coffee table in front of him. The sound of a toilet flushing above reminded him that he should be upstairs making amends for his earlier tardiness, but his mind was too occupied to sacrifice his thoughts to an argument with Nancy.

She'd come around eventually. In twenty-five years of marriage, she hadn't ever held the demands of the job against him. Forfeiting their milestone anniversary celebrations in one of the finest restaurants the city had to offer wasn't the smartest of moves, but the moment Marlene mentioned *Alfred Turner*, the name had rattled frantically around his skull.

It took longer than it should have to realize that Alfred was the employee who discovered Maddison Scott's swollen, pruned-up corpse in the hotel swimming pool at Foo Dogs and as soon as it dawned on him, Burt had paid Angelino a visit which resulted in more questions than answers. Either his friend genuinely knew nothing about any possible connection between Alfred Turner and Alan Dutthie, or the man belonged on the stage.

Had they got it all wrong? It wouldn't be the first time Alan Dutthie had been accused of murder, and Marlene's anagram stacked up; Burt had checked as soon as he'd climbed behind the wheel of his car. Added to which, Dennis Boyd had called and confirmed that their John Doe had been formally identified as Edward Dutthie before he even had chance to turn the key in the ignition.

Nothing was making any sense—so many variables nagging in the recesses of his mind and his head hurt just thinking about it. He reached for the bottle of bourbon, his eyes settling on the deck of playing cards on the table next to it; yet more clues to a puzzle that was so far eluding them.

The creak of a floorboard directly behind him startled him and Burt automatically reached for his gun as he turned to the source of the noise. *Nancy.* He instantly relaxed.

"If the mountain won't come to Muhammad," she said, sidling barefoot around the side of the couch. "Room for a little one?" He smiled. Nancy was larger than life in more ways than one, and the fact that she didn't feel the need to torture herself daily with strict diets and exercise regimes had been one of the first things to attract him to her.

Without waiting for an answer, she squashed herself in beside him, curling up and resting her head on his chest. It felt good, and Burt closed his eyes and leaned back in the seat as he pulled her closer to him and gently massaged her scalp with his fingers.

"You missed a fantastic meal," she purred, inching closer to him as his fingers worked their magic.

"You went without me?" Burt opened one eye to study his wife more closely, unsure whether to be pleased or affronted although the fact she had enjoyed her evening despite the odds was certainly making his life easier now.

"Shame to waste it," she replied. "Place like that gets booked up months in advance." She idly stroked her thumb back and forth on his belly and it growled in retaliation.

"So, who was the lucky guy?" A tiny flicker of jealousy seared his gut, but in truth, he was so ravenous, it could just be hunger pangs and it was difficult to say what he resented more. The fact that another man got to spend the evening with his wife while he had to work, or whether he simply envied him such a fine meal that he had no doubt paid for.

"Paul…a," she grinned, enjoying teasing him.

"Paula?" *Must have been a bit jealous,* he reflected as he felt the tension drain from his body.

"Paula," he repeated, suddenly jerking upright as a thought occurred to him.

"Yes, Paula, who else?" Nancy smacked his thigh playfully.

Why hadn't he thought of her sooner? Before he and Nancy had even met, she had visited a fortune teller —Paula—who predicted from a deck of cards that she would be swept off her feet by a police officer. Days later, while chasing a suspected shoplifter, Burt—who had been in better shape back then—had rushed around a blind bend and done exactly that. Shocked but relatively unscathed, Nancy had later agreed to allow him to take her out for a drink by way of an apology. The rest was of course history, but Paula had been maid of honor at their wedding and she and Nancy had remained friends ever since.

"I need to speak to her." Burt shuffled in his seat and gently pushed Nancy aside as he reached for his iPhone. "Tell her it's urgent," he said, passing the phone to his wife.

"Can't it wait 'til morning?" She eyed his empty glass warily.

"No," he shook his head. "She might finally be able to help us shed some light on what the cards mean and it's the least she can do since she ate my dinner," he joked, remembering the necklace in the side pocket as he put on his jacket.

"And this is for you." He kissed her tenderly on the lips as he passed her the box, his eyes flickering guiltily to the wasted bottle of bourbon as he picked up the deck of cards and car keys from the table and promised to make it up to her the second he got home.

CHAPTER FORTY-ONE

Tuesday, August 27, 2019 (23:30)

BILLY

THE DISTRICT WHERE ALFRED LIVES STARTS OUT WELL enough, but once I've passed the weekly motels and low-stake casinos things start to take a dive. As I keep going, past a gun store and boarded-up fuel station, I can't get Alice out my mind. I get the vibe Bo doesn't really like the kid. Granted, she's high maintenance but I still don't want to see her get hurt because her father's an asshole. I hope he can hold his temper in check until I've finished with Alfred and made my way back.

I reach a payday loan center and stop to catch my breath. A sign sticks out the grass verge in front of the building:

NEED MONEY FAST? WE CAN HELP!

I smile grimly at the clumsy scrawl underneath:

DESTROY YOUR LIFE.

There's no real difference between the legal loan centers and Mario's operation. Either way they'll bleed you dry. I cut through a pitch-black alley, shuffling slowly through the discarded trash that scatters around my feet.

"Fuck you, you piece of shit." A couple—and their argument—spills into the alley and I jerk sideways, my back hugging the wall as they pass.

"You come 'round here with your funky-ass stories and think I ain't wise to the truth?" she screeches. *Careful what you wish for, honey. Sometimes, the truth can lead to a heap more trouble.*

Once I'm sure they're gone, I push forward, out the alley and across the street into another passage which leads to a derelict yard full of old furniture and junked-out cars. I'm pleased to see Bo's kept his side of the deal and my ride home—a scrapped Nissan Altima—is parked exactly where it should be. Neither of us really knows how tonight will play out, but I sure as hell don't want to hang around once I'm done.

I squeeze through a gap in the chain-link fence and creep around an abandoned pool filled with garbage toward the deserted motel. A decomposed sign boasting vacancies hangs by a thread near the entrance and the once-unblemished exterior is now streaked with grime. Most windows are busted out or crudely boarded up with bits of old wood but then others—including room 102—have proper windows; evidence that the occupiers take pride in the cesspit they call home.

I take my time as I approach, mindful of the noise grit makes as it crunches beneath my feet when I move. I'm almost there, just a few feet from the door to room 102, when I hear the rattle of a chain followed by a high-pitched whine. *Alfred has a dog?*

"Sssh!" I step forward on bended knee and try to soothe it. "Sssh," I try again but as I edge closer, it gives out a low growl from deep inside its throat followed by a succession of disturbingly loud barks. Stupid mutt is going to wake the whole neighborhood if I don't do something, and my eyes scan the junk in the yard for something to shut it up before it's too late. A set of lights flick on in the block to my right, and curtains twitch in the room that adjoins Alfred's. *Come on, come on.* I spot a slab of steel, pausing only to lift the metal above my head before I slam it down as hard as I can.

Silence. One hit was enough, and the chain is released. Me and the dog eye each other warily as we wait for the other to make their move. The dog breaks the spell first and as it scuttles into the undergrowth, rage bubbles in my chest as I watch its ribs jutting out at awkward angles as it disappears. What kind of mother-fucker leaves their dog chained up with only a crappy container of dried-up water and nowhere to sleep except in its own piss and shit?

As I step toward room 102, I can't think further than slugging my balled fists into Alfred's skull until he screams in agony and begs me to stop. Scabby fuck is going to wish he was never born by the time I'm done.

About to bust down the door, the sound of barking in the distance burns into my brain. *Not now. Please, not now!* I should have figured the dog would come back, but I only need a few minutes. It doesn't let up though, the yowling getting closer and more determined until I've no choice but to try to calm it if I'm going to finish what I've started. I turn and head back in the direction of the noise until finally, I spot it cowering behind a burned-out car in the yard I passed through previously. As I approach, it turns and darts into the adjoining passage and it's only as I round the bend to follow that I realize I'm not alone.

CHAPTER FORTY-TWO

Wednesday, August 28, 2019 (10:30)

A HUSH DESCENDED AS SERGEANT BURT MYERS ENTERED the room and strode purposefully toward the charts displayed at the far end. Wasting little time on formalities, he pointed to a photograph of a middle-aged woman whose fixed smile didn't reach the striking green eyes that stared back.

"Elizabeth Angel was trapped almost a week in that damned elevator," he turned to address his team who were seated around a table littered with paperwork, "and initial estimates suggest that Edward Dutthie and Lorraine Jackson's remains had been swilling around in sewage for at least two weeks."

"Meaning there may be others we don't know about?" Detective Dennis Boyd asked.

"It's possible," Burt nodded. "We have no way of knowing how many more there could be."

"Could the killer be working their way through the deck?" Detective Noah Mason suggested, referring to the presence of the playing cards that had been discovered with the victims.

"I damn well hope not," Burt said, balking at the prospect of so many related homicides within his jurisdiction.

"But there's no pattern so far as I can tell," Noah replied.

"Unless the number's the pattern?" The thought had occurred to Detective Karl Andrews as he sat in rush-hour traffic on his way to the station. "Thirteen cards per suit…"

"Indicating a possible eight further targets," Burt finished.

"Some who could already be dead if our culprit's working in numerical order."

"I did have a slight breakthrough with the cards." Noah reached into his pocket and produced a deck of cards. Shuffling them dramatically as though about to conjure a magic trick, he then handpicked a selection and fanned them on the table, face up in front of his attentive audience. "What do you see?" he asked.

"Our killer's calling cards?" Dennis reached for the jack of diamonds and picked it up, flipping the card between his fingers before studying the front, an impressive night aerial image of the Strip taken from some 10,000 feet above.

"Every souvenir shop on the Strip sells identical packs." Karl extracted the eight of clubs from the pile and turned it over to reveal a photograph of Betty Willis' "Welcome to Fabulous Las Vegas" sign. "Locating who sold packs will be impossible, let alone who might have bought them." He dropped the card back down on the table.

"Not necessarily." Noah picked up the discarded card and held it between his thumb and forefinger as he slowly moved it in front of each of them so they could look at it more closely. "See those numbers?" He placed it on the table and pointed to the tiny print beneath the photographic image. "If the code on any of the cards is still legible, the manufacturer should be able to tell us when they were printed and where the deck was dispatched to."

"How will that help?" Karl frowned. "They probably sell hundreds of packs a week and there isn't a shopkeeper alive that would remember who they sold packs to, let alone be able to identify them or their whereabouts."

"True," Noah acknowledged, "but it will help narrow down the search area for where our culprit hangs out."

"Get yourself over to the evidence room and have someone check." Burt felt a flutter of excitement in his chest at the first sign of a potential breakthrough. "Follow up whatever we've got with the manufacturer. Even if it's only a partial, it's worth a try.

"The rest of us are going to focus on the meaning of the cards," he continued, as Noah gathered his belongings and hurried from the room.

"Could the perpetrator be telling a story?" The idea that the killer could be trying to communicate with the police had come from Becca. Determined to make amends for putting his work first the other evening, Dennis had confided in her far more than he should have, and he now just hoped she could resist gossiping about it with her friends; otherwise, he would be in a heap of trouble with his superiors.

"Last night, I paid an old friend a visit." Burt reached forward and selected the remaining cards from the splay on the table. "Paula is a fortune-teller, and while some of us might like to dismiss the practice as a load of old baloney," he raised his voice in protest as he observed Karl roll his eyeballs, "every card within the deck can be translated to mean something specific."

Retrieving the jack of diamonds from Dennis' clutches, he held it up in front of them and waved it back and forth. "Remember the 'Laughing Boy'?"

"If you draw it, you laugh," Dennis answered.

"Good to know someone was paying attention," Burt grinned. "As you all know, I've had my suspicions about Billy Jackson for a while and last night Paula solidified those suspicions." He reached into his pocket and produced a newspaper image more suited to a Hollywood slasher flick than reality.

"I don't follow." Dennis shook his head in confusion as he studied the picture and accompanying headline:

FORGIVE ME FATHER,
FOR I HAVE SINNED!
Regular churchgoer gunned down
by his own flesh and blood

"During the early hours of January 1, 1998, Billy Jackson murdered his father in cold blood," Burt replied. "A neighbor—local Law Enforcement Officer Edward Dutthie—witnessed the shooting and issued a written testimony that secured his conviction. Despite initially professing his innocence, Jackson pled guilty, and the case never made it to court. There were, however, critics who argued the press had branded him culpable and that he'd had no choice. Jackson served twenty years—during which time his wife hooked up with Dutthie—but with no institutional violence or escape history, he was granted parole a month ago."

"And next thing you know, Dutthie's remains…"

"Partial remains," Burt interrupted. "We've yet to locate the hands."

"Wind up with the ex-wife in a cesspit at a vacant building," Karl blew out a huge breath of air as he finished his sentence.

"The marriage was never actually dissolved." Burt had no wish to be pedantic, but there was no room for misunderstanding or errors in a case of this magnitude.

"The laughing boy," Karl spoke slowly as the relevance sunk in. "Maddison dubbed him 'the laughing boy.'"

"Exactly! And in fortune-telling, the jack of diamonds is said to warn of an individual who brings news." He returned his attention to the corkboard and rested his finger on the face that was better known to all of them for her tenacious and unorthodox approach to reporting. "Bad news," he added solemnly.

"And the others?" Dennis asked, struggling to keep up with events that had occurred when he was still sporting diapers.

"According to Paula, the ten of spades wedged between the elevator doors could indicate unwelcome news or imprisonment."

"Can we assume he thinks Elizabeth Angel failed him as a lawyer?" Karl asked.

"I don't think we can overlook the possibility," Burt acknowledged.

"What about Mario Brown, though?" Dennis asked. "Where would he fit into all of this?"

"The card found in Mario's pocket could just be a

coincidence," Karl responded. "We know he was playing the tables in the Lucky Plaza that night."

"And we also know that Billy followed him out the casino," Burt countered.

"There was no wallet, money, or cell on him when the paramedics arrived though," Dennis said. "We have to consider a mugging gone wrong, surely?"

"Perhaps," Burt conceded, "but it certainly shouldn't form the focus of our investigation. Particularly," he jabbed his finger toward the corkboard on the wall behind him once more, "when one considers the identities of the other victims… and the fact that in Paula's opinion, the eight of clubs found in Mario's pocket could signify a love of money that turned to greed."

"One thought did occur to me," Karl said, shifting in his seat and resting his elbows on the table. "We know Billy's dad had an electrical repair shop at the retail outlet on Paradise Road, right?"

"Paradise Emporium," Burt confirmed.

"What if Mario leant the dad money to fund it?"

"And true to form, Mario's levels of interest were so high they couldn't make the repayments," Burt finished as a crucial piece of the jigsaw fitted into position."

"It could explain Billy's grievance with Mario," Dennis nodded, "and we now know that Yorkie was Mario's debt collector."

"Which would explain Billy's gripe with Yorkie except that Billy was nowhere near the Paragon on Monday night," Karl said.

"I don't believe Yorkie's death is unrelated," Burt massaged his eye sockets as he spoke, "but in the absence of a playing card, we have to concentrate on the deaths of those that are obviously linked."

"What about the cards found with Edward Dutthie and Lorraine Jackson's remains?" Dennis asked.

"Partial remains," Burt reminded him, a little pedantically this time, but it was too important to be ignored since they were yet to locate either Dutthie's hands or Jackson's head. "Paula suspects the five of spades could indicate interferences that interrupt your daily routine to include changes in the way that you live," he continued.

"So, he's holding Dutthie responsible for his imprisonment?"

"Perhaps," Burt shrugged.

"And Lorraine?"

"Broken promises apparently," Burt replied, tossing the last card back onto the table. "The seven of hearts is considered to be a warning that someone will be unfaithful."

CHAPTER FORTY-THREE

Wednesday, August 28, 2019 (11:00)

BURT GLANCED AT THE CLOCK ON THE WALL, KEEN TO wrap up the meeting so they could get back on the streets and hunt down their main suspect.

"Do we have an address for Billy?" Dennis asked as though reading his mind.

"The authorized address was the mother's," Burt replied. "Yesterday, I also took the liberty of paying her a visit and she apparently doesn't know where he's living, and his parole officer hasn't been able to locate him. According to Marlene—Billy's mother—Billy has been working at a bakery, although she doesn't know which one. I've checked with his previous employer, but he—and I quote—'wouldn't touch Jackson with a shitty stick,' which means we're going to have to wade through treacle to find him."

"Marlene also claims," Burt continued, "that it was Alan Dutthie—Edward Dutthie's son—who killed her husband and that Dutthie framed Billy to save his own son from incarceration."

"Surely, we aren't going to give that any credibility?"

Karl scoffed. "A mother will do anything to protect her child."

"And perhaps a father," Burt retaliated, briefly recounting Marlene's suspicions about Nate's suicide note and the meaning behind it.

"It's hardly incriminating though, is it?" Karl said. *"He isn't guilty, he didn't do it."*

"The anagram stacks up, though," Burt argued.

"Any chance Edward Dutthie could have ID'd the wrong brother?" Dennis asked. "They were twins, right, so maybe Nate's way of confessing was casting blame elsewhere?"

"It's possible… anything is possible in this goddamned case," Burt slammed his curled fist on the table in frustration, "but unless we get to the bottom of what's driving Billy's anger, we're never going to find out."

"Well, if I'd served twenty years in prison for a crime I didn't commit and then found out who did it, I think I'd be pretty pissed," Dennis countered.

"We need to make speaking with Alan Dutthie a priority," Burt said.

"Should we bring him in?"

"No," Burt shook his head. "Go in all gun's blazing within hours of the discovery of his father's corpse and the press will crucify us if the allegations turn out to be false."

"What then?" Karl asked. "We can't do nothing."

"You're going to pay him a visit, that's what," Burt responded. "Issue your condolences on behalf of Metro and give the necessary assurances that we're doing all we can to find out who's culpable."

"But surely it makes more sense for Dennis to go?"

he argued. "If Alan Dutthie is using Alfred Turner's paperwork, Dennis interviewed Alfred and would know if they were the same person."

"Which is precisely why Dennis can't go," Burt stood his ground. "If Dutthie is using a false identity, we can't risk scaring him."

"Is it worth pulling up the initial mug shots of when he was arrested to see if there's any likeness between him and the man I interviewed on the night of Maddison's death?" Dennis asked.

"That was over twenty years ago. The kid would have changed beyond all recognition by now," Karl said, dismissing the idea out of hand.

"No stone should be left unturned," Burt replied. "I want as much information on both men as physically possible—from where they do their weekly shopping to the color of their underpants. Any hint they're the same person, I want to be the first to know… Any other questions?" he pressed, tidying the papers on the table in front of him and eager to draw the meeting to a close.

"There was one thing." Karl shifted awkwardly in his seat, unsure of how to broach the subject.

"Spit it out, we've got a shedload to get through today as it is."

"Should we be placing Angelino Vitriano under surveillance?"

"Any particular reason?" Burt raised a curious eyebrow at his subordinate.

"Despite the absence of a playing card, I think we're all agreed that Yorkie's death is somehow related. Well, as you know, I checked the CCTV myself," he continued, "and while Billy Jackson seemingly never went near the Paragon that night, Angelino definitely did."

"As did a million and one other people, I don't doubt," Burt shook his head. "Your point?"

"Angelino wouldn't take kindly to Mario stealing from him," Karl licked his lips. "What's saying he didn't know about the arrangement between Mario and Yorkie —and his own staff come to that—and decide to punish the pair of them?"

"You think Angelino is responsible for the attack on Mario *and* Yorkie's death?" Burt sneered. The suggestion that Angelino was involved was completely absurd.

"Angelino is connected to pretty much every single incident," Dennis chipped in, keen to air his concerns now the floodgates had opened.

"How so?"

"Maddison's body was found at the bottom of a pool in one of his resorts, Elizabeth's in an elevator at an apartment block his company owns. Mario was attacked after an evening fleecing one of his casinos. He was caught on CCTV at the Paragon at around the time Yorkie was killed, and now we have the *partial* remains of two more bodies dumped in a cesspit on a plot of land that he owns," Dennis tapped each reason off against his fingers as he spoke.

"Midas is one of the largest landowners throughout the state," Burt replied dismissively, keen to defend his friend despite the odds stacking up against him. "It's not exactly damning in the grand scheme of things."

"Maybe not," Karl conceded, "but I don't think we can overlook the fact that Angelino entered the Paragon shortly before Yorkie's death and left shortly after."

"It's what he does with his evenings," Burt replied through gritted teeth, irritated that they were wasting precious time targeting an innocent man. "He checks out the competition and spies on his staff."

"Nor can we ignore the intelligence that Angelino was one of Jacob Jackson's biggest customers," Karl pressed on, warming to his theme.

"An allegation that is currently unsubstantiated," Burt snapped. "Look," determined not to let his exasperation show, he was careful to maintain eye contact with both men, "if it should transpire that Angelino is in anyway involved in any of this, you have my word I'll come down on him like a ton of bricks."

CHAPTER FORTY-FOUR

Wednesday, August 28, 2019 (13:00)

THE LAST-KNOWN ADDRESS ON THEIR RECORDS FOR Alan Dutthie had turned out to be a complete waste of time. The luxury vehicles parked on the driveway had been more than enough to add a certain value to the property and convince Detective Karl Andrews that he could eliminate it from the equation. Nonetheless, he had approached the front door, careful to keep to the path and away from the immaculately manicured lawn for risk of upsetting the occupants.

"Must be almost ten years now, officer," the smartly dressed man who answered the door had explained as he shrugged his shoulders into his suit jacket. "Got a good deal, as it goes." He pocketed a cell phone and picked up a set of car keys from the stand beside him. "Nothing like an acrimonious divorce for picking up a bargain," he winked, handing him a business card with the words *"ELITE REAL-ESTATE"* emblazoned across the front. "Mandy," he called up the stairs. "I'm running late, I'm afraid," he smiled apologetically at Karl, "but, my wife will be happy to answer your questions. Mandy?" he called again when she didn't respond.

Apologizing for any disruption, Karl had politely confirmed that there was no need to disturb his wife and extracted himself from the situation. With hindsight he should have realized that Alan Dutthie's former family home would have been sold when the marriage was dissolved, and his father had hooked up with Lorraine Jackson.

Karl then decided to visit the registered address on Alfred Turner's witness statement that had been taken on the night of Maddison Scott's death. If there was any truth to the claim that Alan Dutthie was using Alfred Turner's identity, it was as good a place as any to start.

When he arrived at the address in question, however, Karl realized that things were about to get more complicated. A large chain-link fence surrounded the abandoned motel and a quick walk around the perimeter was enough to confirm his initial suspicions. Some windows were busted out altogether, others patched up with pieces of wood or plastic sheeting and even from a distance he could see multiple extension cords running the breadth of the yard feeding illegal residents with power stolen from law-abiding citizens in the vicinity.

It wasn't an uncommon problem, the legacy of the global financial crisis still visible on almost every block. Recovery had been a lot slower than the press would have the public believe and, in an economy that created some big winners, there had been many more losers. As the real-estate bubble burst, a toxic combination of frenzied buying and predatory lending had followed. Levels of national debt soared, as did the number of default notices and foreclosures, and unable to repay loans that far outweighed the value of their properties, many had surrendered their homes.

As the properties sat vacant, the squatter's market started to take shape. "How-to" classes and fake leases became commonplace, as did "cash for keys" schemes where individuals took on a property and then refused to leave until the banks paid them to go. While local news channels bragged about a recovery, claiming that prices in the area had risen almost three times as fast as the national average, incomes had barely budged, and consumer debt was now once more on the rise. The average person simply couldn't afford to buy, and those that could were wary of getting back into a market that had previously burned them so badly.

Pulling out his iPhone, Karl placed a quick call to Burt to update him. Deciding to take a closer look, he then squeezed through a gap in the fence and slowly made his way toward the derelict building.

Maximus Hernandez, meanwhile, studied the man from behind the small pane of plexiglass above his portable stove. Heavily coated with a film of grime, visibility wasn't good, but he could still sense exactly what he was looking at. There wasn't much demand for men in suits around the estate and the cop wore his role like a uniform.

He peered closer, watching intently as the officer reached down to pet Al's dog. He was still curious how it managed to escape the strict chain that Al shackled it to so it couldn't roam the yard and wondered if it had somehow managed to break free during the scuffle that had obviously taken place. He would have to make a call to Animal Control tomorrow. Arrange for them to come and collect it.

Padding barefoot down the corridor, Maximus opened the exit door that led directly into the yard and quietly observed the officer. Now on bended knee, he was assessing the hose that provided the residents with water.

"Pssst," he hissed, his eyes scanning beyond where the officer stood for any sign that he was being watched. "Over here."

Distracted by a length of hose that appeared to be running between a large steel barrel of water and one of the adjoining properties, Karl flinched. Reaching to his belt, he felt for his pistol for reassurance as he turned to face the source of the noise. Squats tended to bring a trail of crime with them, so he needed to be prepared for any unexpected ambush.

"You looking for Al?" the voice whispered urgently.

"Al?" Karl inquired innocently, trying to ignore the flash of excitement that flared in his chest.

"Alfred," Maximus replied. "Lives in 102." He gestured with his thumb to a door farther down the block on the right that looked as though it had recently been kicked in.

Casting a glance over his shoulder Karl slowly approached the man, his hand resting on the handle of his gun, ready to pull it at a moment's notice. "You know him?"

"Uh-huh." Maximus gave a curt nod, clearly on edge as he shifted from foot to foot, his eyes swinging erratically back and forth.

"Can I come in?" Karl asked, studying the man in front of him as he stood barefoot in the open doorway. Mid-to-late 30s, he wore a vest top and shorts and little else, except for an abundance of facial hair that would fill many a man with envy… not to mention, a look of dread that bordered on fear.

Several minutes later, sitting on the only available chair in the tiny space, Karl started to relax. He had to hand it to the guy. With only one room to do everything from cooking and eating to washing and sleeping, the place was immaculate. It wasn't what he had been expecting and his eyes travelled around the room, taking in the vanity unit, portable stove, and a table covered in papers, before finally resting on what looked like a relatively new flat-screen television that was attached to the wall in front of the bed.

"You'd be amazed what some of the hotels chuck out," Maximus' eyes tracked Karl's. "I found this mattress in a dumpster," he bounced almost childlike on it as he spoke. "Wheeled it all the way back from Planet Hollywood on top of a shopping cart."

"You wanted to talk?" Karl nudged. Now that he knew which room Alfred—Alan Dutthie too, if they really were the same person—resided in, he was keen to investigate further.

"Al's not there," Maximus replied, as though reading his mind. "That's the thing. He should be, but he's not."

"Care to expand?" Karl asked, raising an inquiring eyebrow at his new ally.

"It's like an unwritten agreement," Maximus answered. "Whenever we both work the graves, we catch up for a beer at the end of the shift. Helps to unwind and all that, only last night…" He left the sentence hanging in the air.

"Last night?" Karl prompted.

"He didn't show up. At least, I didn't think he did. Sometimes, he's showering when I get there… we do wash, you know," he sniped, observing Karl's cynical look. "So, I tried the door and sure enough it was open. I let myself in, and…"

"And, what?"

"Place was a wreck, that's what," Maximus continued. "Busted-out drawers strewn all over the floor, upheaved furniture… he's been kinda weird of late."

"Mind if we take a look?" Karl brushed down the cotton of his pants as he stood up. "Weird how?" he asked, as he opened the door and gestured for Maximus to lead the way.

"I dunno really, just shifty, I guess. Going on about something bad in the past catching up with him."

Interesting, Karl thought as he sidestepped an old vending machine thick with dust as they walked down the corridor. "Would you say you knew Alfred well?" he asked, desperate for any clues about a potential dual identity.

"As well as anyone knows anybody in this town," Maximus replied. "Even talked about getting out this dump." He pointed at the mildewed patterns that fought for pride of place with the nicotine that stained the walls as they moved. "Renting something better together."

Wouldn't be too difficult, Karl thought as he concentrated on not breathing through his nose. The corridor stank of piss, stale tobacco, and weed, and the once proud shag carpet was now littered with dirt and cigarette burns.

"It's this way," Maximus said, directing him left as they progressed down the passageway. "Whoever broke in busted the other door, so I blocked it up."

As they walked, the stench worsened, and Karl

found himself struggling with his gag reflex. "What the hell is that smell?"

"It gets worse," Maximus commented as he opened a door which led directly into a small, partitioned-off kitchen area. As Karl's eyes scanned the tiny worktop camouflaged with opened packets of food and a garbage bag overflowing with waste, Maximus pointed out the window to the German shepherd pacing the yard that Karl had been petting earlier. "That's the cause of the stink. It's normally always caged outside but it somehow got trapped in here last night. There was piss and shit everywhere."

CHAPTER FORTY-FIVE

Wednesday, August 28, 2019 (13:30)

"Tell me about Spun," Sergeant Burt Myers cut to the chase as Marlene begrudgingly invited him over the threshold.

"Just another of Jacob's crazy assed ideas to make his million," she replied over her shoulder as he followed her into the kitchen.

Burt's eyes scanned the room. Used dishes still crowded the worktop and no effort had been made to deal with the trash that spilled from the garbage container. Grabbing the only available seat, he motioned for Marlene to take it, but ignoring him she crossed the room, so he sat himself down instead.

"Financed by Mario Brown?" he inquired innocently.

"Financed by us," she spat, swinging on the soles of her feet, and glaring indignantly at him. "What we borrowed we paid back tenfold. We owed that man NOTHING!" Fumbling in the drawer beside the sink, she retrieved a packet of cigarettes.

"What about Angelino Vitriano?" he asked, studying

her carefully for any telltale signs that he might be close to the mark.

"What about him?" After wrestling with the cellophane, she finally managed to extract and light a cigarette, and had Burt not been looking for it, he would have missed the erratic shift of her eyes and the spark of fury that flashed through them.

"Did you owe him money?" He watched her eyes jerk once more to the right, then left, before they finally settled on his face. It looked like he might get to hear the truth after all.

"Desperate people do desperate things," she sighed.

"Go on." He leaned forward and rested his elbows on the worktop in front of him.

"Jacob should never have got into bed with Mario," she said. "We couldn't afford to put food on the table, let alone make the repayments."

"And so, you approached Angelino?"

"Other way around. He approached Jacob with a proposition." She paused, considering how much to disclose.

"I'm all ears," Burt nudged.

"He wanted Jacob to reprogram the machines in favor of the casino."

"And did he?" A small ripple of unease travelled the length of Burt's spine.

"Nate did," she nodded, "and he added his own code while he was at it."

"A code that could be manipulated?" He sucked air through his teeth as he asked the question.

"I'm not saying what my boys did was right," she continued, "but Angelino stood to make a fortune out of cheating his customers. Something he couldn't have done without my Nate, and we couldn't live off thin air forever."

"Did Angelino find out?" Burt asked, despite already knowing the answer deep in his gut. He also knew his friend well enough to know that if someone crossed him, it wouldn't go unpunished.

"Billy was stripped of his winnings and escorted from the premises," she admitted, the confession only serving to confirm Burt's worst fears. Why the hell hadn't Angelino mentioned any of this to him? *Because he couldn't,* the logical part of his brain reminded him.

"Next thing you know, Jacob's dead and my Billy's serving time for the murder."

"You can't think Angelino had anything to do with your husband's death?"

"No, sergeant, I don't *think* any such thing," she grumbled bitterly. "I *know.*"

"But, yesterday, you were pointing the finger at Edward Dutthie's son?"

"Oh, he killed him all right," she declared vehemently as she lit yet another cigarette from the stub of the last one, "but you'd need to speak to the organ grinder about all that."

"You believe Angelino put a contract out on your husband?" He winced as his toes cramped in retaliation to being so fiercely curled into the soles of his feet.

"Why have a dog and bark yourself?" She approached the door in a silent gesture that indicated it was time for him to leave.

Taking the hint, Burt tidied the chair under the kitchen table and picked up his keys. He needed to speak to Karl and ascertain whether he had managed to locate

Alan Dutthie or Alfred Turner or whatever he was currently calling himself.

"Angelino must have thought all his birthdays and Christmases had come at once when he realized they could frame an innocent bystander for the crime."

Innocent! If it wasn't so serious, Burt would have laughed. Irrespective of Marlene's allegations, Billy was no longer innocent and the sooner she came to terms with that, the better. "Failure to disclose your son's whereabouts is a criminal offense," he reminded her as he followed her to the front porch.

"I've not seen hide nor hair of him for weeks." She turned and glowered at him. "This is the last place he'd come with you all sniffing round."

"Well, if he does contact you, make sure you call me." Burt handed her a card with both his home and cell number printed on it. "I can help him," he tailed off, bowing his head remorsefully. Who was he kidding? He couldn't help Billy. Nobody could.

You created a monster, he scolded himself as he thanked Marlene for her time and proceeded back down the walkway. If there was any truth to her allegations, he had helped put the wrong person behind bars. Maddison, Elizabeth, Edward Dutthie, Lorraine Jackson, possibly even Yorkie... all of them would still be alive if it weren't for him.

And, what of Angelino? Carefully closing the gate, he was deep in thought as he exited the small yard and approached his vehicle. Was it really conceivable that his friend was caught up in all of this? Despite knowing him half a lifetime, it now seemed that he might not really know him at all.

Turning the key in the ignition, he tapped his fingers

impatiently on the steering wheel as he waited for the hands-free to kick in and download the list of numbers from his iPhone. He'd missed two calls from Karl while interviewing Marlene and locating Dutthie's son was now a matter of urgency.

"Well?" he said when Karl picked up.

"Shit," he cursed, slamming his foot on the accelerator as Karl detailed the ransacked room that had greeted him when he finally tracked Alan Dutthie down.

"Make hunting him down a priority." He swore again under his breath at the sight of heavy traffic up ahead. "Oh, and Karl?" he swerved past the stationary vehicles, "you were right about tailing Angelino. I'll explain when I get there—*if* I get there, traffic's dreadful —but we need to tread carefully for now. I guarantee his guard will already be up."

CHAPTER FORTY-SIX

Wednesday, August 28, 2019 (14:00)

As the sergeant sped away from the house, Nigel stepped from his hiding place behind a parked truck and studied the building across the street. *"Don't get angry, get even."* Billy's words to him seconds before he chased Mario Brown out of the Lucky Plaza blitzed his skull. It had taken a week of failed efforts to locate the correct address—hundreds of householders in the city boasting the "Jackson" name—but the detective's presence here today told him all he needed to know.

He approached the house and gently knocked on the door, the wood in such a state of disrepair he almost expected it to crumble beneath his touch.

"Is Billy home?" Nigel asked moments later as Marlene cracked the door ajar and stared at him vacantly.

"Who wants to know?" Her gnarled fingers gripped the edge of the door as though she might need to stop him from forcing his way inside.

"My name is Nigel Goodman," he replied. "I'm a friend of Billy's."

"I've never heard him talk about no Nigel," she said, studying him suspiciously. "Are you a reporter?" She tried to shut the door, but Nigel stopped it with his foot. "Why can't you all just leave my boy alone?"

"Please," he begged. "I want to help him."

"Lies," she snapped bitterly. "That detective said the same thing but look where trusting the cops got him last time."

"I'm a lawyer," he said.

"Is that so?" she growled. "Well, now I know you ain't no friend of Billy's. He wouldn't know any lawyers, nor would he want to after what happened. Turns out they can't be trusted either, so please remove your foot and leave me in peace."

"OK." Nigel held up his palms in a gesture of surrender but left his foot in place. "*Friends* might be overplaying it, but I do know him… and I am a lawyer," he added, pulling a business card from his jacket and passing it to her.

"You aren't even from Vegas." She eyed the card doubtfully before giving it back to him. "How does a lawyer from Connecticut think he can help my son?"

"I'm in no hurry to go home." Nigel cast his eyes to the floor as the memories of his wife's indiscretions that he'd worked so hard to put to the back of his mind resurfaced. He didn't want to go into details. Not here on the doorstep, not ever.

"If Billy instructs me as his lawyer, I can act on his behalf," he said, keen to keep the conversation on track.

"We can't afford no fancy lawyer from out of town," Marlene sighed. "I almost wish we could."

"I don't want money. I owe your son Mrs. Jackson and just want to repay the favor."

"A stranger knocks my door wanting to give my son free legal aid and I'm supposed to think there isn't a catch?" She tried to push the door again, but Nigel's foot held firm.

"Can we do this inside?" he asked. "Just five minutes of your time, that's all I ask." He really didn't want to divulge his private business on the doorstep, but he would if he had to.

"We do it here or not at all," she answered, as though she could somehow test his integrity by how willing he was to confide in her so impersonally.

Nigel sucked in a large breath of tepid air as he tried to compose himself. "I came to Vegas to kill myself," he eventually found the courage to speak. "I caught my wife—well, I guess you don't need to know the sordid details—but with my marriage ended, I kind of lost my way, but then I met your son the other night at the Lucky Plaza and everything changed."

Marlene watched him in silence. When Nate had died, a part of her had died too. The tragic waste of his life as raw now as it was all those years ago—the guilt and knowledge that she had failed to recognize his misery, the indescribable pain at losing her child so unnaturally, even anger that he could do something so selfish until finally, she had understood. She even considered taking her own life so many times she'd lost count; something only someone who had been that low could ever understand.

"I don't believe your son attacked that man, Mrs. Jackson," Nigel continued, "but if they pin that on him, there's a good chance he'll go down for these murders.

"The press annihilated him before and they'll do it

again if you let them," he pressed when she still didn't speak. "I just want to help him."

"You'd best come in," Marlene finally spoke, brushing at a stray tear as she stepped aside and opened the door.

CHAPTER FORTY-SEVEN

Wednesday, August 28, 2019 (17:00)

THE URGE TO SPREAD HIS FINGERS AND TWIST HIS clenched fists around Alfred's neck until his lungs deflated like a spent balloon had been immense, but if he killed him he might never see his daughter again.

Instead, Angelino had him *exactly* where he wanted him... out cold on a shelf made from unforgiving slats in the dungeon-like basement that once served as a luggage store for the thousands of guests that checked in and out of the now-derelict Angelino's Hotel.

Being back had brought back a lot of memories: some good, some bad; all of them serving as a painful reminder of the hotel's faded glory. In its day, it had been *the* place to hang out—the type of place where everybody knew everybody, and trouble was limited to the occasional drunken brawl. More recently, however, the only guests to grace the premises had been good-for-nothing freeloaders and even they were few and far between, the risk of being caught on private property outweighing the appeal of a temporary refuge.

Boards warning trespassers to keep out covered all

accessible windows and doors, camouflaging the gutted interior that lay behind the disintegrated façade. It didn't stop them all, but it helped—those sober enough to pay attention, aware that unauthorized entry would result in a battle they could never win.

Confident there were currently no uninvited guests lurking in the wings, Angelino had taken a walk around for old times' sake but soon regretted it. Even the water in the five-acre swimming pool now festered beneath the overgrown and neglected landscaping in sunken, murky green puddles.

The developers were to blame. Descending like a swarm of plague-infested fleas, they had wasted no time expanding the Strip into a grossly oversized theme park and the hotel's death warrant had been signed. The location alone made it impossible to compete. Neglecting the old hotel in favor of more popular, prime development land had been a necessary evil and Angelino was proud of his achievements. The Midas Touch Empire now controlled a larger percentage of real-estate than any of its competitors.

The hotel's closure hadn't come without unexpected benefits as it turned out. It was after all, the perfect place to house a prisoner without intervention. *Scream as much as you like—nobody's going to hear you here.* The fact that Alfred had given him nothing useful since his capture was, however, disconcerting. The more Angelino thought about it, the more convinced he became that Alfred had spilled his guts about Jacob's death. How else would Billy know the truth?

Maybe the time to stew had loosened his tongue? With that in mind, Angelino made his way back to the basement, pausing only briefly outside the door to listen before pushing it hard against the hinges and bursting into the dingy space.

"Where's my daughter?" he hissed, his face so close his breath tickled Alfred's skin.

"I don't know." Alfred shifted uncomfortably as the strips of timber and bindings holding him in place dug into his skin. "Please," he begged, "you have to believe me."

"Why would I believe a word you say?" Angelino's eyes glittered with fury. "We had a deal!"

"I never told a soul about Jacob. I swear."

"You never told a soul you murdered him, or you never told a soul who put you up to it?" Angelino retrieved the scalpel sheathed to his leg and gently caressed the blade.

"Neither… both." Alfred forced his knuckles onto the slats and tried to lever himself up, but it was useless. The shackles were fixed solid, and his wrists were bound so tightly together, there was no way to fight back even if he could release them.

"So how does Billy know?" Angelino calmly swiped the blade back and forth against Alfred's throat as though using his skin to sharpen it.

"I don't know," Alfred grunted as he collapsed in defeat. Determined to ignore the fire that raged across Angelino's face, he concentrated instead on a spider twice the size of a quarter as it carefully weaved yet another web across the slats above his head.

"The police then, how do they know who you really are?" Burt's unexpected visit yesterday had riled Angelino more than he cared to admit.

"I… don't… know!" Alfred cried again, and he honestly didn't know. He hadn't told a soul about what he had done all those years ago. Why would he? But if the police had worked out who he really was, it wouldn't take long for them to solve the rest of the puzzle.

"I'm going to untie you now." Angelino suddenly sprang to his feet and for a split second Alfred dared to hope that the worst was over; that his employer had finally come to his senses and realized he was telling the truth.

"This might hurt a little bit," he cackled, tugging sharply against the fabric with the blade and shredding the bindings in one swift movement.

It didn't, but Alfred's gratitude was short-lived when he realized he was referring to what would happen next.

Extracting Alfred's arm from beneath his body, Angelino slowly massaged his index finger, paying particular attention to the knuckle and surrounding bone before meticulously snapping it back. A crack and the splinter of broken bones filled the air. *LIAR!* the voice in his head roared.

"One down, seven to go," he announced in a manic, sing-song voice that drowned out Alfred's muffled howl. Billy wouldn't have taken his daughter unless he knew, and the only person who could possibly have told him was the scum in front of him.

As he reached for another finger, Alfred focused on the deadweight of his other arm, slowly releasing it from beneath him and aiming a punch directly at Angelino's face. Restrained for too long beneath the weight of his body, however, and with his shoulders still pinned to the boards with rope, his arm refused to do as instructed and he sank back against the slats in frustration.

Another snap filled the air as Angelino cracked the next bone in much the same way as the first. Was it also

Alfred who deleted the footage of Billy stalking Mario in the Lucky Plaza? Maybe he was protecting him? As for the police, how long before they connected the dots and dragged him into the whole sorry mess?

"I gave you *one job*," Angelino growled as he pressed on, shattering the bones of each finger as though shelling shrimps at a eat-all-you-can buffet. "One measly job to guarantee my silence, but you couldn't even get that right, could you?" Well, now it was his turn to silence Alfred and there was no way he was going to mess it up.

As the last bone splintered beneath his grasp, Angelino carefully splayed Alfred's hand on the bench beside him. Reaching for his scalpel, he then calmly pressed the blade against Alfred's index finger and slammed his fist down hard on the weapon's spine.

As the metal slid through the flesh and bone like butter, the roaring in Alfred's ears intensified and a high-pitched sound like air being released from a balloon left his throat. Spurred on, Angelino sliced faster, oblivious to the blood as it pumped from Alfred's stumps as he chopped manically with the speed and expertise of a butcher carving freshly slaughtered meat.

"**WHERE IS MY DAUGHTER?**" he yelled, as the soft thump of another severed finger hit the floor.

CHAPTER FORTY-EIGHT

Wednesday, August 28, 2019 (18:30)

Nigel was deep in thought as he walked back to the hotel and didn't even notice the rapidly darkening sky until the first spots of rain settled on his skin. Glancing up, he increased his step. He hadn't packed a single item of winter clothing for his trip. In fact, he hadn't packed much clothing at all since he hadn't planned on being around long enough to need it. As soon as the heavens opened and released enough rain to fill Lake Mead, however, he deeply regretted not investing in some more suitable attire once he'd made his decision to hang around.

In the distance, he could just make out the unlit neon sign at the entrance to his hotel and he pushed on determinedly while everyone around him ran for cover. *"We're not charity,"* Marlene Jackson's words as she refused his offer of free legal aid for her son, echoed in his ears as he swerved to avoid a young couple rushing toward him holding plastic bags over their heads to protect themselves from the downpour.

When he reached the hotel, a scorching heat had replaced the rain and, as steam rose from the asphalt, Nigel paused outside the revolving doors and inhaled deeply. *"Hugo Boss," eat your heart out,* he thought to himself as he closed his eyes and savored the scent. Most expensive colognes smelled like goat's piss in comparison and one day he was going to figure out a way to bottle and market the stuff.

Marching mechanically into the foyer behind a group of tanked-up teens, he felt an instant hit of regret at his lost youth. What he'd give to be high right now on whatever illegal substance they were on. Instead, champagne and nibbles served by the in-house butler as he soaked in the oversized bathtub was about as exciting as his evening was going to get, and even that was debatable since, if his memory served him right, he was supposed to give at least 24-hours' notice if he wished to benefit from such luxuries.

All thoughts of his forthcoming pampering session soon evaporated, however, as he spotted the big CEO himself—Angelino Vitriano—standing directly in front of him, arguing it would seem, with a member of his staff. *Not very professional,* but the man was under a lot of pressure, he supposed, what with the police connecting all these recent murders to the dead body that was found in the hotel pool on the day he arrived.

Neither Angelino nor the employee noticed him as he approached, giving Nigel the opportunity to study them both in more detail. Back pressed against the wall as Angelino towered over him, the employee looked nervous. There was also something about Angelino's body language and the way he was holding himself as he leaned into his employee's personal space that was arguably threatening and open to interpretation.

Drenched from head to toe courtesy of the recent downpour and keen not to draw attention to himself, Nigel tentatively approached the large bronze statue of two lions that stood sentry in the center of the lobby. At almost 20-feet tall—mouths wide-open in mid-roar—the sculpture was admittedly impressive, if a little garish for his tastes. It did, however, provide the perfect cover for him to eavesdrop unobserved as he pretended to admire the artwork in more detail.

"I need the location of that drain and I need it NOW!" Angelino hissed, louder than intended and he glanced over his shoulder, his eyes roaming the room like an eagle searching its prey.

"And I already told you, I need more time," Ethan lied. His software had picked up Billy's cell phone again earlier and determined to find out what was going on without being seen or followed, he'd taken the bus across town to check things out. Never again! Full of the city's most prolific window lickers all demanding attention, the journey had taken forever but it hadn't been without reward. Sure enough, the entrance to an underground tunnel lay only meters from where the signal was being emitted.

"And if he kills her in the meantime?" The palm of Angelino's right hand rested against the wall above Ethan's head giving him no opportunity to escape. "We had him, but you let him go," he snarled.

Nigel risked a sideways glance at the two men, slowly shuffling around the statue as he pretended to admire the bronze work in more detail while searching for a better vantage point to observe. As he moved, all the while keeping his eyes on his target, something inside him quietly shifted, and a plan to help Billy slowly hatched in his brain.

Beyond all reasonable doubt. Everyone knew that with doubt, it was hard to prove guilt. All along, he had focused on using his legal expertise to defend Billy, but what if he was able to find enough circumstantial evidence to put any suggestion of Billy's guilt into doubt? Marlene Jackson had been adamant earlier that Angelino Vitriano was responsible for her husband's murder—a suggestion he hadn't paid much heed to at the time, but what if the man was somehow involved?

What if there were witnesses to the unfortunate incident in the hotel pool? What if Angelino only seemed familiar to them because of the hotel's marketing materials strategically placed around the resort to persuade guests to spread their money lovingly between all the casinos within the Midas Touch empire?

As Nigel eyeballed Angelino, straining to see through the limited gaps in the lion's posture, he studied his stance as he towered menacingly over his employee in more detail. Yes. It was perfectly credible for a witness to come forward and describe a man fitting Angelino's description arguing with a woman in the pool area on that afternoon... the same woman who was later found submerged at the bottom of the pool.

"Where's Alfred?" Ethan had been trying to get hold of him all day, but his cell was continually diverting to voicemail.

"Excuse me?" A fire of fury flared in Angelino's eyes as he spoke. "Billy Jackson has my daughter, and you think I'm going to concern myself with the whereabouts of that creep?"

A feeling of unease settled in Nigel's gut. He had a good track record and could get most criminals off even the tightest of charges, but child abduction? *Beyond all reasonable doubt*, the voice in his head echoed. *You just need a witness to stir the pot.*

"I know," Ethan whispered, his voice faltering despite his outward bravado. Angelino might not be able to hurt him here—in front of people—but it wouldn't stop him coming for him later.

"You *know*, what?" Angelino scoffed, each word oozing the confidence of the untouchable.

"About Billy's dad," he breathed, his eyes darting around him before settling on Nigel who was now making an exaggerated attempt to photograph a close-up of one of the lion's heads. "I know you made Alfred do it."

Nigel froze, phone in hand as he pretended to photograph the lion. Marlene had claimed the same— that it was Angelino Vitriano who issued the instruction to kill her husband—and now here he was, hearing the exact same thing. This was gold dust, and he somehow needed to find a way to speak with the employee and gain his trust.

"I'm going to let you in on a little secret." Angelino's face was so close Ethan could decipher exactly what he'd last eaten by the stench on his breath. "You won't be seeing Alfred again." A twisted smile played on his lips. "Unless you fancy joining him that is?" Ethan's body stiffened at the underlying threat.

"The clock's ticking," Angelino said, tugging him

into a faux embrace. "I want the location of that drain by morning."

Neither Nigel nor Ethan moved as Angelino swiveled on his heel and strode purposefully toward the exit, both men lost in thought as to how best to tackle the situation.

CHAPTER FORTY-NINE
Wednesday, August 28, 2019 (22:00)

THE AIR WAS HEAVY WITH A HUSHED QUIET EXCEPT FOR the scratching of razor-sharp claws on the concrete floor as the rats skittered to and fro. Alfred lay motionless, the bindings that manacled him to the fabricated bunk tearing into his skin.

"The night is about possibilities, wouldn't you say?" A door closed behind him with a soft thud that bounced across the floor toward him.

Night-time. Alfred had lost all sense of time hours ago and the small slice of lucidity was reassuring.

"Wait until dark and the mood is always right." As the rhythmic clunk of footsteps approached, Alfred wriggled in vain, desperate to extract himself from the fastenings that glued him to the shelf.

"What's the matter, cat got your tongue?" Angelino dragged a chair across the room and calmly sat down, but Alfred didn't respond. He couldn't. The thirty-two short stitches that drew his lips together in a tight line of swollen flesh made it impossible.

Angelino leaned over to study his work more closely,

his top lip curling against his teeth in a tight, but delighted smile. "It's not that difficult to keep your lips sealed after all, is it?" He chuckled with pleasure at his little joke. He'd really enjoyed stitching him up. The needle had penetrated his skin far easier than he'd imagined, the whole procedure reminding him of the embroidered tapestries that his Grandma Erika used to make. He closed his eyes a moment to briefly savor the image of her in his mind's eye; the quiet, yet comforting sound of the needles clicking and clacking in synchronized succession as she worked diligently on her latest masterpiece bathing him in instant calm. If she were still alive, he was confident she would have been proud of his capabilities.

"Bit off more than you could chew, didn't you?" Amusement gurgled in his guts. Before sewing Alfred's lips together, he had methodically extracted all his teeth with a pair of needle-nose pliers that he had purchased specifically for the task. The first had been the hardest. Alfred's screams had made it hard to concentrate, but once he'd zoned out and focused on the job in hand, he'd found the melodic harmony of teeth tinkling on the concrete floor quite cathartic.

As Angelino did his best to provoke him, Alfred concentrated on the chaotic tapestry of cobwebs that sagged down from the ceiling. A silhouette from one of the candles danced inches from his face and highlighted the large spider as it carefully weaved yet another web.

"That big mouth of yours might cost my daughter her life," Angelino growled, watching carefully as Alfred used his tongue to gently explore the fleshy, soft tissue where his teeth had once been.

"I can't decide what to tackle next." He placed

enough pressure on the blade to draw blood without causing too much damage as he slowly carved a circle around each of Alfred's knees. He needed to make him talk; scare him into revealing Alice's whereabouts, and yet that wouldn't happen now, would it? It couldn't, because he'd been so angry—so frustrated—he'd rendered it impossible, but he needed to do something. He couldn't just sit back and let him protect Billy while her life was in danger.

Maybe he could take some photos—a video even—of Alfred's injuries and send them to Billy? A warning that he'd be next if he didn't let her go? Yes. It was too late for Alfred now—if he didn't bleed out first, he'd die of dehydration, so what did it matter? At least he would die knowing he'd finally done something worthwhile with his life.

Encouraged, he returned his attention to the job in hand. "Ugly, aren't they?" he commented as he scraped the knife slowly across his toes. "Pretty pointless too, and yet it's almost impossible to walk without them… especially these ones." He tapped the steel against Alfred's big toe. "These beauties cope with twice as much weight as all the others combined," he advised as he smashed the blade down and carved it off in one swift movement.

"Hnghhh." A thousand tiny invisible knives stabbed at Alfred's throat as the real knife carved through the bone.

"These little guys aren't so important." Angelino smirked as he set about a couple more. So far, Alfred had shown a disturbing resistance to pain, so it was good to witness the agony screaming out from his eyeballs as his resolve finally started to crack.

"Hungry?" he asked, the tell-tale, pitter-patter of

paws on concrete as he crossed the floor and swung open the door leaving no doubt as to what was about to happen.

"Hnghhh," Alfred howled again, wriggling desperately against the fastenings but they held firm. The son-of-a-bitch intended to feed him bit by bit to a dog... His dog? A wave of nausea smacked him in the guts, and he closed his eyes as he desperately fought the urge to heave.

"Gently," Angelino admonished in a childlike voice, acutely aware of the dog's tendency to grab food as he crouched down and offered it the small treat. Ever since he was a pup, Murphy had eaten too fast, but having not fed him anything since Alfred's fingers, he was pleased to see that he had developed an appetite for what Mother Nature had intended. Strictly vegetarian, Alice certainly wouldn't approve of this new diet, but she need never know.

As the dog crunched on the small bones, Angelino retrieved his cell and began to record a small video to send to Billy as a warning. Alfred, meanwhile, felt strangely calm as a mirage of shapes flashed in front of his eyes seconds before everything went completely dark.

CHAPTER FIFTY

Wednesday, August 28, 2019 (23:15)

PUSHING HIS HANDS FIRMLY INTO THE DEPTHS OF HIS pockets, Ethan pulled the jacket tighter to his body. As the latest storm moved out of the Pacific, the torrential rain had been replaced with a fierce wind that had brought an unprecedented chill to the air for the time of year. Standing a short distance away from the neglected building, he was obscured by the trunk of a large tree that he could duck out of sight behind if his employer made a sudden reappearance.

Swarming with activity in its heyday, it was hard to believe that the derelict property in front of him was the once thriving Angelino's Hotel and Casino. Graffiti encrusted boards shielded every window, scarring the once shimmering jewel like a mouthful of decaying teeth. The tropical landscaping that surrounded the estate was either dead or overgrown, and the only remaining proof of the hotel's previous success was a faded, broken sign, which hung precariously from the front of the building.

Stepping out from his hiding place, Ethan tentatively

approached the metal fence that surrounded the plot, pausing briefly to observe a crudely attached notice that warned trespassers that they would be prosecuted. Legal action would be the least of his problems if Angelino caught up with him, and he quickly checked his cell again to make sure that the little green dot on the map that signaled his employer's current location hadn't moved. Satisfied, he glanced one final time over his shoulder to check for anything untoward and then squeezed through a tiny gap in the fence.

Using his cell as a flashlight, he crept slowly toward the main entrance. Grit and debris crunched underfoot as he moved, each step amplified against the otherwise silent backdrop. Littered with dirt and weeds and potholes brimming with rainwater, the once grandiose driveway was barely recognizable from the days when uniformed valets would have lined the sidewalk to relieve arriving guests of their baggage.

He followed the track as it curved to the right, passing a dilapidated fountain with an ugly, winged figure that loomed almost ten-feet-tall and cast a shadow on the ground as it glared down menacingly at him. It took him a moment to realize that the statue was, in fact, supposed to be an angel; an upturned chalice in each hand where fresh water would have once flowed into the now stagnant reservoir below.

As he reached the front of the building, he aimed the light from his cell at a large padlock that seemed to be securing the boards to the doors. Sure enough, it had just been made to look as though it was fastened. Quickly removing it, he shoved the wooden sheets aside and hastily pulled them back as best as he could behind him as he entered.

Bathed in darkness, Ethan stood stock still, the only sound, his own pulse as it hammered in his ears. What business could his employer possibly have here except for the video he'd witnessed of Alfred that had been sent to Billy's cell phone? Added to which, according to the location history on Angelino's cell, he hadn't been near the place for months and yet, in the past twenty-four hours, there was no keeping him away.

The images of Alfred, his lips sewn firmly together in an amateur cross-stitch, played over in his mind like an aggressive worm. What kind of a person could inflict that level of suffering on another? He wondered yet again, whether he shouldn't have just called it in and let the police deal with it, but how, without admitting he'd broken the law and been snooping?

A pained groan interrupted his thoughts as it drifted toward him from the bowels of the building. *Alfred?* A proper flashlight would be safe now. The boards plastered across the windows and doors would protect him from being seen from the outside, so he reached into his coat pocket for his flashlight.

Rapidly flicking it on, Ethan fired the light around the gloomy space, his eyes skittering between the thick film of dust that covered the surfaces to the stained walls where pictures used to hang, before finally settling on an array of cobwebs that hung almost decoratively from the ceiling.

"Alfred?" he called out as he jerkily directed the light around him. "Alfred?" The floorboards creaked ominously beneath his feet as he moved. "You know this place stretches for miles, right?" he tried again. "So, if you're here, you need to give me a clue."

"Nnngggh." Ethan stiffened at the confirmation, his

body and mind on high alert as he slowly made his way toward a set of warped steps that would lead him to the source of the noise.

"Are you alone?" Ethan hated himself for asking, but Angelino couldn't be trusted and there was no way he was willingly walking into a trap.

"NnnggGH!" *Yes, or no?* Ethan had no idea, but still, he inched his way toward the old stairway. "If you're alone, stay quiet, otherwise I need you to talk to me as best you can."

Silence. Ignoring the bitter stench of damp, mold, and something else he couldn't decipher, Ethan pressed on. One rickety step at a time. *Slowly, does it.* Was this a trick? Was his employer waiting for him down below? Pressuring Alfred to respond accordingly? *He'll kill you if he catches you.* Ethan paused mid-step, the anxious knot of dread tightening in his chest at the prospect.

"The cops are on their way," he lied, hoping that the tremor in his voice wouldn't give him away. *Should have called them*, he mentally scolded himself. *And told them what?* If he'd been wrong, he'd have been fined for the false call out, and Angelino would be baying for his blood.

Ethan checked his cell once more. The little green dot still hadn't moved. He was also pleased to see that he still had two bars of signal. Returning it to his pocket, he slowly continued his descent, wrestling against the overwhelming sense of foreboding. As he reached the last step, his eyes fixed on a large metal door that separated him from whatever lay on the other side. Directing his flashlight around the edges, he noted that there were no locks, just three large barrel bolts secured to the adjoining frame.

"Alfred?" Ethan held his breath as he listened for a response, but the only sound he could hear was the rhythmic, thumping of his own pulse in his ears. *If you're alone, stay quiet,* he remembered his earlier instruction. Taking a couple of deep breaths to calm his nerves, he carefully released the bolts, the strained metal of the heavy door squealing ominously as he slowly wrenched it open.

"Al?" Ethan staggered clumsily toward the lifeless form, his legs refusing to function properly as he moved. "Oh, Jesus, what has he done?" A thin layer of bile coated his tongue as he stared in horror at the blood that oozed through the slats beneath Alfred's body and pooled onto the floor below.

This was so much worse than any stupid recording. He reached forward and grabbed Alfred's arm to feel for a pulse, instantly dropping it in shock as his eyes locked on the bloodied fist that hung limply from his arm. "What the fuck?" He heaved as another wave of nausea hit him, the bitter taste of vomit burning the back of his throat.

He stepped forward again, this time placing two hesitant fingers on the man's neck. Congealed blood had seeped from the heavily swollen and punctured wounds, clinging to his chin. Struggling with his gag reflux, he looked away as he concentrated on listening for a pulse.

Nothing. He moved his fingers and tried again, holding his own breath to be sure that he wasn't missing a beat until finally he found what he was searching for. It was weak, but it was a pulse. Unable to put off the inevitable any longer, he turned to look at Alfred once more, his eyes glued to the thick, black cotton that firmly held the man's lips together.

"Hang in there," he begged as he dropped to his knees beside Al's lifeless body. Yanking his cell from his pocket, he retched again as his eyes were pulled back to Alfred's hands as though by magnetic force. Brain on fire, he couldn't focus, and he misdialed twice before finally managing to type the three-digit number he so desperately needed.

CHAPTER FIFTY-ONE

Thursday, August 29, 2019 (10:30)

THE GRIFFIN & LEWIS WELLNESS CENTER WAS LOCATED in one of the busier malls on the Strip. Wedged between a top-end designer clothing store and a fast-food chain, the interior wasn't at all what Sergeant Burt Myers had been expecting.

More homely than clinical, the space had been carefully designed to create a public yet private place of solitude away from the chaos of the outside world. Subtly lit with scented candles that filled the air with a pleasant but not overpowering aroma, the waiting area was furnished with comfortable couches laced with scatter cushions. A plush, cream carpet covered the floor, and a large flat-screen television on the wall displayed a repetitive, hypnotic image of a waterfall, the soothing sound of the water enhanced by speakers that quietly breathed into the room from their strategically placed positions.

"He's still in *there*," the receptionist whispered, jabbing her finger in the direction of a door to her right. The waiting area was so peaceful—Burt and Detective Karl Andrews, the only occupants of the room—and yet, she was behaving as though she was afraid to disturb other clients. Burt's eyes followed the direction of her determined digit, drinking in the words that were clearly imprinted on the door:

DR. JOSEPH. GRIFFIN
LICENSED CLINICAL PSYCHOLOGIST
Confidential, non-judgmental therapy in a safe & comfortable environment

"It's most unlike him to overrun," she apologized. "Perhaps I could get you gentlemen a drink while you wait?" The receptionist adjusted the air conditioning even though the room was already the perfect temperature. "Or a snack?" She seemed flustered, almost eager to enhance the informal atmosphere that her employer had clearly worked so hard to create.

Despite having not yet eaten today, Burt shook his head. Unable to rid his mind of the images of Alfred Turner that had been forwarded to his cell phone, the thought of any food right now was enough to give him heartburn.

"Penny for them." He turned his attention to Karl, who had barely uttered a single word throughout their journey across town.

"I initially thought the message to Edward Dutthie was to keep his hands off his wife," he answered, referring to the fact that Dutthie's hands had been hacked off prior to his death. "But now…" he tailed off, leaving the unfinished sentence hanging in the air.

"If Alfred is in fact Alan Dutthie, the culprit's set to work on his son's hands," Burt finished.

"And stitched up his mouth. Whoever did this

wanted to stop him from talking, but if Billy Jackson is our perpetrator and there's any truth to the allegations, it makes no sense."

"Because, if he can't talk, he can't confess, and if he can't confess, he can't clear Billy's name," Burt concluded.

"Exactly," Karl agreed. "Whoever did this wanted to silence him."

"Quite possibly, the others too," another voice interjected and both Burt and Karl startled. Neither had heard the doctor enter the room, and they eyed him curiously as he spoke. "These recent murders are quite a jump for a young man who survived twenty years inside a top security prison without a blemish on his record, wouldn't you say?"

Burt stood and shook the doctor's hand, introducing himself and then Karl. "You don't think that Billy is capable of this?" he asked, unable to disguise his surprise.

"Please," Joseph swiveled on his heel and gestured for them both to follow. "I am expecting another client shortly." He paused and tapped his finger against the word *"confidential"* on the placard affixed to the consultation room door. "No offense, but I would prefer to have this conversation in private."

"None taken," Burt replied, as the doctor stepped aside to let them pass and closed the door gently behind them.

"Can I offer you any refreshments?" Joseph gestured toward a cluster of easy chairs arranged in a semi-circle in the corner of the room and invited them to sit.

"Thank you." Burt gently raised the palm of his hand and shook his head in polite refusal. "You were

Billy's appointed psychologist for the duration of his incarceration, is that correct?" he pressed on, eager to obtain as much information as he could before the arrival of the doctor's next client.

"It is," the doctor confirmed, taking a seat opposite the two men.

"One of Billy's parole conditions was that he attended weekly sessions with you, here at this clinic. Has he kept those appointments?"

"He did at first, but more recently, no," Joseph frowned. "But that's not all that uncommon, I'm afraid,' he continued. "Supervision of such matters is surprisingly slack on release."

"Overworked, understaffed, not paid enough to babysit offenders." Karl's tone dripped with sarcasm as he echoed the excuses previously given to them by Billy's parole officer.

"As pressure increases to reduce the number of inmates, so the number of ex-offenders grows," the doctor argued in defense. "Resources are stretched to the limit and so yes, many officers struggle with the number of ex-felons allocated to them."

"You recommended against Billy's early release to the parole board," Burt commented, keen to glean both further insight into Billy's character and potential state of mind.

"Billy was carrying a lot of anger," Joseph said, leaning back in his chair as he reminisced. "He was, how shall I put it? He was so tightly strung, I was concerned that with very little pressure, he might snap."

"You don't think that could be what happened here?" Burt asked. Joseph Griffin was one of the most highly respected and sought-after experts in his field, and he genuinely valued his opinion. "You don't think he snapped and sought revenge on everyone he held responsible for his imprisonment?"

"It is possible," the doctor conceded. "But no, I don't believe that's what happened. Prisoners," he continued, "particularly, long-term residents such as Billy, struggle to adjust to life on the outside. Nothing is as they remember it. People, places, technology, everything has changed. I didn't think he was ready to be let loose as it were, but I also don't think he is capable of the levels of violence you are looking at."

"We can't just ignore the fact that all of the victims are connected to him and the events surrounding his father's death," Karl interjected.

"Or the fact that all the evidence so far points to him," Burt agreed.

"In my business—yours too, I'm sure—the most obvious answer is rarely the right one," the doctor said, refusing to be swayed. "Besides, Billy had no reason to want Maddison Scott dead and the idea that he would have killed her doesn't stack up."

"You have read the historical news reports relating to the case, I assume?" Karl asked. "Maddison had it in for him from the start. Some might even argue that by turning the world against him, she helped secure his conviction."

"She was also more recently working to clear Billy's name." Joseph stood and retrieved a bottle of mineral water from a small fridge located at the other end of the room.

"She was?" Burt glanced at Karl, concerned they had missed something so crucial to the investigation.

Passing a glass of ice-cold water to each of his

guests, the doctor sat back down. "I didn't pay much attention to her, at first," he admitted, picking up his drink and taking a sip. "When Billy was released, journalists were calling our offices around the clock, all desperate to secure an interview with him, but this time it was different."

"Different, how?" Burt asked.

"Well, for starters, I had to ask myself why this journalist—who had been so utterly convinced of his guilt from the beginning—was now suddenly, equally keen to prove his innocence." Joseph paused in thought for a moment, before proceeding. "She had some pretty damning evidence," he continued, "so I decided to hear her out."

Burt's eyes drifted to the large file on the table between them and the doctor. The so-called evidence that would help them identify their culprit? He certainly hoped so.

"For the first time in years, Billy had an energy about him that I had never previously seen," he continued. "He truly believed he was finally going to show the world that he was innocent all along. Why would he risk that by murdering the one person who claimed to have the proof to substantiate his claims?"

"Billy admitted his guilt," Karl reminded him.

"To the courts, and at his parole hearing," Burt added.

"Indeed," Joseph acknowledged. "Convicts aren't stupid. They know the rules and they know how to play the system. It's in the internal handbook, so to speak."

"You think he said what they wanted to hear so he would be released?"

"I don't doubt it," the doctor replied solemnly.

"Offenders admit guilt all the time in exchange for a lighter sentence and parole is no different. Prisoners will say whatever they need to if there's so much as a hint of freedom at the end of it."

"You said that Maddison Scott claimed to have proof of Billy's innocence?" Karl reminded him, giving Burt a doubtful look.

"It came to light that Billy's public defender had accepted several hefty payments from a man named Angelino Vitriano," Joseph replied, crossing one leg over the other as he spoke.

"Angelino Vitriano?" Burt shifted uncomfortably in his seat.

"The casino mogul," the doctor prompted, unaware of Burt's personal relationship to the man he was discussing. "Maddison claimed that the lawyer was on his payroll, and that she had the bank statements and transcripts to prove it."

"She believed that Angelino Vitriano paid Billy's lawyer to persuade him to plead guilty?" Karl asked for clarification.

"In exchange for a lesser sentence that he didn't receive," the doctor confirmed.

"Why would he do such a thing? It makes no sense," Burt queried, determined to ignore the nagging doubts.

"I suggest that you read this." Joseph picked up the file from the coffee table and passed it to Burt. "Make copies, do whatever is necessary, but I would like it back. It would also be preferable if the contents were kept away from the press. It will destroy my reputation if it gets out that I have breached my confidentiality clauses so shamefully."

"What is it?" Burt accepted the folder, suddenly

reluctant to open it for fear of what incriminating evidence against his friend might be inside.

"Billy had trouble talking about what happened," Joseph answered, "but then finally the dam burst. As part of his ongoing therapy, I thought it might be helpful to him if he wrote everything down for me to assess before our meetings. He did as I asked. Sent everything to me in the post, but that was the last I heard from him. Read it," he encouraged. "Draw your own conclusions."

Karl reached for the file, which Burt happily relinquished, and gently thumbed the contents.

"Now, forgive me," Joseph looked at his watch and gestured to the door, "but I am going to have to ask you both to excuse me. My next appointment will be waiting."

CHAPTER FIFTY-TWO

Thursday, August 29, 2019 (16:00)

"Alfred's talking?" Detective Karl Andrews inched his stool closer to the table and meticulously carved his blueberry muffin into four segments.

"Not exactly," Detective Dennis Boyd replied, gently blowing the top of his Americano to cool it down.

"You said he pointed the finger at Angelino?"

"Toe would be a more accurate description—he thankfully left some of them intact." Dennis put his untouched coffee back on the table. Some things couldn't be unseen, including Alan Dutthie—Alfred's—mutilated hands and feet, and the biting zip of stitches that secured his bruised and bloated lips together.

"He spoke to you with his feet?" Karl didn't know whether to be more impressed at Dennis' ingenuity, or worried that any so-called evidence would be dismissed by the court.

"It was Noah's idea." Dennis took a sip of his coffee, hoping it might help to dilute the acid coating his tongue. "Luckily, he was left with enough toes for the experiment to work."

"So, what did he say?" Karl tucked into another slice of muffin. It took more than the image of a butchered body to make him lose his appetite—twenty years of working for the Coroner's Office had seen to that.

"Not a lot, but you try writing with a couple of toes and see how you get on."

"Any hint of what happened the night Jacob Jackson was shot?"

Dennis shook his head. "The fact that it was Angelino Vitriano who attacked him was as much as we could get."

"Corroborated by Ethan Gardner and yet Burt is still refusing to authorize an arrest," Karl replied irritably. "He claims it could compromise everything, but what if he's not done? What if he strikes again?"

"Oh jeez, don't even go there!" Dennis rubbed his hands over his face, massaging his eye sockets with his fingers as though the action might erase the images. *Hi, I'm Chucky, wanna play?*" he said, imitating the creepy porcelain doll from the *Child's Play* movie. "He's sick in the head to do what he did."

"Asshole's that crooked he can't even lie straight in bed," Karl agreed.

"What if we went over Burt's head?" Dennis suggested, secretly hoping that Karl might agree to do the honors.

"To the lieutenant?" Karl asked, surprised. "Burt's the best sergeant we ever had. No way I'm throwing him to the sharks."

"What then?" Dennis asked. "He'll drag us all down with him, and I need this job." He drained his coffee and put the empty cup back on the table. "I've got a wife and maybe even a kid to support."

"A wife *and* a kid," Karl spoke slowly, deliberately emphasizing the words as they rolled from his tongue. "You finally did it then?" he grinned, reaching across the table to give his shoulder a friendly squeeze. "Seriously, man, I'm happy for you."

"Thanks," Dennis blushed, declining the offer of a refill from the waitress. "That kind of brutality, though?" He rapidly changed the subject as the image of Alfred in his hospital bed crawled to the forefront of his mind. "Extracting teeth, amputating fingers, force-feeding razor blades. This wasn't just about securing silence, and Burt seems to expect us to pretend that none of it even matters if it links back to his friend."

"How many did he swallow?" Karl asked, pushing away his plate.

"Three," Dennis answered, eyeing the last piece of muffin on Karl's discarded plate. He knew he needed to eat something to line his stomach, but right now he couldn't muster the appetite. "He's lucky they didn't cause internal damage."

"Irony being, they'll more than likely pass of their own accord."

"They did." Dennis cringed as he spoke, all thoughts of eating the last bit of cake instantly forgotten.

"Were you able to ascertain if the victim was the same man you spoke to on the night of Maddison's death?" Karl changed tack.

"No doubt in my mind," Dennis nodded. "Alan Dutthie and Alfred Turner are definitely the same person."

"Which brings us back to Angelino." Karl signaled to the waitress for the check. "He must have known that his employee was using a false ID, so *why* was he was prepared to overlook it?"

"Exactly," Dennis agreed. "Unless the allegations are true."

"The doctor's right." Karl pulled out his wallet as he saw the waitress approach. "Why would Billy want to shut up the one person who could have vindicated him?"

"Did you have chance to read the file he gave you?" Dennis smiled politely at the waitress as she thanked them for their business and wished them a good day.

"Bit of bedtime reading for you." Karl reached under the table and retrieved the copies of the file that Joseph Griffin had given them earlier. "See what you make of it, but in my opinion, Angelino Vitriano is guilty as charged."

"Any chance we could obtain a DNA sample from Angelino without either him or Burt knowing?" Dennis fidgeted in his seat as he flicked through the papers.

"A guy like him won't roll over and have his belly tickled without good reason," he replied, doubtfully.

"He needn't know, though," Dennis countered. "According to Burt, he's always on the floor of one of his casinos keeping an eye on his profits… a discarded bottle of beer, a smoked cigar, it wouldn't take much."

"It wouldn't stand up in court," Karl instantly dismissed the idea.

"An official sample would be taken as a matter of course later though, when—if—Burt finally allows us to make an arrest… and if we already have the evidence to nail him…" Dennis grinned at Karl as he observed him warming to the idea.

"Get a sample without raising suspicion, and I'll get

the results fast tracked through the lab." Karl picked up his iPhone as it vibrated on the table and scanned the incoming message. "We're needed back at the station."

"What's happened?" Dennis pushed his stool away from the table and picked up the file that Karl had given him.

"They've finished interviewing Ethan Gardner. Billy Jackson's abducted Angelino's daughter."

CHAPTER FIFTY-THREE

Thursday, August 29, 2019 (19:00)

"I TOLD YOU, NO COPS," ANGELINO GROWLED, HIS FISTS clenched so tightly that his palms bled as his fingernails dug into the flesh.

"How many times?" Ronnie sidestepped him and flicked on the television, instantly regretting it as it sprang to life and Billy Jackson's face filled the screen. She risked a glance at her husband, before forcing her eyes back to the television. "They already knew, and I could hardly deny all knowledge with a police officer standing on our doorstep, inquiring about her whereabouts."

Ignoring his wife, Angelino glared at the scum who currently held his daughter hostage. What happened if they found her before he did? The truth would come out, that's what, and he couldn't allow that. Never in his life had he been so torn between wanting and dreading the same outcome.

"The LVMPD has upgraded the manhunt for Billy Jackson to an urgent status," the newsreader announced. "Jackson is wanted in connection with several unexplained deaths, including well-known reporter Maddison Scott and highly regarded attorney Elizabeth Angel. Considered to be extremely dangerous, the public are urged not to approach him under any circumstances, and anyone with information regarding his whereabouts, should call (702) 385-5858.

"Detectives are yet to confirm whether they are linking the latest discovery of a further victim—found yesterday, badly beaten and on the brink of death at an unnamed location—to the recent murders. More reports on this story to follow as they come in."

As the screen flicked to a story about a robbery at a local pharmacy, carried out by three youths who had since been detained, Angelino slowly exhaled. No mention of Alice was good news. The odds of ever seeing her again, except perhaps to identify her corpse on the mortuary slab, would be vastly diminished if they alerted Billy to the real reason the search had been elevated.

The suggestion that they might connect the attack on Alfred to Billy was also promising but did nothing to alleviate the unwelcome mix of emotions that gurgled in his guts. How the hell had the police found Alfred so soon? And what if he recovered and set the record straight? *Impossible*, he attempted to reassure himself. He had seen to that, but it was still an added complication he could do without.

Angelino also couldn't understand why the police hadn't been in touch with him and he wondered about contacting Burt, but what could he possibly say without implicating himself? Until they publicly disclosed the location that Alfred was found—or pulled him in for questioning—he was going to have to sit it out and keep his shit together. *Easier said than done.* Ever since he heard the news bulletin on his car stereo, he had been on tenterhooks and coming home to find a detective in his home had really unnerved him. It was only a matter of time.

"So, what *exactly* did you tell them?" Angelino strode across the room to the cocktail cabinet and poured himself a hefty measure of bourbon.

"I played dumb," Ronnie snapped, struggling to contain the rage that had been quietly brewing since the officer had left. "According to you, I'm good at that."

Angelino's cell phone pinged with an incoming text, and he lunged across the room and swiped it from the table. Ethan. His eyes hurriedly scanned the contents of the message:

THEY'RE IN A FLOOD CONTROL CHANNEL.
TROPICANA AVENUE, WEST OF I-215.

"Don't wait up." He threw his wife a filthy look as he pocketed the phone and picked up the dog's leash.

"Where are you going with him at this time of night?" she asked in alarm as he attached the leash to the dog's collar.

"Out," he replied obstinately, tugging the dog toward the door, and slamming it behind him.

Ronnie listened to the roar of the engine as he accelerated out of the driveway. Angelino never took the dog out. At least he never used to, but this was the second time in as many days. *Alice's dog,* the warning sounded in her ears. Should she call the police and notify them of this latest development?

The police...

Three firm raps on the door, and she had known immediately. A "cop's knock," her mother would have called it; years spent dealing with the trouble her father regularly brought to their door.

"Does the name Billy Jackson mean anything to you?" The heel of the detective's shoe tapped the floor in rhythm to his jigging leg as he leaned against the kitchen counter and took a sip of steaming coffee from his cup.

It was stupid—absurd—that she hadn't instantly made the connection. Jackson's mugshot had filled every newsstand and television screen over the past few weeks, and yet, it wasn't a name she instantly associated with her daughter, and so, she had shaken her head in denial.

"Billy is wanted in connection with several crimes that have recently been committed," he hinted, producing a copy of the same picture that had been plastered all over the news.

"What's this got to do with Alice?" The high-pitched squealing in her ears was soon accompanied by a throbbing pressure behind her eyes that threatened to escalate into a full-blown migraine.

"Did your husband ever mention his past relationship with Billy Jackson and his family?" the officer inquired gently.

"Alice's abduction has something to do with my husband?" Ronnie struggled to breathe, the unhappy combination of fear and fury colliding in her chest and pressing down so hard on her lungs that they refused to inflate.

The tirade of accusations aimed at her that had tumbled from his mouth over the past twenty-four hours like a river that had burst its banks clattered through her brain: *Irresponsible; inconsiderate; selfish; neglectful; unreliable*; and all the while, Alice's disappearance was his fault? She shivered involuntarily.

"You think a suspected murderer has my daughter?" she squeaked, and the officer had remained ominously quiet; a silence that told her everything she needed to know.

How dare you, Angelino? There's far more to being a good parent than buying a child's affection through lavish gifts and the refusal to right their wrongs for fear of recriminations. Bad mother! The implication had been rammed down her throat so often that she had almost started to believe it.

"There's no bond like that of a mother and child," her friend Bella always reminded her. Despite her friend making no secret of her dislike for her husband, Ronnie knew deep down that she was right. A mother's love was irreplaceable; the scarred navel, a symbolic reminder that never went away of the lifeline that would tie her and Alice together, forever.

Angelino hadn't been present at the birth, but Bella had. Weighing over twelve pounds, and almost twice the size of an average newborn, they had both stared in awe at her full head of blonde hair and striking blue eyes.

"She's got teeth," Bella had finally whispered in surprise. The doctors had soon removed them of course, to prevent her from choking or cutting her tongue, but she had still been the most beautiful thing that Ronnie had ever clapped eyes on. Her heart swelled at the memory, crushing her ribcage, and threatening to suffocate her.

The bitterness she now felt for her husband, however, coated her tongue and she was struggling to compose herself in front of the detective. All she really wanted to do was retire upstairs to bed and scream into her pillows. It wouldn't be the first time. If Angelino was somehow responsible for all of this, it was bad enough, but to allow her to believe that it was in fact her who was to blame was unforgivable.

"What is it you need?" she eventually asked, unable to make eye contact with the officer for fear she would talk herself out of it at the last minute.

Angelino's suite was situated on the first floor, Ronnie herself, relegated to one of the spare rooms on the floor above. "We have separate sleeping arrangements," she commented as he followed her up the stairs, quietly questioning why she felt the need to explain her private business to a stranger.

"In there." She pointed to a door at the end of the landing and as he walked deliberately toward it, she had stood a moment and watched—curious—despite knowing deep down exactly what he was looking for.

He took his time, his eyes sweeping between the marble-clad walls, oversized backlit vanity tub, and separate walk-in shower, before finally settling on the flat-screen television that was embedded in the mirror above the two sinks directly beneath it.

"Please don't be long," she'd urged, glancing nervously over her shoulder, half-expecting her husband to walk in at any moment. "If he catches us," she tailed off as she heard the distinct bang of a car door closing on the driveway outside.

The officer must have heard it too as he moved fast then, stretching his hands into latex gloves, and quickly scraping samples of hair from Angelino's comb into a clear evidence bag. Noting her sense of urgency, he then grabbed a toothbrush from the rack and held it up to her as though seeking approval before chucking it in another evidence bag and following her downstairs to the kitchen.

Just so long as she remembered to replace it with a fresh one as soon as the detective left, Angelino wouldn't think to question it...

Snapping out of her trance, Ronnie rushed from the room and up the stairs as she remembered that she needed to do just that.

CHAPTER FIFTY-FOUR

Thursday, August 29, 2019 (20:30)

DETECTIVE DENNIS BOYD STARED AT THE MOUTH OF THE tunnel, trails of sweat tracking down his spine and forming small pools of damp on his shirt. The specialist Task Force was less than ten minutes away and he had heard the instruction loud and clear on the radio that all officers were to hold back until they arrived. Sergeant Burt Myers, however, had other ideas.

"We're going in," he muttered under his breath.

"But…" Dennis attempted to argue.

"But nothing," Burt snapped, interrupting him before he even had chance to form a sentence. "If the intelligence from Ethan Gardner is correct, he's got my godchild in there." Adjusting his belt so the gun holster was sitting more comfortably, he stepped forward and gestured for both Dennis and Detective Karl Andrews to follow.

"Hold on," Karl wrestled for time. "How sure are we they're even in there?" Entering the drainage channels against advice and without back-up was a crazy idea.

"We're not," Burt replied. "Ethan never thought to mention his software in the initial interview. Claims he 'forgot,' which I find as hard to believe as you, make no mistake, but since his conscience seems to have finally got the better of him, I don't plan on wasting any more time."

"How do we know it's Billy's cell phone he's been tracking, though?" Karl pressed.

"We don't, but one thing's for sure. He's been tracking whoever took Alice—our tech guys checked it out and everything stacks up."

"How long since it last gave off a signal?" Karl asked.

"Almost two hours, so either he lost reception or it's switched off."

"So what's the hurry?" Karl raised a restraining hand and talked over Burt as he tried to respond. "I understand your urgency—we all do—but what's a few more minutes in the grand scheme of things? Much better we reach her alive, surely?"

"Ethan Gardner has sat on this knowledge too long already," Burt grumbled. "Anything could have happened to her."

"And anything could happen to us," Karl said, hoping to make him see reason. "You won't even let us use a flashlight." At Burt's insistence, it had been agreed that no artificial light would be used in the tunnel unless strictly necessary.

"We can't alert him to our presence," he argued, trying to tamper down his irritation at being challenged.

"Oh, come on!" Karl scuffed the end of his boot on the ground in frustration. "If we can't even see the end of our noses, he'll hear us from a hundred paces, and will these even work?" He waggled his radio in front of Burt's face. "What if we lose signal?"

Moments later, the three men slowly pushed their way through the first cobwebbed tunnel, guided only by the strips of faint neon light that filtered through the grates above their heads.

"It stinks," Dennis complained, burying his nose and mouth in the collar of his shirt to filter the stench.

"I'm guessing when the tunnels were built, the budget didn't stretch to restroom attendants," Karl whispered back, covering his own nose and mouth as he spoke.

"Sssh," Burt warned, all confidence he initially felt dissolving fast as he blindly groped his way through the maze of underground chambers. Back-up should have arrived by now, but would they even find them? He had lost all sense of direction within seconds of entering the pitch-black shaft.

"You hear that?" Dennis asked, reaching for his gun, and releasing the safety catch.

"We've got company," Karl replied, concentrating on the shuffling sound as it penetrated the silence. Clutching his flashlight as a weapon—powered off, as per instructions—he inched forward.

"Critters?" Dennis suggested, as the strange scuffing noise he had heard was drowned out by a frantic tapping on the concrete floor.

"What the hell they been eating?" Karl jibed. The acoustics might be somewhat skewed in the enclosed space, but whatever they could hear was a lot bigger than the average sewer rat.

"You ever see that video on YouTube when a guy gets caught releasing an alligator into Lake Mead?"

Dennis struggled to swallow the lump that had formed in his throat.

"Would you quit with this nonsense?" Burt snapped, instantly lowering his raised voice. "I've lived here my whole life and never seen a single alligator."

"First time for everything," Dennis mumbled, his finger poised over the power switch of his unlit flashlight in case he should need to turn it on in a hurry, "and it sure looked like a croc to me."

"And if the drains run into Lake Mead, who's saying something from Lake Mead can't run into the drains?" Karl agreed.

"Enough!" Burt growled, swiping at his face as a large cobweb that hung precariously from the ceiling attached itself to him.

"Hello?" Karl called out, struggling to disguise the anger he felt at Burt for putting them in this predicament. Disobeying instructions and carrying on without back-up was madness. Clicking on his light in a final act of rebellion, he waved it back and forth in front of him as he delved deeper into the culvert.

"Hello," the voice echoed in the hollow space.

"Idiot," Burt hissed, squinting as his eyes adjusted to the bright light being directed at his face. "Now he knows we're here." Pulling his pistol from its holster, he released the safety catch and held it at arm's length in front of him as he crept toward the complex labyrinth of tunnels that lay ahead.

CHAPTER FIFTY-FIVE

Thursday, August 29, 2019 (21:15)

"HELLO." THE VOICE REVERBERATED FROM THE WALLS like a pinball that had been flipped too hard, but Angelino was focusing so hard on the dog, he barely noticed. Locating his daughter was his only priority now, and as he studied Murphy's body language, he was confident the dog had picked up a scent.

Ears pinned flat against his head, a thousand miniature hackles stood to attention on his back as Murphy slowly prowled into the next culvert, his every movement as fluid as the muscles that supported them. He faltered, his tail held high and spine curved outwards as his ears now pricked on high alert.

"What is it, boy?" Angelino crouched down on bended knee, massaging his fingers through the fur beneath Murphy's ears. The dog released a low growl and lunged forward, tugging the leash from Angelino's grip.

"Murphy," he hissed, scrabbling to catch up with the dog as it motored down the corridor in front of them. Water dripped from the walls and formed murky puddles on the tunnel floor, sloshing beneath his feet as he moved, but he kept going. "Murphy!"

BILLY'S BODY STIFFENED AT THE UNMISTAKABLE CLICK OF a gun as it was released from its safety catch; the sound amplified in the cavernous depths of his hideaway. Pressing the tip of his forefinger gently against his lips, he gestured for Alice to remain quiet as he crept forward, his eyes straining in the dark as he struggled to identify which passage the noise had come from.

"Murphy." He froze as the unfamiliar voice ricocheted from the walls of the hollow cage and raced toward him.

"Daddy?" Alice whispered, her bare feet slapping against the dirty water as she climbed from the makeshift bunk and approached the spot where Billy stood.

Daddy? Billy's skin crawled, his nerves tingling as though a thousand tiny insects were cultivating beneath the surface, and he scratched irritably at his arms in a feeble attempt to alleviate the sensation. How? With hundreds of miles of underground channels to choose from, how was it possible that Angelino had found him so soon?

"Is Alice in trouble?" Alice asked, the whites of her eyes reflecting the dull orange glow of a flashlight as it bobbed buoyantly toward them.

"We gotta stick like glue, baby girl." Billy grabbed hold of her hand, grateful of the feeling of solidarity it gave him. "Daddy's not well right now and it's making him real angry, but do what I say and everything's gonna be just fine."

A<small>S THE DOG POWERED AHEAD,</small> A<small>NGELINO ROUNDED THE</small> bend on legs of jelly. His lungs were on fire and his chest so tight with stress and overexertion he was scared he might combust. Leaning against the tunnel wall for support, he gulped urgently at the stale air as he tried to stave off the stifling breathlessness. How could he have let this happen? First, his daughter, and now he had managed to lose her dog too. He slammed his fist against the wall in frustration, instantly regretting it as his knuckles burned in rebellion.

"Murphy!" Alice collapsed to her knees and threw her arms around the dog's neck as it scrabbled into the camp.

Alice? At the sound of his daughter's voice, Angelino slowly turned and began to inch his way along the pitch-black passage, his fingers groping the wall for guidance as he moved.

"Alice?" he breathed, unsure whether the adrenaline hurtling through his veins was playing tricks on his mind.

"Sssh," Billy whispered, dropping to the floor and grabbing Alice from behind. "He can't know we're here."

"Alice?" Angelino's voice was more urgent this time, the sound hugging the walls and pulsating in his ears. "Are you there?" His nose curled in disgust as the stench of sewage intensified the farther into the gully he got.

"Is this another game?" Alice giggled, as Billy crouched behind her and hugged her in a vice-like grip.

"Get the fuck away from her," Angelino snarled, his face contorted with rage as he stumbled into their hideaway, the light from the torches hanging above his head highlighting the good-for-nothing, low-life snake that clung to her as though she were a suit of armor.

"Daddy swore!" Alice gasped in shock, her eyes bulging at the gun that was directed at them both.

"I won't tell you again," Angelino threatened, spittle spewing from his lips as he brandished the weapon at them.

"You won't shoot, you wouldn't dare." Billy increased his grip on Alice, the only thing standing between him and the revolver that Angelino wouldn't think twice about using if she wasn't directly in the firing line.

"You've got to the count of five to let her go."

"Uncle Burt is going to be so mad at you if he finds out you took his gun," Alice whistled, clucking her tongue against the roof of her mouth in disdain.

Billy studied her profile in wonder. Up until now it had all been a game, he had seen to that. He would never hurt Alice. Angelino just needed to believe that he would and yet, even now, as she stared down the barrel of a gun, she showed no fear, as though she was somehow immune to the gravity of the situation.

"One—two…" Angelino began to circle around them, picking his way through the trash on the floor. As he moved, Billy also slowly maneuvered himself and Alice around so he couldn't get a clean shot.

"Three," he growled in anger as Billy mirrored his own movements. With him sticking to her like an aggressive skin condition, the risk of catching Alice in the crossfire was too great.

"Four," he glared at the dog, trying to will the useless mutt to do its job.

"What's the alternative?" he continued. "Rot on Death Row while you wait for them to press the switch?"

"Or maybe, Alan Dutthie tells the cops the truth," Billy replied with far more conviction than he felt.

"Haven't you heard?" Angelino feigned surprise. "Our mutual friend is being remarkably *tight-lipped* about the situation," he cackled raucously at his little joke. "He's not going to tell them anything."

"That's where you're wrong, Angelino." Burt stepped out from the shadows, his finger poised on the trigger of his firearm as he directed it at his oldest friend. "Alfred—Alan Dutthie—has told us more than enough." In all his career, Burt had never faced such a difficult decision, but right now he wouldn't think twice about shooting if he needed to.

Angelino's eyes flickered between the two men; one, who he would happily die for, and the other, who he could happily kill. "You need to leave now," he warned Burt.

"I can't do that," Burt murmured, the sound of approaching feet pounding the floor in the adjoining tunnel and vibrating the ground beneath them. "Back-up," he whispered, raising his eyebrows knowingly at Angelino as though confiding a secret.

Billy stayed silent, scared to even breathe as his brain raced through the catalogue of drainage channels. *Too late*, the voice warned as the footsteps hammered the ground behind him. Four more cops, maybe five? It was impossible to guess from the rapid staccato beat that threatened to bring the walls crashing in around him, but one thing was for certain. There would be no escape.

"Put down the rifle and face the wall." Burt's finger gently stroked the trigger of his gun as he spoke.

"Just stay still, sweetheart," Billy whispered, squeezing Alice tightly to him as she started to whimper with fear. "Nobody's gonna shoot."

"Don't you *dare* pretend you care about her," Angelino roared with anger as he bent down on his knees and placed the gun on the floor. The battle was over, the risk of his daughter getting caught up in the fight too great. He gazed at her one last time, willing her to look at him so he could silently reassure her, but as the scumbag gripped her from behind, her face remained stubbornly buried in the dog's fur.

"Hands where I can see 'em," Burt growled before turning his attention to Billy. "Now, you. Let the girl go and get your ass over there with him."

"It's gonna be OK, baby," Billy whispered in Alice's ear as he slowly released his grip and approached the wall as directed. "I promise."

"Get them cuffed and out of here," Burt instructed to the flurry of boots that thudded on the concrete behind him. Approaching his godchild, he then carefully extracted her fingers from the dog's neck and pulled her into an embrace.

CHAPTER FIFTY-SIX

Thursday, August 29, 2019 (23:15)

"My lawyer isn't picking up," Angelino grumbled into the handset, oblivious to the late hour. "You need to get your ass down here, pronto."

Nigel stared at the screen as Angelino cut the call. He didn't *need* to do any such thing. In fact, most lawyers wouldn't even pick up a call after hours, let alone traipse halfway across town to pander to a potential client's every whim. Used to people revolving their lives around him, it was time for Angelino to learn his first lesson about life behind bars. From now on, time would be defined and controlled by others, and he was no longer able to bark orders.

Nigel stripped naked and entered the bathroom, filling the tub with water and a generous dose of foam from the selection of free toiletries, but it was a pointless exercise. He was far too wired to relax, his mind working overtime as he tried to figure out the implications of acting for Angelino.

He had previously toyed with the idea of offering Angelino his services, but had soon dismissed it, and had only mentioned his legal status to him in the hope it might secure him the room upgrade he had so desperately been angling for at the time. Now, however, the beginnings of a new plan started to hatch in his mind. It could cost him his reputation, but it would at least even the score. Finally, he would be able to thank Billy properly for saving him from himself.

Settling instead for a quick splash under the arms and between his legs, Nigel pulled the plug and twenty minutes later, he joined the taxi queue in front of the hotel. The line was long and as a fight broke out directly behind him, he stepped aside to allow the squabbling, drunken duo to take his place. Eventually, when he could hold back no longer, he moved toward a fog of car fumes as the doorman ushered him into a waiting cab.

"South Central. I'm not sure of the exact address but head for the Bellagio—the scenic route—and we'll take it from there." He slipped a dollar bill into the doorman's hand and settled into the passenger seat.

"Round-the-world trip, huh?" The driver chuckled as he accelerated out the lot. "You've come to the right place. We got Egyptian pyramids, volcanos, medieval castles, a taste of gay Paree, and if that don't satisfy your appetite, we've even got ourselves a Roman Empire that would make Julius Caesar envious."

Traffic was heavy and it would be quicker to walk, but that would defeat the purpose. The only thing giving him any pleasure right now was the thought of making Angelino sweat as he took his time to arrive. He would wait until they were south of Mandalay Bay, and then admit his "mistake" and ask the driver to turn around; the Detention Center where Angelino was currently being held, a good fifteen minutes in the opposite direction.

Nigel turned his attention to the sights as they swept past the window. Signs of liquid fire illuminated the sky and the Strip bustled with an indefinable energy. On both sides of the street, the sidewalks were choked with tourists as they spilled out the bars and restaurants with their suicidally, calorific takeouts. *The city that never sleeps,* his lips twitched into a smile. The more time he spent here, the less he wanted to return home to his old life, which was kind of a shame since according to his sources, all was no longer perfect in paradise. His so-called best friend had apparently already bored of his wife and returned to his own, so there was nothing really to stop him from returning to his. Except, that time had moved on. He had moved on, and he was no longer sure what he wanted from his life. What he did know was that it didn't include working all those hours to keep his wife comfortable in a lifestyle she had become begrudgingly accustomed to.

As the cab paused at the traffic light in front of the Bellagio, Nigel instructed the driver to keep heading south as he leaned against the glass to get a better view of the fountains. The final show of the night was always the best. As onlookers craned their necks to watch and photograph the waters as they swayed and twirled above the artificial trees that dotted the hotel grounds, the cabbie lowered the window, and the vehicle was instantly filled with the sound of "Lucy in the Sky with Diamonds."

"Take you more than a year to fill that lake with a garden hose," he commented. Nigel just wished he'd shut up and let him enjoy the show.

"It don't look all that big," he continued, "but it's the equivalent of eight football fields. 17,000 gallons of water in the air each time… would you look at that?" Suddenly distracted, the driver pointed to the Arc de Triomphe on the opposite side of the road. Not quite a full-size replica, it was still impressive.

"Who in their right mind thought foul mouth Ramsay's ugly mug belonged on such a significant building?" The cabbie jabbed his finger at the huge billboard that was attached to the front of the building, promoting the famous chef's Hell's Kitchen at Caesars Palace.

Nigel zoned out and eventually, having performed the desired U-turn, his ride pulled up outside the Clark County Detention Center. Designed by local architects, the building was far more salubrious on the outside as it turned out than what was hidden behind the precast concrete walls. Every internal aspect seemed to have been devised to make it as uncomfortable as possible, but then he supposed that was the idea.

"No formal interviews now until tomorrow." Engrossed in a James Patterson novel, the disinterested desk sergeant didn't even look up from the page as he spoke.

"I can still meet with my client, though?" Ice-cold air blasted from the air conditioner grill above his head, the space as cool as a refrigerator, and any previous itch to further delay his meeting with Angelino was rapidly evaporating.

"No visits allowed after 11:30 p.m. It's the rules." Finally, he looked up from his book and eyed Nigel suspiciously.

"Aw, c'mon," he glanced at his wristwatch. "I'm not that late and my client wasn't even arrested until almost

10 p.m. I came as quick as I could." Having been in no hurry to see Angelino up until now, he suddenly found himself desperately wanting what he couldn't have.

"Wait over there," the sergeant sighed, pointing at the waiting area. "I'll make a call and see what I can do."

A few minutes later, he called Nigel back to the serving window. "Your conversation will be recorded and monitored," he informed him. "Anything incriminating will be used in court."

"I thought any consultation between client and attorney was strictly confidential?" Nigel queried.

"It usually is," the desk sergeant shrugged. "But *your client*," his tone dripped with sarcasm, "gave two names, neither of which match yours so right now, until the paperwork's been checked, you'll be treated like any other visitor."

Useful. Very, useful indeed. Nigel couldn't wait to get started.

"You took your time," Angelino bitched as he entered the room. Dressed in a cheap prison-issue suit with sandals on his feet, his new client was restrained with leg shackles and handcuffs that linked to a belly chain at the front. If Nigel wasn't so amused, he could have almost pitied him and he struggled to suppress a smile. Gone was the air of superiority; the man sat in front of him, barely recognizable from his former arrogant self.

"How are you finding it?" he asked, taking a seat opposite him, and doing his best to look sympathetic.

"Well, you know," Angelino attempted to make light of the situation. "The accommodation and amenities aren't that great, so I don't think I'll hurry back."

"You'll be here for a while yet," Nigel warned, enjoying the look of concern that settled on his face.

"Over my dead body!" The metal of Angelino's shackles rattled as he tried to raise his hands in protest. "I'm paying you good money to get me the hell out of here."

"All in good time." Nigel relaxed into his seat, intertwining his fingers and cracking the knuckles. It was always the financially privileged clients who gave him the most bother, as though their monied backgrounds gave them the right to preferential treatment. "We have to follow protocol."

"You don't know what it's like," Angelino complained, and Nigel had to concede that no, he didn't. But then, he had never reneged on so much as a speeding ticket, let alone committed the type of atrocious crimes that his client was accused of.

"The place is a goddamned zoo—I can't even pee in private," Angelino plowed on.

"I need you to be entirely honest with me." Nigel's eyes flickered to the camera in the corner of the ceiling. He couldn't rely on the desk sergeant to be paying attention, but hopefully the recording would be checked by authorized personnel in the morning. "Why did Billy Jackson take your daughter?"

"How would I know?" Angelino grimaced as he shifted in his seat and the shackles dug into his skin.

"I can't construct a solid defense if it's built on lies," Nigel cautioned.

"You can't reason with crazy." Angelino refused to make eye contact and concentrated instead on a stain on the wall.

"OK," Nigel deliberately made a point of stretching

and crossing his legs. It must be such a nuisance for his client to not be able to perform such a simple action, but nevermind. "Talk to me about Alfred."

"Nothing he didn't deserve," Angelino snarled. "His big mouth almost got my little girl killed."

"How?" he asked.

"Forget it," Angelino replied.

"But you don't deny inflicting his injuries?" Nigel's eyes fluttered once more toward the camera.

"It's all circumstantial; they can't prove jack," Angelino mumbled in response.

"You want to know something?" Nigel leaned toward his client, as though about to confide a secret. "I think," he pressed when Angelino didn't respond, "that Billy took your daughter as a trade for something. The truth, maybe? And so, you decided to silence the only other person who could have revealed it."

"Truth about what?" he snapped.

"You tell me," Nigel shrugged, leaning back in his chair. "It's the only hope you've got of getting out of here."

"Alfred killed Billy's father," Angelino sighed, resignedly. "Tried to implicate me and say I put him up to it, but I swear to you I knew nothing about it."

Nigel was deep in thought as he studied his client. If Billy had served much of his life in prison for a crime he hadn't committed, why would he now turn to murder and risk imprisonment again when he finally had the chance to clear his name?

"I saw you arguing with the reporter on the eve of her death." Nigel's lips twitched in mirth at the look of horror on Angelino's face. He hadn't seen any such thing, but this was going to be far easier than imagined.

Please, God, let them survey the recordings in the morning. "Obviously, I won't deliberately disclose the fact, but I should warn you that I won't lie either, if the question should arise."

"I didn't kill her," he growled. "Jesus, you're supposed to be on my side."

"I am," Nigel lied. "But you must see how it will look to the prosecution if it comes out, so tell me, what did you argue about?"

"I don't remember," he muttered, and Nigel chose not to pursue the matter. It had been a very productive first meeting and, just so long as they did monitor the conversation as promised, Angelino had already provided more than enough information to hang himself.

"My advice to you?" Nigel stood to leave, rapping his knuckles on the door to indicate to the guard that he was finished with his client. "Sleep on it. Figure out how truthful you want to be with me, but if it turns out they have any evidence placing you at the scene of these murders, you'll do yourself no favors in denying it."

CHAPTER FIFTY-SEVEN

Friday, August 30, 2019 (10:30)

Burt's eyes were fixed to the glass that separated him from the suspect as he fumbled in his pocket for a lighter and retrieved a cigarette from the pack with his teeth. He wouldn't light it; it was a non-smoking building and he had supposedly quit, but sometimes going through the motions helped calm the cravings. Not always though, and right now he would happily trade a kidney for the instant rush that only nicotine could provide.

There was no law prohibiting him from supervising the interview, but his friendship with the accused could muddy the waters further down the line if the case went to court. Keen to avoid any conflict of interest, it had been agreed that Detective Karl Andrews would lead the interview, which was why Burt now found himself seated in the unlit observation room watching proceedings through the two-way glass.

"Tell us about Maddison Scott." Karl studied the swollen, red welts on the prisoner's wrists where the cuffs had been applied too tight and cut into his skin. It wasn't a rookie error and was intended as an early warning by the arresting officer—which just happened to be him—of how much trouble he was in.

"What about her?" Angelino had clearly been a good boy overnight and his prison jewelry was now applied with more slack, enabling him to lean forward and wipe a bead of perspiration from his cheekbone with the back of his hand.

"We have reason to believe that you argued with her at around the time of her death," Karl hinted.

"So, it's an offense to argue now?" Angelino was clearly agitated, the veins in his neck throbbing in rhythm to his fingers as they played out a tune against each other.

Determined not to express any pleasure that they had monitored his conversation with Angelino the previous evening, Nigel meanwhile made a point of pretending to make some notes on the pad in front of him.

"What did you argue about?" Karl pressed.

"No comment," Angelino replied, his eyes flicking toward his attorney. For guidance? Burt wasn't so sure. He'd known Angelino long enough to recognize certain facial expressions and right now it was clear that he was furious with his counsel.

Nigel Goodman also wasn't at all what Burt had expected. The man had an impeccable track record, and his credentials boasted an impressive lack of convictions for his past clients, and yet his manner was remarkably bereft of the aggression required of a successful court-room defender.

"It could harm your defense if you don't mention something now, which you later rely on in court." Karl turned his attention to the lawyer, keen to see how he intended to handle the fact that he may be required to testify against his client.

"My client is exercising his right to silence," the lawyer warned, apparently unfazed. "I suggest you respect that."

Burt leaned forward and rested his elbows on his thighs as he studied Nigel Goodman more closely. Inferred guilt was the worst type; the reluctance to tell the truth when given the chance, far more incriminating than any actual proof. Any self-respecting lawyer would discourage a 'no comment' response to such a crucial question, and yet Angelino's attorney seemed to be actively encouraging it.

"We have CCTV footage that shows you leaving Foo Dogs that night at around the time Maddison met her death. You returned shortly after 9 p.m., only to then leave again just past 10 p.m. Where did you go?" Karl asked.

"The first time or the second?" Angelino smiled pleasantly but it was clear to Burt that his friend was uncomfortable with the question.

"The latter," Karl replied. "Where did you go when you left Foo Dogs just past 10 p.m.?"

"Home," Angelino lied. He knew what was coming, and there was no way they were setting him up for the attack on Mario Brown.

"Did you stay there all night?" Karl asked, despite having evidence to the contrary.

"No." It was pointless denying it since even the poor excuse for a lawyer who sat next to him could place him at the Lucky Plaza later that night.

"Where did you go?" Karl asked again.

"To the Lucky Plaza," he grumbled furiously. Locked up in a concrete box that was a fraction of the size of his own bathroom with about twenty other inmates, he'd had plenty time to think. It was Ethan who had informed the police of Billy and Alice's where-abouts—having gone to the trouble to place him at the scene first—he was sure of it. And it didn't take a genius to figure out that it was Ethan who deleted the footage that could have proven he was nowhere near the Lucky Plaza at the time Mario was followed and attacked. The second he discovered that his employee was Mario's tenant, he should have known he couldn't be trusted and dealt with him.

"To the Lucky Plaza," Karl repeated as though this was news to him. "What time would that have been?"

"Midnight."

"So, you left Foo Dogs at just past 10 p.m., and you went straight home and didn't leave until you decided to visit the Lucky Plaza around midnight?" Karl reiterated the point deliberately. If he was right and Angelino had in fact attacked Mario, it would aid the prosecution in their efforts to prove Angelino's lack of integrity if the case went to trial.

"Yes," Angelino snapped. "Were you dropped on your head as a child? I left Foo Dogs and went straight home until much later that night. Why is that so difficult for you to grasp?"

Nigel's lips twitched with pleasure. Antagonizing the interviewing officer was never a good idea and he should be warning his client against it if he wanted to protect him. Which, of course, he didn't.

"Can anyone corroborate that fact?" Karl ignored his outburst as he sipped from his bottle of water.

"My wife." *At least she'd better if she knows what's good for her.* Angelino shifted in his seat and studied his reflection in the mirror. God, he looked like shit, and the sooner he got out of here and cleaned up, the better.

"Do you know what I think?" Karl didn't wait for an answer, and Burt exhaled as his friend returned his scowl from the mirror to Karl. For one horrible moment, he had been convinced that the lighting wasn't working properly, and that Angelino had observed him watching from the other side of the glass.

"I think you knew that Mario was stealing from you, and I think it was you who attacked him that night. I think you attacked him, and then you took back what was yours. I think you deleted the footage in the hope we wouldn't find out that Mario was in the Lucky Plaza stealing from you just moments before someone tried to kill him."

"What? No!" Angelino licked his lips, his mouth so dry they had turned numb.

"Stealing from right under your nose," he made a tutting noise with his tongue against the roof of his mouth, "that must have really riled you."

"Ask Burt. He'll tell you; I knew nothing about Mario until later."

"Tell us a little more about the CCTV that went missing from the Lucky Plaza on the night of Mario's attack." Karl had no intention of informing him at this stage that it had been retrieved… assuming he wasn't already aware, since it was somewhat convenient that the footage highlighting Billy's potential guilt was bought to their attention by one of Angelino's employees as soon as they received intelligence about Mario's presence at the Lucky Plaza that evening.

"Somebody deleted it and, trust me, I'm as eager as you to find out who," he growled.

"Bit unfortunate, isn't it? The recordings that could have confirmed that you weren't in the vicinity of the Lucky Plaza until later that night as you say, going missing like that?" Karl was enjoying toying with him now. Billy Jackson had confirmed during his interview that he followed Mario out of the casino but denied attacking him and Karl was inclined to believe him.

Angelino had a far more likely motive, and he certainly wasn't at home like he claimed when Mario was attacked. To the contrary, they had evidence placing him around the block from the parking garage at the time of the assault and Karl casually now placed that evidence face down on the table in front of him.

"Uh-uh." He waggled his finger as though admonishing a naughty child as Angelino attempted to turn the photograph with his restrained hands. "All in good time."

"It's not too late to tell us where you really went when you left Foo Dogs that night," he pressed, but as the silence stretched and it was clear that Angelino wasn't going to change his story, Karl finally turned over the photograph and slowly pushed it across the table toward the suspect.

"That is you, isn't it? Leaving the casino at the Paris," he made a show of checking the timestamp on the picture, "at exactly 23:08 last Wednesday."

"I didn't lay a finger on him," he growled. "He was already out for the count when I got there."

"A-ha," Karl goaded. "So, you *were* there that night?"

"A mere oversight, that's all," the lawyer finally

spoke up, and Burt shook his head in bemusement. The man was completely useless and how he had managed to gain such a good reputation was beyond belief. "My client denies any involvement in the actual assault, so if you have no further questions?"

"Oh, but I do." Karl flicked through the pages in the folder in front of him. "On the morning of August 12 of this year, officers were called to attend the discovery of a corpse in an elevator at the Amathus Resort."

"I don't have to listen to this." Angelino's chair toppled to the floor as he bucked against his shackles in his haste to stand. "I hand you the culprit on a plate, and this is how you repay me? *America's most wanted,*" he sneered. "What's the matter? Now you've got him, you don't know what to do with him? I should have shot him when I had the chance." His cuffed fists shoved Nigel's hand away as he tried to pull him back into his seat.

"If I might ask you to disregard that last comment," Nigel said, deliberately drawing attention to Angelino's threat. It would be a shame for it to get lost in the moment when it could be used against him later. "Tensions are clearly running high, and of course, my client didn't shoot anybody."

"If you've got nothing to hide, you've got nothing to fear," Karl responded calmly.

"The only thing I'm *afraid* of," Angelino snarled, bitterly, "is that you're so busy trying to frame me, you're going to let that snake go free."

"I should inform you that your fingerprints are currently being compared to those found in both the elevator and the electrical closet," Karl replied. "If you're as innocent as you say, we'll have you eliminated in no time, now *sit down.*" He barked the last two words, leaving no doubt that he wouldn't tolerate any further disruption.

"I own the damned building." Angelino reluctantly sat back down as his attorney straightened his chair. "Of course my prints will be present."

"How convenient," Karl muttered.

"What's that supposed to mean?"

"Almost all the crimes either took place on premises you own or are somehow connected to you."

"Oh, come on," his nostrils flared in fury, "my company owns half this city."

"I'm not sure if your lawyer has advised you," Karl smiled pointedly at Nigel as he spoke. The man was a waste of space, and any bystander would think he was working for the LVMPD, not Angelino. "The DNA sample taken at the time of your arrest will be checked against certain items found at the crime scenes. It will also be added to CODIS—the national database—where it will be kept indefinitely." Karl didn't see any point telling him at this stage that his DNA had already provided a positive match. To do so, would also mean explaining—and attempting to justify —how they came by it without a warrant in the first place.

"And I shall look forward to a formal apology prior to my imminent release." Angelino leaned back in his chair, apparently relaxed for the first time since the interrogation had begun.

Burt had to hand it to him. Despite the mounting evidence against him, Angelino was remarkably calm. *The best type of defense is good offense,* he reminded himself as he studied his friend through the glass.

"Ask him why he thinks Billy Jackson would have

abducted Alice," Burt mumbled urgently into the microphone that was attached to Karl's earpiece.

"You're the detective, so how about you do some detecting?" Angelino bit back as Karl repeated the question. "Or ask the scum responsible instead of wasting your time interrogating me with this bullshit."

"We did," Karl locked eyes with Angelino. "He claims that he wanted to force you into the truth. That you were responsible for his father's death… a fact, that your employee Alfred Turner has also now confirmed," his voice rose as Angelino made to interrupt. "It was a good effort, I'll give you that, but it turns out that Alfred is more resilient than you might have hoped."

"Cut it there," Burt instructed through the earpiece. He could spot a mile off that Angelino's invisible barriers had been raised. They wouldn't get anymore from him right now. Much better to give him time to sweat it out in his cell, and it was certainly clammy enough today for that.

CHAPTER FIFTY-EIGHT

Friday, August 30, 2019 (14:30)

"How's Alice?" Detective Dennis Boyd asked as he hurried into the room and took a seat. Courtesy of the recent flash floods wreaking havoc on the highway, he was running uncharacteristically late.

"Missing her *friend* apparently. Can you believe that?" Burt muttered, unable to disguise the bitterness. "If we hadn't got to her when we did," his eyes flickered toward the window and the rain pounding against the glass, "she would have died in those flood channels."

"Interesting how she's missing Billy, but not her father." Detective Noah Mason, who had also been caught up in the heavy traffic, grabbed the nearest available chair and sat down. "Makes you wonder what kind of a relationship they shared, for her to prefer the company of a convicted killer."

"A convicted killer who is about to be exonerated of any such guilt," Burt reminded him. "Billy's lawyer is suggesting he could be looking at as much as six figures in compensation."

"At least she escaped unharmed," Karl tried to focus

on the positive. Burt looked washed out, the recent scare over his goddaughter and charges against his friend clearly taking their toll.

"Physically perhaps, but who knows what damage has been done up here?" Burt tapped the side of his temple with his index finger. "Or what harm could be done if they sentence her father to death?"

"Did Billy say why he took Alice?" Dennis had been at the hospital, collecting as much information as possible from Alfred in case he didn't pull through, and so he was yet to be updated on the latest events.

"Reckoned he wanted to force Angelino into telling the truth," Burt replied. "Except of course, Angelino would never take a threat like that lying down."

"What about Billy's DNA?" Dennis asked, helping himself to a cup of water from the cooler in the corner.

"Clean," Karl replied. "Which is more than can be said for Angelino. We're still waiting on the formal results, but the rapid machine returned a positive for the flakes of skin found under Yorkie Fletcher's fingernails. Ethan Gardner has now also provided us with the messages his tracking software picked up. Whoever stole Mario's cell sent messages to both Yorkie and Angelino engineering a meet at the Paragon. Next thing you know, Yorkie's been murdered, and we find footage of Angelino leaving the Paragon shortly afterwards."

"If Angelino attacked Mario, it makes no sense that he would then send a text to himself," Burt challenged.

"Or that's what he wanted us to think," Karl replied. "I think he used it to cover his ass… he needed a reason to be there if caught and that text message would provide the perfect alibi."

"What about the discarded cigarette inside the sewage pit?" Dennis asked.

"Angelino's DNA also gave a positive match."

"Anything connecting either of them to Mario?" Dennis drained the contents of the cup and fired it into the trash can before returning to his seat.

"Only Angelino's slip of the tongue under interview and the CCTV placing him in the right place at the right time," Karl answered.

"I still think Billy's caught up in all of this," Noah was skeptical. "If the fortune teller's right about the meaning of the cards, it makes no sense for anyone else to have placed them at the crime scenes."

"Unless it was a deliberate ploy to put Billy in the frame," Burt replied sadly as the reality about the man who he had considered a lifelong friend finally hit home. "Angelino always was a devious little shit when the need arose."

"But why kill Billy's ex-wife," Noah pressed, still unconvinced, "and decapitate her?" he added with disgust.

"To cause a diversion?" Dennis suggested. "Push suspicion away from himself? We now know he's capable after what he did to Alfred."

"Or maybe she was just in the wrong place at the wrong time?" Burt shrugged. "Or she knew too much? We'll never know, but two positive matches for Angelino's DNA at separate crime scenes—including Lorraine Jackson's—is pretty damning."

"His fingerprints also matched those found on the elevator doors and in the electrical closet at the Amathus," Karl added.

"Too easy to dismiss," Burt shook his head. "Given

his relationship to the building, any good attorney will rule that out as permissible evidence within minutes."

"Lucky, he doesn't have one of them," Karl quipped. "What is it with the lawyer? Angelino could afford the best that money could buy, but he employs an unknown from out of town who's about as much use as a solar-powered flashlight."

"Damned if I know," Burt smiled ruefully. "According to Ronnie, his usual lawyer refused to defend him when he heard the gruesome details."

"A defense attorney with morals?" Karl joked. "Give that man a medal."

"Next thing you know, Nigel Goodman's stepped in. His credentials certainly come up good but at this rate it'll be a decision Angelino will regret."

"What about the restroom attendant's creams at the Paragon?" Dennis asked. "There were other unidentified prints on them."

"Now identified as Karl's," Burt threw him a look of disdain. "Unfortunately, there was too much cross-contamination to get any other match, but we now have more than enough to prove Angelino met with Yorkie at the time of his death."

"We'll still press charges against Billy for Alice's abduction though, yeah?" Noah asked, struggling to suppress his frustration that they were about to let him walk free when he was so obviously involved.

"No." It wasn't a decision that Burt had made lightly, but Alice was his number one priority.

"What? Why?" Stunned at this latest revelation, Noah couldn't believe what he was hearing. "By your own admission, he could have killed her."

"Any subsequent punishment would have to account

for the time that Billy has already served for a crime he didn't commit," Burt said, massaging his temples with his fingers.

"Billy would walk from court a free man, regardless," Karl nodded in understanding.

"But he would at least still have a criminal record," Noah protested.

"And Alice would be forced to take the stand. Not only would she have to face *that man* all over again, but she would also have to relive the events that led to the arrest of her father. Five people are dead and if we win this case, I can't see him escaping the death penalty, can you? I'm not having that on her conscience for years to come."

"Can I have a quick word?" Dennis approached Karl as the meeting ended.

"Sure." Karl studied the younger man quizzically.

"The lawyer," Dennis hissed. "I've had this feeling for a while I'd seen him somewhere before and then it came to me."

"Go on."

"Nigel Goodman is in the CCTV with Billy at the Lucky Plaza that night. They're playing the same table and he watches him leave and follow Mario. Which got me thinking and when I listen to the Crime Stoppers tape, I think it's him. I think it's the lawyer who gives us the tip-off that Mario was in the casino that night. No mention of Billy, though. Then later, we've got Nigel Goodman and Angelino having a heated discussion in the casino."

"If the lawyer told Angelino about Mario's antics and Billy's presence, it would explain how the footage came to disappear if he decided to get his revenge on

Mario, but that was later, wasn't it? Mario was already bleeding out on the asphalt when Angelino returned to the Lucky Plaza."

"True, but the lawyer knows more about what happened that night than he's letting on. Him and Billy were thick as thieves, whereas later, his dislike of Angelino is evident from his body language alone."

"You think the lawyer might secretly be acting in Billy's favor?" Karl grinned. "It sure as hell would explain why he's making such a mess of Angelino's defense."

"Should I mention my concerns to Burt?" Dennis asked.

"Why? We know Angelino's guilty. Who cares if his lawyer knows it too? I'd call that justice served, myself."

CHAPTER FIFTY-NINE

Friday, August 30, 2019 (15:00)

ALFRED LAY MOTIONLESS IN THE HOSPITAL BED, HIS EYES gazing vacantly at the ceiling. Attached by tubes and wires to machines designed to keep him alive, a thin sheet covered his torso and his heavily bandaged hands lay limply by his sides. He didn't need to turn his head to know the police officer was still stationed at the door, the persistent knuckle cracking either a deliberate attempt to goad him or a habit he wasn't even aware of. He suspected the latter. This one was far friendlier than the last, and he would be sorry when his shift ended.

"You're lucky to be alive," the nurse had informed him earlier as she cleaned and dressed his wounds. Was he? Right now, he didn't feel all that fortunate, the idea of death far less terrifying than the prospect of returning to prison. He squeezed his eyes closed in an effort to block out the memories, but it was impossible.

Tuesday, May 3, 1993: Aged just 15 and weighing in at only 120 lbs, he had entered adult prison. The smell hit him first; a noxious combination of cleaning agents that masked a multitude of sins. It hadn't taken long for the unwanted attention to follow.

However hard he tried to keep to himself and out of trouble, it wasn't easy. Smaller and weaker than his fellow inmates, he was easy prey. He even tried to seek help, but it turned out the prison officials didn't really care if a felon was screwing another. Several transfers later to other parts of the prison, and he had learned that it didn't matter where you ended up, there would always be someone waiting in the wings to get you. The only solution was to keep his head down and accept the inevitable.

The detective who had interviewed him the night of Maddison's death had visited again today, promising him impunity if he agreed to testify against Angelino. He didn't believe him. His father had taught him from an early age that to trust a police officer was one of the most single-handed, stupid things that a person could ever do. A manipulative bully, who systematically gained compliance through threats and violence, it was no loss to him when he learned of his father's demise.

"Somebody had to protect you from going back to prison," he had growled when Alfred asked why he lied under oath about Jacob Jackson's murder. Protect his precious reputation, more like. God forbid people found out that he was capable of what his father had spent his whole lifetime conditioning him to be.

"Before you were even born, I knew you were a bad egg." He had reached for another bottle of beer from the cooler and cracked open the lid with his teeth. *"I told your mother to get rid of you, but she refused."* He spat the small metal cap into his hand, rolling it between his thumb and forefinger before flicking it directly at his head. *"Stupid woman wouldn't even let me deal with you when you murdered our baby girl."*

It was the internet that finally educated Alfred as to the real cause of his sister's death. Sudden infant death syndrome: there was nothing he could have done, and he certainly hadn't been responsible. It didn't stop him from punishing himself, though. He would always believe that he could have done more to save her.

"Can you think of anyone who would have wished your father harm?" seemed to be a standard question at first. *He was a cop—hardly short of enemies.* Even his own mother had wanted rid of him. *"I could kill him,"* she continually threatened when he had left her for "that whore." Alfred was glad someone had saved her the trouble.

He concentrated on a stain on the ceiling again, wrestling against the never-ending slideshow of images that played over and over in his mind like a frantic Wurlitzer at the fairground. *His sister's arctic flesh glued to his own; the gurgle of blood flooding Mannequin Man's lungs; twisted flesh and bits of Jacob's brain strewn around the stairwell; Nate's lifeless eyes staring back from the noose.*

How many lives would be ruined because of his stupid mistakes? He had been determined to right the wrongs, to face up to what he had done but now that day had come, he was still searching for the easy way out. He killed a man. He deserved everything he got, but not prison. He couldn't go back there.

His eyes flickered to the machines beside the bed. Would an alarm sound if he knocked out the tubes and wires so they were no longer feeding life into him?

"Everything OK?" As though reading his mind, the police officer tasked with guarding him approached the bed. "They can do some incredible surgery these days, check this out." He pressed the play button on his cell phone, the sound of Beethoven's "Für Elise" filling the room as he held it over his face. "This guy lost all his digits in a machine at work but look at him now. With the help of toe implants and prosthetics, he can play the keyboard better than anyone." He placed a reassuring hand on Alfred's shoulder. "When you're up to talking, you should ask the doctors about it."

Alfred turned his head to face the window. He didn't want to be rude, but neither did he deserve kindness given what he was planning to do. The hospital air conditioner had turned the space into an icebox, and he closed his eyes again and basked in the heat from outside as it burned through the glass onto his skin.

"I'm going to get myself a coffee and pay a visit to the little boy's room," the officer accepted the hint gracefully, "but I'll be right back." He wasn't supposed to leave the prisoner unattended, but he couldn't see how it mattered. It wasn't as though he would be going anywhere, anytime soon, and he'd be back before anyone even noticed his absence.

Alfred lay still and listened to the incessant beeping of the machines and the shuffling of feet in the distance as doctors, nurses, and visitors all went about their business in the corridor beyond. Only once he was satisfied there was no risk of being caught did he lift his arms and start to tug and shove with his bandaged, mangled hands at the necessary tubes and wires.

The fleeting pang of shame that he was about to destroy yet another life when the officer had to explain why he had left his prisoner unattended was soon replaced with an overwhelming sense of calm. Every breath that he now took, a determined step toward death.

SIN CITY

2022

EPILOGUE

BILLY

IT WAS A FELLOW PRISONER THAT GAVE ME THE IDEA.

"You deliberately planted evidence to implicate yourself?" The guy was a special kind of crazy, and I shook my head in confusion. "Why?"

"Stupid fools were supposed to think I'd been stitched up," he grumbled, chewing furiously on his fingernails. "Concentrate their efforts on finding the *real culprit*."

"Even though that culprit was you?" I was starting to think he needed locking up in a mental asylum, not prison.

"If they thought I was framed," exasperation leaked from every pore, "they would ignore any other so-called evidence on the basis it was probably also planted."

I barely slept a wink that night, the pathetic excuse of a mattress sagging beneath my weight with every toss and turn. How could I make people sit up and listen when everyone involved were filthy liars, happy to see me rot in prison if it meant they walked free? I had to grab people's attention, but how? Eventually, I collapsed back in defeat as the flimsy fabric swallowed me up, but by morning the start of a plan had formed in my mind...

Our ma was always superstitious. Forever knocking on wood or crossing her fingers and a zillion other things she swore prevented bad luck, she sure did her level best to avoid the wrath of the universe. Once a week without fail, she used to visit this old bag who me and Nate nicknamed *"Psycho Lady."* Psychic Sadie lived on the Westside, an area plagued with crime. Most the neighborhood had given up trying to keep their houses looking nice, but not Sadie. She always did her best, but it didn't matter how hard she tried to sugarcoat the turd, it was a battle she would never win.

There was a sign outside Sadie's house boasting her 'gift' and I think even she believed she could predict a person's destiny just by looking at them. In truth, the old bat couldn't see anything through her high prescription lenses, but our ma still lapped it up like a dehydrated dog.

"The cards all have meanings, dear," Sadie once told me, her gnarled fingers clutching mine so hard, I thought they might snap under the pressure. "This card here," she said as she let go of my hand, "tells me you're going to have a lot of luck with money." My eyes followed the direction of her finger as it settled on the ten of hearts. "And this one," she continued, as her finger moved to the three of clubs, "promises a successful marriage, full of love and happiness."

If I didn't know at the time that the old girl was full of shit, I sure as hell did a few years later when I was jailed for Father's murder after I was caught pocketing hefty profits from the rigged machines. The fact that my wife then left me for the man who secured my conviction only added fuel to my fire. The idea that a story could be told through the cards was interesting though. I had a story to tell, and thanks to Sadie, I realized that I could finally make people listen to it.

I started to spend time in the prison library, reading up on people and what drove them to kill. The Zodiac Killer got my attention. He sent messages to the cops, so I figured there was nothing stopping me. If I played the cards right, the cops would piece together my story and I could finally punish those who took my life by taking theirs *and* I could punish the biggest perpetrator of them all.

Removing the crumpled piece of paper from beneath the blanket I was using to support my head, I pressed down the folds with my fingers to iron out the creases.

DISCARDED CIGARETTE HELPS NAIL KILLER!

Beneath the headline was a full-page spread detailing the most recent advances in technology, and exactly how crimes were being solved through forensic DNA testing. Over the weeks, months, and years that followed, I made it my business to study every daily newspaper available and kept anything that might prove useful to me in the future.

I'll never know for sure if Maddison Scott had the evidence to prove that Elizabeth Angel received a substantial payout from Angelino days before she hung me out to dry. Nor will I know if she would have been successful persuading Alan Dutthie—Alfred—and his good-for-nothing dad to tell the truth. It didn't matter, anyway. I couldn't trust her. Not after what she'd done, and no amount of backtracking could take away my need to finish what she started.

Maddison was going to save my ass. It was the least she could do, and as Doctor Joe pointed out: why would I kill the one person who was determined to prove my innocence? Angelino, on the other hand, had good reason to silence her.

I can't believe how close I came to killing Alfred! My gloved hand was actually gripping the door handle when the crazy mutt started barking at me. I saved the dog from him, and I think it wanted to save me right back. If it hadn't alerted me to Angelino's presence, it would have been too late. I would have killed him and worse still, Angelino would have witnessed the whole thing and made damn sure I paid the price. Of course, Alfred died anyway. He wasn't as stupid as he tried to make us all think. I can't say I'm sorry. He'd only have rotted in jail if he hadn't killed himself and I'm not sure he deserved that.

That other officer—Detective Karl Andrews— adopted the dog in the end. I'm glad. I hated leaving him there that night, but I could barely look after myself, let alone Alice *and* a dog.

I never took Mario's money, by the way. Maybe the tourist who found him did that? Well, good luck to him. Mario's dough never bought me nothing but trouble. Either way, it did me a favor. By relieving him of it, the police had gotten a nice incriminating motive on Angelino's part and when he then did what he did to Alfred, well, I never saw that coming. It just goes to show that whatever gamble you take in life, you're still going to need some luck to come out on top.

Alice didn't take things so well, but she's a clever kid and she'll soon realize she's better off without me.

"What do you mean, I'll never see you again?" she cried, her lip quivering as she fought the tears. Unsure how to proceed, I glanced at the detective—her godfather—for guidance.

"I did something bad, Alice. I should never have taken you like I did." I replied, in response to his gentle nod of encouragement.

"But you didn't," she whined, her face flushing as the tears she was desperately holding back escaped. "I wanted to come. Uncle Burt, tell him," she begged as she grabbed the sleeve of his jacket and tugged at it, but he merely shook his head. We had a deal. I had served more than enough time inside for a crime he now accepted I didn't commit, but if I was to be released with no further charge there was to be no more contact with Alice.

"Liar, liar… LIAR!" she screamed at me, her face contorted with anger as she was dragged away. "Friends forever, you promised. Daddy's gone, and now you're going too. I HATE YOU!"

Hurting Alice was never part of the plan, you must believe that. Letting her go without telling her the truth was probably the hardest thing I ever had to do. You can't protect people from it though, can you? One day, not so long from now, she will become curious. She'll want to learn more about her father, and when she does dig a little deeper, she'll discover who—and what—he really was. I don't envy her that day. In the meantime, she's fine. She has a family. A mother—and godparents —who would do anything for her.

Angelino, on the other hand, gets to learn what it's like to lose someone he loves. Just like I had to do when my brother killed himself because of what he did. They haven't fried him yet—a global pandemic hit the world not long after his trial and as the universe shut down and millions died, the last thing on anyone's mind was distributing a dose of lethal drugs to scum like him. At first, I hoped he might catch the deathly disease that was overpowering the world. Social distancing wasn't going to be an option in an overcrowded prison, and there'd be zero priority for inmates when it came to healthcare and vaccinations.

No such luck, although now I'm glad he survived. Death would have been too easy, but the fear of death is a whole other level and this way he gets a taste of what he deserves every single day.

I never heard from Bo again. Lucky son-of-a-bitch always was in the right place at the right time and that night, when the cops flooded the drains, he was out getting supplies. We had a deal that when the time came, we'd part company with no questions asked, so that's what we did but it doesn't mean I don't think about him or hope he finally put his demons to bed. I couldn't have seen none of it through without him.

Lorrie's formal burial went without a hitch. Her folks had since passed and she had no close family to object, so I was able to give her the sendoff she deserved. I didn't think the Little White Chapel would agree but as it turned out, they'd been doing more divorces than marriages of late and liked the idea of expanding their little empire into funerals. We could have been happy me and her if she hadn't had to go and spoil everything. I did try to reason with her that night, but she got all tricky like she always did and nothing I said would shut her up so in the end, I did the only thing I could to silence her.

Nigel never did return to Connecticut. It turned out he had a taste for Vegas, which was just as well. As a state of emergency was declared in response to Covid-19 in March of 2020, he couldn't have got a flight home even if he wanted to. For almost a year, the city came to a standstill as the disease paralyzed the nation, but somehow, he still managed to find himself a new lady friend to fill the lonely days and nights.

We still talk on the phone sometimes. He always says he owes me his life but in truth, I owe him just as much for mine. The news reports at the time were full of snide remarks about what a bad job he was doing, but I disagree. You could do a lot worse than have Nigel on your side! Nigel Goodman is exactly that… a good man!

I perch on the end of my bed, an inch of dirty water covering my feet. I don't need to be here anymore. The game is finally over. I'm free to go and do whatever I want and yet, as the minutes turn into hours in a darkness that shows no sense of time, the drains are harder to escape than prison.

THE BAKER'S DOZEN

Is a card game of patience. It is a game that can only be won with careful planning from the outset.

ACKNOWLEDGMENTS

Once again, heartfelt thanks to Matthew O'Brien… for planting a seed in my head, for not running a mile when I messaged him out of the blue to ask for his help and editorial expertise, and for his early and ongoing input into this book.

Also, to my first readers, in particular Zoe Wasley, who gave me just the encouragement I needed while throwing some brilliant ideas at me. Zoe also introduced me to Elisabeth Phillips, an avid reader of the genre who kindly read my effort within twenty-four hours and returned with more great advice and suggestions. I am eternally grateful to them both… Ian Hobbs (Devon Book Club)—who was subjected to a very early version and managed to rein in my evil sense of humour. (Apparently, a reader shouldn't be doubled up laughing during a torture scene). Also, to Helena Rapps and fellow author Stevenson-Olds.

Huge thanks also to my friend and fellow author Julie Archer, who frankly deserves a medal for her patience and perseverance. Julie not only advised me how best to convert and upload to e-book format, but also spent hours of her life she will never get back, deliberating with me over the title and dreaded "blurb". If contemporary romance is your thing, I highly recommend my talented friend, so please do visit her website: juliearcherwrites.com.

Emmy Ellis for the fantastic cover, Morag Fowler for her eagle-eyed proof-reading, Mickey Wadeson for the (often bizarre) brain storming sessions, and my parents for their continued support in everything I do.

Ernest Hemingway once said that "writing, at its best, is a lonely life," but I was fortunate enough to have Boost, Scooby, Tinker and Pickle, who spent endless hours quietly supporting me throughout the process.

Finally, I'd like to thank my readers… without you, a writer can't exist, and I really hope you think this book is worthy of the time you have invested in it.

ABOUT THE AUTHOR

When she's not plotting her next murder, L.E. Willetts runs a B&B on the South Coast in Dartmouth, Devon, UK. (Occasionally, the two interests collide).

She has a weekly column in her local newspaper. Passionate about animal welfare, she also undertakes writing projects for "Rehoming Cyprus Pointers"—an organisation close to her heart as they rescued two of her dogs.

In her free time, she likes nothing better than to snuggle under "blankie" with her dogs and a good psychological thriller.

You can follow L.E. Willetts on Facebook and Twitter or contact her via her website at: lewilletts.com

facebook.com/lewilletts

twitter.com/lewilletts

Printed in Great Britain
by Amazon